A Cask of You

A BUTLER'S WHISKY ROMANCE
BOOK ONE

AMBER COOPER

malted
mouse
press

Foreword

Hello!

Welcome to Butler world, part one. You have joined at the very beginning of what I hope will be a truly memorable and wonderful journey for both you and me. I truly hope you love Cal and Bea's story as much as I do. Before you read, just a word about the content and steamy bits.

This book touches lightly on the topics of terminal illness, coercive control and feelings around not being a mother. It is a subtle touch but I feel it best to put it out there to give you the option of turning back now if you feel this would not be for you.

Predominantly, however, this story is about Cal and Bea and their developing feelings for and attraction to each other, and desire to 'you know what'.

Which leads me onto the sexy bits...

FOREWORD

There are several open door, steamy scenes in this book. The characters do occasionally swear, because Scottish people tend to swear a fair bit.

And with that all said, I'll let you get stuck in. I hope you love it!

Amber xx

P.S. Cal has four brothers and two sisters, so if you love this book, you're in luck as there are more Scotsmen on the way.

P.P.S At the end of the book there is an opportunity to sign up for a secret scene which goes in between chapters forty four and forty five. This scene tells a bit more of Cal's backstory and gives spoilers to the prequel to the series, thus is not included in the novel. But, if you wish to have it to read as part of the story then you can use this link: https://BookHip.com/LRZFRTQ or download it here.

The link to download the prequel is available at the end of the book or at my website www.ambercooperbooks.com.

Email sign up is required for both of these, you won't be added to the list more than once, and unsubscribing is easy.

To Chris and the real Amber.

Chapter One

Bea Gracie peered out the grimy window of her Edinburgh apartment. Rain was thundering onto the ground and the dark skies were sinking lower. Back in her home of New York City, Scotland's capital had seemed the perfect place to spend three months getting over her ex and writing her next novel, but now she was here, Bea wasn't sure that those three months wouldn't feel like three years.

Plus, the apartment was awful. After the taxi breaking down on the wrong side of The Meadows, resulting in a quarter mile walk in the rain, and now damp to her core, Bea met dirty wallpaper, equally filthy floorboards and furniture that was new in the late 1990s – not what she'd pictured when she chose Scotland as writing inspiration.

Bea's late father was Scottish and had grown up in Edinburgh. He had told her stories of ghosts that lurked down closes, of rogue merchants and devilishly charming and tenacious local businessmen who built Edinburgh up from a slum to the thriving city it was today. Fascinated by these tales, Bea couldn't wait to use all the city offered to write a story of her own, but all she cared for at this moment was a shower and a nap.

Perched on the edge of the bed, Bea wondered what her ex, Josh, would say if he could see her now. He'd gloat, no doubt. She could hear him: 'What did you expect, Bea? You have to work if you want a good life and it's only me that knows the meaning of hard work in this relationship.'

Five years Bea had spent with Josh, five years before he'd decided he no longer wanted to be with an unsuccessful novelist whom he claimed leaned on him for money, and, instead, he would be coupling up with a successful trust fund baby whose father owned a highly lucrative shipping company. Josh and his new girlfriend could lean on her father for money instead.

It had all come spitting out in their last argument. Bea was working solidly on her latest romance novel, but every night Josh had come home and asked her what she was going do to ensure that this one would be successful.

'I'm drafting and redrafting,' Bea explained. 'I'm working all day until I go to the bar in the evening.'

'Yes, but nothing's happening, is it? How can you not know how to get readers when there's a mountain of information out there on the internet about how to snag an agent or even self-publish successfully?'

'I have fans, Josh. And maybe with this book I'll get more. It's a marathon, not a sprint. One day, people will realise that they want to read my books, and until that day I'll keep plugging away.'

But Josh had little faith in romance writing (and little understanding of romance, Bea thought) and couldn't see how it might be a career option. He didn't want Bea doing her night job either.

'To be honest, Bea, I don't think you should work in a bar. It's not right for a woman in her thirties. And it's certainly not the place you want to be if you're planning to fall pregnant soon.'

'I had no idea I was planning to fall pregnant soon,' Bea countered. 'I've only just turned thirty.'

'That's exactly my point. Wake up and smell the coffee.'

And that was their last argument. Looking back, Bea couldn't understand why Josh had talked of her falling pregnant when he was clearly cheating on her, as the next week he told her of his decision to leave. A week after that she was on her way to the airport – a flash decision to get out of New York and jump-start her writing in Scotland, maybe even meet a muse. Had it been the wrong decision? Bea wiped away a slight tear, then caught herself.

Don't be ridiculous. You're a grown woman who has chosen to have a working-vacation in one of the most beautiful cities in the world. Why are you crying? Okay, so your apartment is a little grubby, but you have escaped that awful man. You're here to write and you can do that in coffee shops, even parks – if it ever stops raining.

Thunder rumbled outside.

Bea reached for her phone.

'Hey, babe,' the comforting tones of Bea's best friend, Amira, came through the phone, helping to soften the edges of Bea's discomfort. 'How's it going? You got there safe?'

'Well, yes and no,' said Bea. 'I'm here in body. But I'm not sure this was a good plan. This place is so wet. It hasn't stopped raining since I arrived, and my apartment is disgusting. I think I'm running away from things back home, which will mean that when I get back I'll be where I was when I left, but everyone else will have moved on.'

'Ah, come on, it can't be that bad,' Amira soothed. 'Can I remind you how much you wanted to go on this trip. You've put your life savings into getting there and staying there, so I think that's what you need to do. New York isn't going anywhere.'

Bea nodded at her friend's advice. She knew it herself, but it was comforting to be reminded of it by someone else. 'That's true.'

'And besides, how am I going to live vicariously through you snagging a hot, sexy Scotsman if you hop on the next plane because of a little rain? It rains in NYC too, you know, except we don't get wet Scotsmen here. Imagine him, standing in the rain asking if you love him like he loves you. You have a chance to experience that. You're so lucky, Bea!'

Bea laughed. 'That is a good point; the chances are always higher in a place with such a high concentration of Scotsmen. And I guess I did come here to write, rain or shine. But, Ams, in all seriousness, what guy will want me? Poor, lacking in self-confidence, on the rebound?'

'Does it matter if you're on the rebound? You're not planning on staying there forever. If you ask me, the circumstances are perfect for a temporary liaison with a smoking hot Scotty who you can immortalise in between the sheets of your next book. It might do wonders for your self-confidence.'

Amira knew Bea so well. Her confidence was in the gutter because of Josh. 'I guess it might.' She hoped that her friend's optimism was right, as it often was. 'But how do I get one of these smoking hot Scotties when I feel about as attractive as last week's newspaper and people here are walking around staring at their soaking wet feet?'

'Well, I can't stop the rain, hon, but my advice would be to channel old Bea, pre-Josh Bea. Remember her?'

Bea pulled at a loose thread on the bedspread. 'Kinda.'

'I fully do.' Amira's voice was full of the encouragement Bea needed to hear. 'You've got looks and personality in spades, Bea. Only, Josh has kicked the confidence out of you. But you've also got a clean slate. Nobody knows you over there; you'll fly home in a few months. Scotland is your stage. Go out there and flirt and grab yourself that man. If not for yourself, then do it for your readers. Fake it until you...'

'Make it?' Bea suggested.

'I was going to say until you've written the book.' Amira laughed and it sparked laughter in Bea too. She turned her mind to her readers. They were the fulcrum around which her writing career revolved, and that was all she had, so focusing on them would help keep her balanced. People depended on her.

'You know what, Ams? You're right,' Bea tried to soak up Amira's positivity. 'I have to think of the readers. I owe it to the ones I already have, and there are new ones out there that deserve to find me.'

'Exactly! You can do it, Bea. Remember that girl in college who had heaps of self-belief? Be her. And don't think about Josh or any of that stuff. It's all thousands of miles away.'

'Thanks, honey.' Bea wished she could reach down the phone and give her friend a hug. 'Gee, I miss you already.'

'Miss you too, babes. Call me anytime.'

Bea said goodbye, hung up and considered a plan of action. She had to hold onto the good vibes the phone call had given her and make things happen before she could change her mind again. She had to find a Scotsman to be her next hero.

Chapter Two

Cal Butler coasted into shore on the last wave of his morning surf. Not unusually for August in Scotland, the rain was teeming down and the sea choppy and unpredictable, but Cal paddled on. Surfing in the sun was his preference, but surfing in the rain was invigorating – as if you were winning against nature. And Cal needed to score some points on that front.

As he waded through the shallows towards the beach, Cal glanced back to check on his younger sister Eilidh. Eilidh and her triplet sister, Cara, were five years younger than Cal and he was protective of them. Living in the same village outside Edinburgh, Eilidh often joined him on his morning surf, sometimes with Cara, and he always had one eye on the waves and another on his sisters to make sure they were safe.

Eilidh caught the crest of her final wave. Cal turned his attention towards the beach. An older man – possibly around sixty, the age of Cal's own father – was walking his dog. Cal tried to push the worries from his mind and concentrate on the dog and its zest for life.

'Stop it. I know what you're thinking, and it won't help.'

How long had Cal been staring at the dog? Long enough for Eilidh to have had ridden into shore and be standing next to him reading his mind. She knew he was thinking about the phone call yesterday from his mother, about the fact that his father now had a sentence on his life. Motor neurone disease was its name, and it would entail a rapid decline in mobility for Jimmy Butler. Cal couldn't get his head around this.

'It's unbelievable, right,' said Eilidh. 'How is it possible that someone so energetic and dynamic, who runs a multi-million distillery empire, will be confined to a wheelchair and reliant on others for support?'

Cal didn't like it when Eilidh presented things so bluntly, but it was exactly what was on his mind. He would try his best to avoid dwelling on it too much by throwing himself into his work running his bar off the Royal Mile, in the heart of Edinburgh, but it wasn't easy pushing down something as monumental as this. Cal loved and adored his father. Growing up, he had always been his hero, especially considering that when Cal was six years old, a couple of years after his emotionally abusive biological father had died, Jimmy Butler, his father's older brother, had married Cal's mother, Amanda, and taken on Cal and his two younger siblings – Jamie and Niall – as his own. Amanda and Jimmy had one child together – Sean – and then fostered and adopted from a troubled background, triplets, Eilidh, Cara and Nate. There weren't many men who would put their heart and soul into it the way his father had. But Jimmy Butler wasn't any man; he was a powerhouse in so many respects: as a father, a businessman and a person. Cal couldn't bear the thought of seeing him deteriorate.

But there was another reason Cal dreaded going to see his father, and it involved the family business.

When the siblings were growing up, Jimmy Butler had

always talked of his children working for and taking over the family company. So far, Jamie, the second eldest, was the only one following that plan, working as an operations manager in the headquarters in Kinshore on the Kintyre Peninsula. Jamie loved working for BDL, but Cal, as dogged and determined as Jimmy, had wanted to do things differently. Whisky might run in the family, but so did proving yourself. So, at twenty-three, after completing the degree that Jimmy had insisted all his children study for, Cal took a job as a barman and worked his way up through the ranks, first to bar manager, then – having saved and invested ruthlessly – leaseholder, and after that full bar owner at thirty. Cal was now thirty-four and his bar, Butler's, had one branch in Edinburgh's Old Town with plans in the pipeline for further development.

'Do you think this will change things?' Eilidh asked as they walked up the beach. 'Change your mind about being part of BDL?'

Eilidh had hit on the reason Cal had a knot in his gut when he thought about going to see his father. With this news about his father's health, there would be more pressure than ever on Cal to become part of Butler's Distilleries Limited. It would be Jimmy's wish before he passed on to know another of his sons worked for the family business. And with only Jamie employed at Butler's, it would mean more likelihood of outsiders coming in and taking over.

'I don't know, Eils. I'd never say this to Dad but I'm kind of past the point of needing something to fall back on.'

'I think we all know that. It's the elephant in the room, isn't it?'

'Yep.' Any visit home by Cal would be uncomfortable on two levels: seeing his father a shadow of his former self and letting him down by telling him he had no desire to work at BDL. He, therefore, was putting it to the back of his mind for as long as he could.

'Come on,' he said to Eilidh, opting for distraction as today's coping mechanism. 'I'll race you to the road.'

And before Eilidh could register what was going on, Cal was pounding up the beach, surfboard under his arm. Amidst the grey and bleakness, he could create a shaft of light if he ran hard enough, then block the rest out with work.

Chapter Three

The rain lashed the pavement outside the coffee shop. If Bea hadn't been so deeply in the writing zone, she would have noticed that the ferocity of her typing sounded like a mini rainstorm. Two thousand words down in the past two hours. She allowed herself a break, sipped her almond mocha, reached for her phone and let her fingers drift to the Instagram icon. The voice in her head said *don't do it*, but resistance was futile. Ever since Josh had left her for this Avery Delaney woman, Bea sneaked occasional looks at Avery's profile to see what she had that Bea didn't.

Logically, Bea knew the answer. Everything and nothing. You couldn't compare a curvaceous redhead with a penchant for vintage fashion to a gamine blonde whose style was almost always designer. Josh had loved Bea's curves and had said that he was so proud to be seen with this stunning redhead who made heads turn wherever she went. Amira had remarked that it was like comparing a rich red wine to champagne; they were both delicious in their own right, yet entirely different. Still, Bea couldn't help but peek at Avery's profile, maybe to convince herself that the other woman wasn't perfect.

Avery's latest post showed her somewhere in a lush, green landscape wearing a flowing maxi dress. Stunning as ever. Bea sighed. This was a mistake. Why wasn't there a picture of a too thin Avery, or a shot that made her jaw appear a little masculine, or one with pigmentation on her face? Of course, there wouldn't be. The woman's sole purpose was to promote herself through social media. Then Bea noticed something that stole her breath. The curve of Avery's stomach. Was it a little belly fat or was it a bump? A bump bump. Bea glanced at the caption and her fears were confirmed. *Twelve weeks today. Can't wait to meet Little Bean.*

The whole world wobbled under Bea. Avery was pregnant! Twelve weeks pregnant. Josh had only left her four months ago. This was like being blown into the back wall of the coffee shop. It was betrayal all over again – essentially finding out that because she hadn't been keen enough to drop her writing dreams to have children, somehow, she wasn't good enough.

You have to put this baby news to the back of your mind. You will be a mom in time with the right guy. The one saving grace was that Bea felt a little sorry for Avery. The woman had fallen for Josh. *At least I don't have a douchebag for a partner and I'm not tied to one for the rest of my life due to sharing a child.*

Bea pulled up her own Insta profile. Maybe she should update it with something exciting. The last post was of her trying on a spotted hat at JFK. It was quirky and some of her readers had commented 'cute' and how they couldn't wait to read the writing that her travels inspired, but Bea didn't have the inclination to create visually stunning social media posts with her face front and centre. She communicated with her readers but preferred to put all her efforts into chatting to them and the actual writing. What was important to Bea was the development of the characters in her novels, not the development of a glossy image.

Besides, she had made it known that she would be away

for three months and that her interaction on social media would be minimal. Amira was tending to that side of things, monitoring to check there weren't any urgent posts that needed attended to, reminding those unaware that Bea was busy in Scotland researching and writing her next novel – the first in a series set in the country – but that she promised them the silence would be worthwhile.

Secretly, Bea hoped that this novel would be the one that did it for her. The one that people sat up and took an interest in. She wasn't expecting *Fifty Shades* type interest – that storm only came along once in a while – and her small but loyal group of readers were what kept her going, but she wanted her books to be known by more than a hundred people and she wanted to pay her bills without worry. And now a little voice told her it would be an excellent way to show Josh that if only he'd stuck with her a little longer – had more faith – then he would have reaped the rewards.

'Okay, stop that now; you're tempting fate,' Bea spoke out loud as she put her phone back on the counter.

'Pardon,' said an old lady sitting at the table behind her.

'Oh, nothing.' Bea smiled at the old lady. 'I was talking to myself.'

'First sign of sanity,' said the lady, and Bea chuckled at the woman's humour. In conjunction with her sing-song accent, it was comforting. And Bea needed all the comfort she could get right now.

Chapter Four

Butler's bar was situated down one of Edinburgh's many closes – narrow, sometimes cobbled, alleyways that ran perpendicular to the main streets of the Old Town. This secluded location meant that in the early morning there weren't many people passing, and there were never any cars – only the view of two residential properties with pretty, coloured doors across from the bar entrance.

Cal sat at a table in the bar scrolling through his LinkedIn feed, but it was all drivel. He pushed the phone to the side, sipped his coffee and meditated on the bucketing rain. The bar would get busy at night with locals who knew about it through reputation, tourists who'd found out about it on a review site or those who happened on it by chance. But for now, particularly because of the weather, it was quiet. Cal inhaled the silence.

On the table, his phone vibrated, his sister Cara's name flashing up on the screen.

'Hi, Cara.'

'Is it true?' As usual, Cara wasted no time in getting to the point.

'You might need to give me more to go on here. Is what true?'

'That I'm going to be an auntie.'

Cal froze. 'What are you talking about?'

'You mean you don't know? How can you not know? It's all over the socials. And besides, you're the dad, so you should know.'

'I'm the dad?' Cal thought for a second. The last person he was intimate with was his former girlfriend, Elisabetta Angelsey, a socialite and social climber/leech. They'd dated for about six months and Cal couldn't believe they'd lasted so long. Elisabetta's desire to appear at the opening of every door with Z-list celebrities was in direct contrast to Cal's desire to appear nowhere and to have as little to do with celebrities as possible. Elisabetta had dragged him to social events where photographers from society magazines had pointed cameras, so they'd be sure to end up on the social pages with captions under the photos saying things like: *Elisabetta Angelsey and Cal Butler, CEO of Butler's bar and heir to the BDL empire.* Photos next to people whose names meant nothing to Cal but when in print next to her own had made Elisabetta squeal with delight. Cal was entirely faithful to Elisabetta and hadn't slept with anyone else in the three months since they'd split up, so he figured it must be her child to whom Cara was referring. But why was he learning about this from his sister, who had learned about it from social media?

'Well,' said Cara, 'she doesn't say that you're the dad, but Elisabetta is your ex and the timings would make sense, so I figured...'

'Let me get this straight.' Cal put the phone on speaker and massaged his temples. 'Elisabetta is pregnant and shouting about it on social media, but she isn't saying who the father is?'

'Yes, check your socials. You'll see. She's posted a scan and underneath it says, "*I'm not sure who it looks more like, me or the daddy. What do you think?*" And she isn't dating anyone else, so it must be yours.'

Cal held back from swearing. This was so Elisabetta. Each move calculated with an audience in mind, all about likes and followers. Cal didn't even want to see the photo. If he was the father, why hadn't she called and told him?

'Okay, well, thanks for letting me know, Cara, but this is the first I've heard of it, so hold off on telling people you'll be an auntie for now, please?'

'Oh.' A kilo of buoyancy dropped out of Cara's voice. 'Are you going to call her and ask her? You know, this would make Mum and Dad's year.'

Cara had pinpointed a poignant truth, but that couldn't be the only consideration. The fact that this could all be a drive for attention was one of the first things that crossed Cal's mind. One of the reasons he had ended the relationship with Elisabetta was because they had nothing in common. At first, he found her physically attractive; they'd both enjoyed fine dining and sharing superb wine, but even the sex hadn't been good enough to buffer things when their personalities were so diametrically opposed. He, down to earth and protective of his privacy, she, highly strung and socially vivacious. And that was putting it generously. Attention-hungry might have been a better description, and that's what worried Cal about this pregnancy. Sure, it would be wonderful for his father to become a grandfather in the last years of his life, but Cal also didn't want hopes being raised then dashed.

'Yes, I will call her, but you can't say anything to anyone in the family about this.'

Cara reluctantly agreed to do things her brother's way. He knew what a great auntie she'd be. She would love a child of her own, but chose the wrong men, time after time, and was now busy with her work as an in-demand actress.

Cal brought up Elisabetta's number on his phone – this needed sorted and sorted now. His stomach pitched as the ringtone kicked in, but Elisabetta didn't answer and the call diverted to voicemail. Cal redialled.

Again, the phone went to voicemail. Cal tried four more times before leaving a short message.

'Betta, it's Cal. Call me when you get this, please. We need to sort this thing. You know what I'm talking about.'

Cal laid the phone on the table. A baby. He sipped his coffee and considered the possibility for a moment, before deciding it was best not to. The rational part of his brain told him that if he got too attached to having a child and it turned out it wasn't his then he would face disappointment. He also deduced that although Elisabetta was no doubt enjoying the limelight granted by her social media tease posts, her followers would soon grow bored and she'd need to find a new angle. If Cal were the father, she'd probably use that as her next publicity strategy, name dropping her baby-daddy as 'one of Scotland's most eligible bachelors,' as stated by *Scottish Bar Manager* magazine, or something else utterly meaningless if you were of Cal's mentality, but impressive if you were of Elisabetta's.

A shadow moved across the table and Cal glanced up to see Kitty, one of his employees, and Cara's best friend, standing at the window. He got up to let her in for her 11a.m. shift. Could he be imagining it or was there a lightness about Kitty that wasn't usual for this hour of the day? She had a funny expression on her face and was suspiciously jolly as she wished him good morning. He suspected that she had already been on the phone to Cara discussing the baby situation. Kitty and Cara were best friends from primary school and knew each other inside out. Cara had probably confided in Kitty that she would be an auntie before she'd even called Cal to discover if it was true. Well, he wasn't about to confirm or deny to Kitty, no matter how many knowing smiles she might give him. He was her boss and a professional distance was required.

Kitty made her way behind the bar towards the staff area to take off her coat and bag. As she did she hummed a song Cal was sure had the word baby in the title. He tried coughing loudly as a signal that he knew Kitty's game, but she appeared not to notice, instead asking Cal if he had a sore throat.

'Um, aye, a wee bit.' Cal supposed that being grumpy about such a minor detail would draw more attention to the issue and he'd be better taking a step back to let his mind settle. 'Listen, I'm going to pop out for a bit,' he said. 'Get some, um, Lemsip. Are you all right to set things up here? I'll be back before opening.'

'Sure,' said Kitty. 'I can get the Lemsip if you'd rather. I'm sure you've piles of emails and stuff to deal with. Plus, it's bucketing outside.' She pointed out the window as if Cal hadn't noticed the rain.

'Thanks for the offer, Kitty, but it's all in order.' Cal shrugged on his coat. 'And I can cope with a wee bit of rain. Plus, I've got an umbrella.'

A minute later, completely forgetting the umbrella, Cal headed out of the bar, up the close and onto the Royal Mile where he turned in the direction of his favourite coffee shop.

Chapter Five

Bea plucked a napkin from the box on the table and wiped away a streak of condensation from the window. *Give me inspiration from somewhere.* She peered through the clear streak to see if there might be a glimpse of sunshine struggling through the clouds. *Don't let this mission be a complete waste of time.*

There was no sunshine, but Bea saw something else on the street that made her sit up. A tall, striking figure, his collar up against the wind and rain, passing by the window of the coffee shop. This could be her hero, on his way to make up with the heroine. To take her by the rain-sodden hand and lead her up the stony stairs of a dark tenement and into a warm bed, to make passionate love to her while rain battered the window and the fire roared in the hearth. Bea swallowed hard. She should pack her laptop up and follow him. He could be her muse. But what would she do if she caught up with him? In her dreams she would follow some guy, accidentally bump into him, lock eyes and hold his gaze a moment too long: long enough for him to realise he'd fallen in love at first sight. In reality, Bea had little confidence to do this.

Fortunately for Bea, making chase was unnecessary because, moments later, the tall, striking man pushed open the door of the coffee shop.

Bea inhaled sharply as his presence fill the room. He was well over six foot with dark blond hair cut short at his neck, sharply dressed in a light-green tweed coat paired with jeans and brogues. He strode to the counter with confidence. It was like she was being given a second chance. What should she do? A glance at her coffee cup reminded Bea that she'd only drunk a few sips and it wasn't time for a refill. But what if she went up to the counter and got him to notice her? Almost orchestrated a meet cute. It would be super-difficult because it wasn't in her nature to be out there like that, but there could be an amazing story in it for the readers. And not just the novel itself but the story of how she met her muse. She had to do it – for those waiting for her next book. Bea slid out of her chair and headed to the counter, gripping her empty cup.

The man was ordering a latte. Bea noticed the bank card he was ready to swipe across the payment machine. She moved in, stood next to him – heart beating so loud he must be able to hear it – but didn't acknowledge his presence.

'Excuse me.' Bea held her coffee out to the barista. 'I don't think this is an *almond* mocha, and I did ask for an almond mocha.'

'Um...' Bea's commanding voice made the barista forget about her original customer, and the fact that the drink *was* made with almond milk. 'Sorry about that,' she said. 'I'll get you a new one right away.'

As the barista turned to the coffee machine, the man sighed. Bea sensed him tense and bristle. There was an intoxicating energy emanating from him. He also smelled divine: wafts of warm lime and cedarwood filled her senses.

'Oh, and while I'm here,' Bea continued to the barista, her jaw almost shaking, 'is that chocolate cake dairy free also?'

The barista leaned back from the coffee machine and examined the labels on the cakes in the glass-fronted cabinet. 'Yes, it is.'

'I'll have a slice of that as well.' Bea beamed with gratitude and commended herself for holding her nerve. How some people behaved like this daily without thinking twice, baffled her.

'Seriously?' The man's stare was boring into the side of her head.

'Oh, I'm so sorry.' Bea turned, pretending to notice him for the first time, although she hadn't accounted for his eyes being the greenest she had ever seen. She could stare into those forever. 'Were you...?'

'Being served? Aye, but I think you knew that.'

And the deep Scottish accent. It made Bea's core vibrate. She could sail away on those tones, across a loch the colour of his eyes.

'I'm so sorry,' she said. 'I should have noticed you. That's so rude of me. I can only apologise. It's just, when you can't have dairy and they give you dairy, well... it's frustrating.' Hopefully now, if she played it sweet, he would come round.

But the man's gorgeous greens were choppy with annoyance and Bea sensed a reprimand coming. She wasn't wrong.

'By all means, stand up for your dietary rights but do it while waiting your turn.' The man simmered with annoyance. 'Unless you're allergic to that?'

I've riled him. I can't play confident without coming across as arrogant. Now I'll need to get him on side or lose him. 'I'm sorry,' she said. 'I'm not allergic to waiting. And I'm not allergic to apologising either. Why don't you let me buy your coffee as a way of saying sorry? It's the least I can do.'

'I'm all right, thanks.' His voice was terse, which only made it sexier. 'Maybe just pay attention in future.'

'Yes, of course. I'm sorry again.' Bea was a little deflated.

He was a tough cookie. She wanted away so she could blush and cringe in private. 'Look, I'd better get back to my seat. I've left my laptop, but it was lovely to meet you.' Taking her coffee and cake, she lifted her mouth into what she hoped was a softening smile.

'Right. Bye then.' The man slid his coffee off the counter and gave Bea a strange sideways glance. It wasn't what she'd call a softening, more an indicator that he was completely baffled by what had just hit him.

Chapter Six

What the hell was that? Cal sat down with his coffee at the back of the shop. *Or more to the point, who the hell was that? What an annoying woman.* In fact, she was a perfect example of why Cal was swearing off females for the time being. Because so many attractive women were full of themselves and expected the world to revolve around them. Cal could appreciate feminine curves, delicate tendrils of red hair and peachy soft skin as much as the next man, but why did women like that use it to skip out of things like waiting in a queue or having manners? If no attractive women who also valued politeness and grace crossed his radar, Cal would remain single.

There was something about her, though. Cal couldn't help but glance up towards the front window. Irritating as she was, he felt a charge in the air as they locked eyes. *I've never felt that before.*

The woman was wearing a crimson sweater and dark skinny jeans that hugged her shapely thighs, but despite her casual attire, the space between them had sparkled more than with any woman he'd ever escorted out in a ballgown or evening wear. The chemistry was especially strange since she was unaware of other people, a trait Cal loathed.

Cal considered as he sipped his coffee that possibly he'd been a little harsh in reprimanding the woman. *She's probably a tourist, and I've obliterated the friendly Scottish image in one brief interaction. I should apologise. Offer her a free drink at the bar.* He pushed his chair out an inch.

Get a grip, Cal. Don't even go there. For all you know, she could be another social climber hell bent on making your life a misery. Stop letting what's in your pants control your brain. God, but she smelt amazing. Amber and honeysuckle. And it was weird that he only came into this coffee shop about once a fortnight, yet the day did he choose to come, this sizzling-hot woman was here.

Jeez, Butler, you're your own worst enemy. Such a sucker for a pretty face. And since when did you believe in all that fate nonsense?

Cal took his phone out of his pocket and opened his emails for a distraction. There were some about the second bar he would open soon in the New Town. There was also the possibility of expansion into Glasgow, although he didn't want to branch out all over the place without the same care that had gone into the original premises. He valued his reputation as a businessman. The way Cal saw it was that if you took care of details such as customer care and providing a quality service, then the financial things fell into place. Also important was hiring the right staff and treating them properly. Cal could never understand employers who would complain about the rapid turnover of their staff – he knew plenty in the bar trade – but fail to consider rate of pay and working conditions. He tried to be fair to his staff and pay them well, and he believed that this was the reason he'd held on to his best bartenders, Kitty and Zack, for as long as he had.

Admittedly, Kitty was his sister's best friend, but she'd had her fair share of short-term jobs and said she was happy working at Butler's. And Zack was ambitious and had made this clear to Cal, who planned to reward him with a managerial role in the new bar. Things on that front were running as smoothly as expected, so Cal could lay off the worrying, thankfully, since he had enough to think about with his father's health and the baby that may or may not be his.

Cal glanced across the coffee shop again to the almond-mocha redhead sitting at the front window typing away on her laptop. Maybe she was creating a vanity-driven social media post. Since being with Elisabetta, Cal considered an awful lot whether people were taking photos to post online. The bar had an active social media presence, but it was a tightly controlled and professional one. Elisabetta, however, would take photos of Cal doing things like drinking a morning coffee in his boxers and, without his permission, post it online. He knew that, considering he was only thirty-four, it made him a bit of a fuddy-duddy, but he wasn't a fan of the way social media made people behave. And he especially disliked being used for likes. A bar owner didn't need to be a celebrity, however minor. His younger brother, Jamie, who was never going to win any tech innovation prizes himself, found Cal's attitude amusing and backward, often joking that their mother had a sharper grip on modern technology than Cal. 'I can use technology fine,' Cal had said. 'It's the fact that I do know how it works that bothers me.'

Cal was thinking about the creamy skin on Almond-Mocha Redhead's neck when she turned around and caught him watching. He glanced back down to his phone. *Was I staring at her?* Scratching the back of his neck, to give the impression of being busy, he absentmindedly drifted to the Twitter account he rarely used. A dangerous move because when he opened his notifications, he realised someone had tagged him in about a hundred conversations about Elisabetta

Angelsey's baby – or #babybetta as it was being hashtagged. For goodness sake! Elisabetta herself was remarkably quiet, having kindled the fire that she knew would rage on of its own accord. This burned Cal with annoyance.

Cal rubbed across his jaw and glanced back up towards the redhead, who was turned to her laptop screen again, although she'd pulled her hair out of its clip and it was sitting in soft curls across her shoulders. *How can the back of a woman be so damned attractive? Should I offer to buy her a coffee? What harm could it do? At the least, she'll be as annoying as she first was, and I can scratch her from my mind.*

Cal sauntered over to her seat by the door. It was then he noticed the woman had ear buds in and was laughing and chatting to someone on the phone. Her voice wasn't loud enough to reach the back of the coffee shop, but anyone this close could hear it all. This put him off her on two counts: one, she was busy so he couldn't interrupt, and two, people who talked on their phones in enclosed public places were idiots.

'I think I've found him, but lost him already,' the woman said. There was a silence as she listened while the other person spoke, then she laughed. 'But you know what? You were right. It has made me perked me up getting out of my comfort zone.'

Found him but lost him? Cal's brow furrowed. Who was she looking for? Regardless, he'd missed the moment for offering her a coffee and now he had to get back to work.

The woman caught Cal's eye as he walked past, and her face fell a little in surprise. He nodded politely at her and left the coffee shop.

Chapter Seven

Bea hung up the call to Amira. She'd needed to debrief after the strange meeting with the man at the counter. Despite not witnessing events, Amira would help her see that she hadn't made a complete fool of herself. But in Bea's daze of chagrin, she had forgotten about the time difference, so the call was brief and she had let Amira go back to bed mere seconds after the man had left the coffee shop. It was shocking to see him inches away from her as she declared into the phone she had 'found him but lost him', but she had assuaged herself with the insistence that he couldn't possibly know she was referring to him.

Bea decided that even if the man was a lost cause she could use the encounter somehow, so she spent the next hour making notes about the new hero of her next novel, using him as inspiration. But as she wrote, she became more and more intrigued about the actual person behind the cool and some-what grouchy exterior. Was there a way to meet him again? Perhaps she should have followed him out of the coffee shop when she had the chance: let him lead her to his place of work and...

Oh stop, Bea, you sound like a stalker.

But he was so handsome. And there was electricity – wasn't there?

A short while later, Bea packed up her laptop, put on her coat and moseyed over to the counter to ask the barista another question. She was less nervous than last time, due to not having to orchestrate a meet cute with a smouldering Scottish man. This time her objective was simply to find out when he might be back here.

'Um... you know that guy who was behind, or rather, in front of me in the line earlier,' Bea asked the barista. 'Does he come in here regularly?'

The barista gave Bea a knowing smile. 'He's here from time to time.'

'Oh, okay.' Bea was disappointed that she couldn't depend on meeting him here again tomorrow.

'But his name's Cal Butler. He owns Butler's bar on Advocate's Close. Pretty sure you'll find him there most days.'

Bea's face lit up. 'Oh, thank you.' She popped a couple of pounds into the tip jar. 'I'm sorry if I was rude before. I was a little preoccupied. The cake was exceptional though.'

'No problem.' The barista shook her head. 'Good luck.'

The rain had stopped, and the sun was peeking through the clouds, so Bea headed back to the apartment with her head up, past colourful shop fronts and statues with tales to tell and crowds of tourists snapping photographs and soaking everything in whilst walking in the leisurely way that tourists did. There was a vibrant energy that energised Bea, the caffeine pulsing thorough her veins and the thrill of meeting a gorgeous man no doubt assisting it. She wandered into a vintage clothing store and allowed herself to purchase a cute peach cashmere sweater, on account of it being fall soon and the Scottish weather necessitating a warmer wardrobe than she had anticipated.

Back at the apartment, the walls were still dirty and the paintings still hideous, but Bea had a little more buoyancy. She flexed her fingers and read the words below them: *Cal Butler, Butler's bar, Advocate's Close.* A knot of nerves tightened in her stomach at the thought of essentially having to stalk the man if she wanted to see him again. It was not in Bea's nature to be so brazen.

But she didn't have to think about that. This afternoon, she could embrace her introverted side and channel the sexy vibes that meeting Cal Butler had generated into wonderful words on the page. She would write as much as she could, then if she could meet him again and learn more, that would be even better. On top of the story their encounter would become, imagine getting to know him and being able to tell him he was her muse. What man wouldn't love that surprise?

Chapter Eight

At eleven the following day, the bar was cool and silent. In the four years he'd owned Butler's, Cal had never grown tired of the sanctuary of the morning moments spent alone. Kitty and Zack were busy elsewhere, and it would be an hour before the bar opened for lunch.

Cal tried calling Elisabetta again but, as yesterday, the phone rang to voicemail. It was possible she was avoiding him as an attention seeking strategy. He moved his focus to researching motor neurone disease. There must be something that could be done to help his father – to get them all some control over the situation.

Then, as the search listings loaded, something in the doorway caught his attention. Cal glanced up and did a double take. What the hell? Almond-Mocha Redhead from the coffee shop was standing in the door frame. Had he left the door unlocked?

'Oh, hello.' A strange breezy energy blew through the woman's voice and she was wearing an over-the-top smile that didn't quite suit her. It was almost as if she was faking it. Cal's mind flashed back to the words he'd heard from her phone call: 'I've found him'. He spoke without missing a beat, 'We don't do almond milk.'

'I'm sorry. You must think I'm following you,' the woman said.

'Are you?'

'Oh, no, of course not. But, um... this is a coincidence.'

'It's a small city,' Cal said flatly. He couldn't turn away a potential customer, but he was cautious about this woman. It would take a big coincidence for her to have just stumbled upon his bar down this narrow close, even if it was in the busiest part of town. 'Did you want a drink? Is that why you're here?'

'Well, now that you suggest it, that would be lovely.' The woman stepped over the threshold. She was stunningly beautiful; Cal could admit that to himself: curvaceous hips, ample breasts, red hair spiralling tantalisingly around her face. But it wasn't enough to cancel out her irritating nature. Or the weirdness of her presence here.

'Now that I suggest it?' Cal's gaze narrowed. 'You walk into a bar but only think to have a drink when the bartender suggests it?'

'Yes, um ... why not?' The woman's voice was as bright as sunshine. 'What would you recommend?' She moved to the bar and scanned the bottles on the back wall. Cal examined her from behind. Her curves were even more pronounced from this angle; she had a perfect hourglass figure. Then he shook his thoughts from those that caused complications to whisky.

'The *Bruichladdich.*' Cal put his phone in his pocket and got up to serve the woman. He'd get her a drink, then get rid of her as quickly as possible.

'Okay, I'll have one of those. Or two?' She nodded towards him as if to ask whether he would join her for a whisky.

'I never drink before twelve. Or when I'm on duty.' This was true.

'A man who likes to be in control of his faculties. I admire it.' Almond Mocha Redhead arched a perfectly sculpted eyebrow over a glittering sapphire blue. She was right. Cal liked to be in control of things. But he didn't like the way she flirtatiously tried to compliment him. It was too clichéd. Too obvious. He poured a measure of the whisky and placed the drink on the bar in front of the woman, watched as she raised the glass to her lips, took a generous sip of the Scotch, then made a face as if she'd had liquid honey licked from her breasts.

'Mmm,' she said. 'I have no idea who Broo Claddy, or whoever, is, but his whisky is divine.'

Cal's insides stirred at this lustful appreciation of Scotch. He folded his arms in defence.

'Brui-CH-laddy,' he said, placing a forceful emphasis on the 'ch' sound she'd missed. 'Can I get you anything else or will that be all?'

'Broo-ICK-laddy. Ick … ick. I can't get it like you can.'

Cal shook his head. What was this nonsense?

'While I'm here,' the woman said, moving away from the accent offensive, 'I'd like to apologise again for pushing in front of you in the coffee shop.'

'There's no need. Truly. I'm a big lad and I'm over it. Worse things happen in here every night.'

'Well, that leads to why I'm here.' The woman put down her glass. 'Assuming you're the boss. You could just be an incredibly capable bartender.'

Cal stiffened. 'Yep, I'm the boss. What do you want?' He was aware he sounded brusque but he needed to communicate to this woman that he wasn't in the mood for flirting, if that was what she was trying to do.

'Well … 'Almond Mocha Redhead tilted her head to one

side, met him dead on with her sapphire eyes dazzling under lusciously long lashes, and hit him with a question he hadn't been expecting. 'Are you, by any chance, hiring?'

Chapter Nine

This flirting wasn't coming as easily to Bea as she'd hoped. And that her flirtee was one prickly customer didn't help. *The worst thing is, each time he rebuts me, I become a more of parody of someone flirting.* First, she was spurred on by the whisky comment, and now she'd surprised herself by asking for a job. It was awful but she couldn't drop the act mid-scene. That would be even more bizarre. Fortunately, she didn't need to back out of the job pursuit: because of her father's heritage, Bea owned a British passport and had the right to work in Scotland, so she hadn't stepped down a dead-end close. *Except that you've come to Scotland for a vacation and your time should be spent either writing or rejuvenating by taking in the sights. You don't need extra responsibilities. Conversely, working for this Cal Butler guy might not be work at all – rather exceptionally enjoyable research.*

'I'm not hiring,' Cal said flatly, putting Bea's dreams to bed in a clinical manner.

'Oh.' She nodded and tried to perk up to cover her disappointment. 'Not to worry. I'll see if any of the other bars might be.' This was a lie, as Cal Butler was the only drawcard to bartending while here.

'Some will be. A lot of them have a quick turnover of staff. We treat our staff well, so we don't.'

'Okay, thanks for the tip.' Bea made for the door, trying to appear casual but wishing she had another reason to stay and try to get to know this guy. As it happened, she didn't need to.

'You know you need a visa to work here?' Cal said as she turned away. 'I don't mean to assume, but I thought you were a visitor.'

'Ah, yes, well, I am a visitor, of sorts, but I also have Scottish heritage which allows me a passport and the right to work here.'

'I see.' Cal nodded. 'That's fortunate. Well, good luck.'

'Yes, I am lucky.' Bea flipped Cal's good luck comment around to keep the conversation going. 'I'm also a little remiss, because you already think I'm the rudest person on the planet, then I burst in here asking for a job without even telling you who I am.' She held her hand out for Cal to shake. 'Bea Gracie.'

Cal reached out and encased her in his cool, firm grip. 'Cal Butler.'

'Nice to meet you, Mr Butler.'

He creased his brow as if confused at Bea's sudden polite formality.

'Cal is fine,' he said. 'So, you came over here for a working holiday?' Manners must be the way to penetrate Cal Butler's cool exterior, although he wasn't exactly fervent in his inquisitiveness.

'Yes, kind of. I'm a writer, and I came to write. I set my next book in Scotland, but, well ...' Bea laughed to mask her embarrassment. 'I'm not a terribly successful writer, so I thought, why not immerse myself in life here by getting a job and getting to know the locals, learn about Scottish life, and earn a little money at the same time?'

Was Bea imagining it or did Cal sharpen his gaze, scrutinise her? Did he know that this was essentially a lie, that she hadn't come to Scotland intending to get a job? That until she had walked into this bar and asked if he was hiring, the only plan was to write?

'What kind of stuff do you write?' he asked.

'Oh, it's probably not anything you've heard of.' If Bea were to admit that she wrote romance, then he might work out that she wanted to use him as a muse.

'I've maybe not heard of you, but I'm sure I'll know the genre unless it's some new Australian vampire architect love story genre or something.'

Bea laughed. He did have a sense of humour. 'Well, funny you should say that...'

Cal's eyes widened.

'You got the love bit right. I'm a romance writer. No vampires, architects or Australians so far, though.'

For a moment that could have been an hour, Cal examined Bea's face. What on earth was he searching for? Or had he seen something? Worked out that she was tracking down a muse and had her sights on him? Was she that transparent?

'I see,' he said, finally. 'Well, look, Bea...'

Oh goodness, maybe he was going to change his mind and offer her a job. That would be fantastic.

But Cal pulled her empty glass back to his side of the bar. 'I have to get on. We open shortly. But all the best with your job search and time in Edinburgh.'

'Oh yes.' Bea slid off her bar stool thinking she must have been right about him seeing through to her muse plan. 'I'm sorry for taking up your time. And thank you. Look ... why don't I leave my contact details in case anything comes up here? I've several years' experience tending bar in New York

City.' She rifled through her bag for a piece of paper. 'I think I've a paper and pen in here somewhere.'

As efficient as he was gorgeous, Cal pushed a small pad across the bar and passed Bea a pen. She scribbled down her name, her US mobile number and email address.

'Sorry, I don't have a UK cell yet,' she said, 'but I've added my email there too.'

'Thanks.' Cal glanced at what she'd written but gave nothing away about whether he might be in touch. Although he did ask how long she would be in town, which could mean that he was considering her potential as a member of his staff.

'My flight home is three months from now, although it's flexible,' she told him.

'Okay dokes,' said Cal, whatever that meant. If it had a hidden meaning in it, Bea couldn't work it out.

'Well, I guess this is goodbye,' she said.

'Aye,' said Cal as if not remotely bothered by the prospect of never seeing Bea again, which she supposed was understandable. 'Enjoy the rest of your trip in Scotland.' He walked her to the door, opened it and even let a smile inch onto his lips. She mirrored the expression but had no choice but to bid farewell to the perfect Scottish man without having secured a third meeting.

Chapter Ten

Ten days later, early on Saturday morning, Cal and Eilidh were floating on their surfboards waiting for the waves to pick up.

'This might have been a waste of time,' Cal said of the flat waters in front of them. 'Think the best was before sunrise.'

'I agree,' said Eilidh. 'Which is frustrating because I needed this today.'

'Bad week at school?' Eilidh worked as a teacher in a somewhat notorious inner-city Edinburgh school. Cal was in complete admiration of her tenacity and ability to connect with the most difficult of students.

'Yeah, work's been tough. That, on top of worrying about Dad, isn't helping.'

'I understand.' Cal circled his thumb round a lump of wax on his board. 'I've been doing the same. Although we might be doing more worrying than he is; he's probably cracking on with work.' Both his parents were hard workers but Jimmy Butler filled each moment and beyond with industry, although he did know how to stop intermittently and enjoy the good times with his family. Cal and his siblings remembered with fondness the times from their childhood when their father had brought home a signed football and kicked it around with them in the garden or let himself be buried in freezing sand at the beach or helped with their Halloween make-up. It hadn't happened loads, but when it had it made them happier than skylarks.

'Have you spoken to him since Mum called?' Eilidh asked.

'Nope because Mum told us he doesn't want to talk about it on the phone and I don't suppose an email would be his cup of tea either. I'd go over there but during the festival isn't a time I can leave the bar.'

'Same,' said Eilidh. 'I'm flat out with tutoring on the weekends now school is back. I guess we'll see him at his birthday party but I'd like to do something now. I don't suppose he'd appreciate a surprise visit either.'

'I don't think he would,' agreed Cal. 'There is something I'm going to try when I get home, though.'

'Yeah? What's that?'

'I'll tell you after.' Cal motioned to the incipient ocean swell a few metres away that held promise of morphing into a beautiful wave. 'Get this one and forget about your worries for a bit.'

An hour later, Cal's finger was hovering over the call button on his phone. He'd prefaced the number with 141 so it would show up as unknown on his father's end, guilt gnawing at him for doing so, but his father would be more likely to answer a number that might be a business contact. Cal had wondered about calling his mother instead – she would blether away no bother – but it wasn't her he needed to talk to. He pressed the call icon.

After five rings, his father answered the phone with the greeting 'Moshi moshi.' Why was he talking in Japanese?

'Hey, Dad? It's Cal. How are you doing?' Was that a stupid thing to ask someone with a progressive illness? But what else were you meant to ask? *Are you feeling better* wasn't right, was it?

'Oh hello, Callum.' Jimmy Butler sounded surprised to hear from his eldest son, as if he didn't expect him to have time to call. 'I thought you might be Mr Yamamichi.'

'Aye, sorry about that. It's just little old me. How are you?'

'I'm doing away, thanks,' said Jimmy. 'Making the most of life as ever.'

Cal was listening for sounds in his father's voice that would betray his illness, but he heard none. It was still early days, but he didn't want to make any assumptions.

'How are your um … symptoms?' he enquired.

'My symptoms,' Jimmy chuckled throatily, 'are behaving themselves for now.'

Cal pressed his temples. His father could very well be masking. It would be typical of him to hide his struggles. He could be going down on the Titanic and still insist he was fine and dandy. Cal would have to cut to the chase.

'Right, well,' he said. 'I was reading about motor neurone disease, and I saw this story where a guy had managed to stave off the symptoms for longer than the average by getting things like special physio and occupational health as well as an emotional support therapist.'

A momentary silence filled the line. 'Och, I don't need any of that stuff,' said Jimmy, and Cal wondered if it was a mistake to phrase the therapist as emotional support. That wouldn't appeal to his father's masculine pride.

'Anyway, I don't know how much there is at the hospital up there,' Cal went on. 'But I've been doing research and making some calls and I've made a list of top-notch therapists that would be able to see you online. It means you could get access to the best care despite living more remotely.

I think it could help you and I'm more than happy to pay for it.'

Jimmy chuckled. 'Money's not a worry, Son, but I don't think I need any fancy therapists. I'll be fine. I've a nice doctor at the hospital and I've your mother at home.'

Cal tried to sigh silently so as not to reveal his frustration at this statement. Why could his dad not accept help, at the least to ease the burden on Cal's mother? She was still working at the distillery herself in her role as master distiller, a job she loved. However, these circumstances meant she may need to step aside from that position, unless Jimmy would seek support from elsewhere.

'Well, this could help on top of that. Maximise your chances of staving things off for as long as possible.'

Cal could hear his father breathing and some shuffling and he wondered if he was fully focused on the call. He was probably doing paperwork, tidying up his desk or emailing Japan to see what was keeping Mr Yamamichi.

'Look, Dad, I'll tell you what I'll do: I'll email you and Mum a list of the folk I've come up with. If you've got a minute, you could take a squizz at it.'

'Aye, that sounds good, Callum.' More shuffling in the background. 'I do appreciate your concern.'

Cal suspected this amenability to the idea was merely to stop him pursuing it. His father would always do things his own way. But before Cal had time to think of another approach, his phone vibrated. A check of the display told him the call was from Zack: not someone he usually received phone calls from – unless something was wrong.

'Dad, someone else is calling me. I'll need to go.' Cal had got as far as he could with his father on this call. 'I'll send that list through today. Take care of yourself and say hi to Mum.'

'Aye, thanks, Son.' And before Cal had switched to the

incoming number, his father was gone. He shook his head and turned his attention to the new call.

'Hi, Zack. What's up?'

'Morning, Cal. Sorry to call you so early.'

'Not a problem. Nine isn't early. You okay?'

'Aye, well, yes, but no. My sister went into labour seven weeks early last night, so my other sister and I have been at the hospital in Inverness with her. The baby was born, but it's in intensive care.' Zack's voice cracked a little. 'I needed to be here to support her, what with Mum and Dad not being around and her husband leaving her. I hate to do this, but I won't make it in for my shift tonight. I wanted to give you as much notice as possible.'

Cal stopped Zack before he explained any further. 'Say no more, Zack. It's fine. I'll handle the bar. You make sure your sister is okay. Is there anything I can do to help?'

'Nah, it's fine. As long as you're sure it's alright about the shift?'

'Sounds like your sister might need you up there for a while. You'll be needing more than one shift off.'

'Aye, well possibly, although I didn't like to ask.'

'Zack, you're a great barman, but your sister doesn't have a premature baby every day, so take all the time you need. I'll make sure you are sorted for money, too. Just keep me posted, alright?'

'Will do,' said Zack. 'Thanks, Cal. I appreciate it.'

Cal hung up and took a deep breath. Saturday night and the only staff member he had left was Kitty. This left him in a bit of a predicament on the busiest night of the week, not to mention slap bang in the middle of the Edinburgh Festival when the Old Town was heaving with people.

Dressing quickly, Cal grabbed breakfast and made some calls to his other staff to see if they could work a last-minute shift. But Cleo was busy babysitting, Jake had a wedding to attend, and Jas had a gig with her band.

Damn. Cal ended the call to Jas. *Looks like it's me and Kitty.*

With a coffee-to-go, Cal jumped in the car to drive into town. He'd bought a beachside cottage because he would far rather drive to work than drive to the surf. Without surfing, Cal was sure he'd be a lot more stressed out. During a hot and sticky evening shift, he needed the promise of fresh Scottish waves crashing over his head the next morning. But the surfing was done for the day, and the real world was creeping in. He sipped his coffee and thought about how to staff tonight's shift.

A small voice in the recesses of Cal's mind reminded him of the piece of paper in the top drawer of his desk which could solve his problem: a piece of paper he purposefully hadn't thrown away but was ignoring for a reason. *She's too beautiful. A woman that attractive knows it and plays on it. Remember the way she flirted as she came into the bar, wanting something and using her feminine wiles to try and get it. You won't be falling for that nonsense anymore.*

She did say she was an experienced bartender, though. And you need one of those.

After a near hour of driving and deliberation, Cal reached his office, sighed and pulled open his desk drawer to retrieve Bea's details. But the note was nowhere to be seen. A quick rummage didn't bring it to the fore either. He was sure he'd put it there but out of sight – to forget Bea yet reach her if needed.

But then Cal remembered something. The evening after Bea had visited Butler's, he'd enjoyed a drink in his city flat. The whisky had loosened him up and he'd gone online to see the latest on Elisabetta and the baby. His infuriation at her continuing game of cat and mouse had led him to swear that he was done with women, so to prove it to himself, he'd gone downstairs, unlocked the bar and, to avoid temptation, thrown the paper out.

What a numpty. Come on. You're strong enough to resist the eyelashes of a pair of tempting blues when they're fluttered at you. You can work with this woman. Get it together and get in touch to ask if she can cover a few shifts in the bar.

'Aye, that's all well and good,' Cal replied to himself out loud. 'But how are you going to get in touch when you don't have her number, eh? Like I said, you're a numpty.'

Chapter Eleven

Bea was so inspired by Cal that the short story she'd begun – in which an American writer meets a Scottish barman and they end up in hot and steamy circumstances – was flowing onto her keyboard. Her regular writing residence was the coffee shop in which she'd found herself on her first day in Edinburgh, and where good things happened. After all, this was the place she'd bumped into her delectable muse, although in the story she had loosely changed his name to Hal Hunter to protect his identity. The plan was to publish the story to her website as an apology to her fans for not being around during her vacation, and to give them a taste of the novel to come.

Craving another coffee, Bea turned to the counter to see what the queue was like. And that's when her heart shot into her throat. Standing right next to her was Cal Butler, his clear green eyes piercing her own.

'Morning,' he said, in his low Scottish burr that sent a river of warmth like whisky straight through Bea.

'Hey! Good morning!' Bea could barely mask the delight she felt, particularly as she was thinking about Cal so much that he had almost become a fantasy figure in her mind. 'I wasn't sure we would ever meet again. Would you, um ... like a coffee? A seat?' Bea then inwardly cursed herself for being giddily over the top in the face of his reserved coolness.

'I'm not here for coffee.' Cal said flatly.

That's a great line, thought Bea, imagining her protagonist saying it before sweeping up the heroine and taking her to bed. *I must remember to use that.* She gazed at Cal and wondered if he could read her thoughts. Then she remembered the story on her laptop and pulled the lid down gently in case he should spot some incriminating evidence.

'I'm here to see if you might still be available to come and work for me.' Cal shuffled a little. 'I'm having a few staffing problems. It's the busiest time of the year, and I could do with someone experienced.'

Oh wow! This is unexpected yet amazing. Bea wanted to jump up and whoop with delight. *I'll get to work with Cal Butler after all. This will make for some great writing; some wonderful experiences; some amazing... Okay, so I might be jumping the gun a little to expect that I'll sleep with him, but how's a girl meant to not imagine that? He's so utterly...*

'Well?' Cal was staring at Bea expectantly. 'Are you available?'

Bea realised she'd been in a daze.

'Um, yes,' she said. 'I am. I mean, I was planning to spend the evening writing and taking a nice soapy bath, but I can do those things tomorrow night.'

'Right, okay.' Cal did that shuffling thing again. Had the image of her in a soapy bath crept into his mind? Bea hoped so. She'd love to share a big tub of suds with this guy.

'Would you be able to come in around five so I can show you the ropes before things get busy around seven?' Once more, Cal had pulled Bea out of her little fantasy. 'And to do some paperwork. Bring your passport and other ID.'

'Can do.' Bea tried her best to be a little more professional. 'Is there anything in particular I should wear?'

Cal glanced over Bea's skinny black jeans, pastel-lemon blouse and black sneakers combo. 'What you're wearing now is fine. I'll give you a company shirt to wear though.'

A hot pulse thumped through Bea as Cal's eyes hit her chest. He wasn't inspecting her breasts; she could tell that. She'd had enough sleazy men ogling her to know when that was the case. But, for a moment, his vision was right there and it made her flutter with excitement at the thought of his gaze feasting on what was beneath her clothing. Marvellous things really did happen in this coffee shop.

Chapter Twelve

For the rest of the day, Cal did paperwork, dealt with suppliers and helped behind the bar during the lunchtime rush. By the time 5 p.m. rolled around, he genuinely hadn't had a moment to stop and think about anything: not his father, not the baby and not the beautiful, voluptuous redhead who was coming to work bar that evening. So when he looked up to see Bea standing in the doorway of his office, he did a double take, then inwardly cursed himself for behaving like some ridiculous cartoon character. *Try to be professional, Butler.*

'I'll need to take copies of your paperwork,' Cal told Bea as she took a seat on the other side of his desk. 'And then I'll show you around.'

Standing with her passport at the photocopier, Cal tried not to stare at Bea's photo. It was difficult. Few people came out well in passport photographs, but she did. No rabbit in headlights stare or under-eye luggage for her. Her skin was blemish free and her sapphire eyes were as glittering as they were in real life. Cal checked out her date of birth; she was thirty, four years younger than him. All compatible with working in the bar. *Because that's why you have this paperwork, remember? Don't be one of those sleazy boss types who ogles their staff. Keep things professional.*

'So, you've several years' bar experience?' Cal sat down behind his desk again, attempting to focus on an interview and find out a little about Bea's background before officially hiring her.

'Yes,' Bea said. 'I've worked in several of the busiest bars in Manhattan, some of which are popular with high-end clientele. You can contact any of them for a reference.'

'That's excellent.' The experience on Bea's CV was impressive. No doubt there were more demanding customers in NYC than she'd find in Butler's. If her experience was as she claimed, she would fit right into the job and do well – which then begged the question...

'So how long did you say you were planning to stay in Scotland? You're here to write a book?'

'Yes, bartending is my trade and writing my passion. I am hoping to stay for three months, but I could extend, depending on what happens. Scotland is so inspirational.' Bea regarded Cal with a twinkle from under swan-like lashes.

'I see.' Cal shifted a little in his seat. This woman was so beautiful it unnerved him. And what was she getting at about 'inspiration' whilst staring like that? 'Scotland is indeed a beautiful country,' he said, focusing on the sexually neutral part of the conversation.

'It is. I can't believe it's taken me thirty years to come here.' Bea beamed and held his gaze. 'My father always said we should vacation here, but somehow we never had enough money to do so and sadly he passed away before we had a chance to visit together. He used to tell me so many tales about Edinburgh that it's like I know the place.'

'I'm sorry to hear that about your father,' Cal said sympathetically. 'And that's a shame about the vacation, but nice that you're at home here.' He shuffled the papers into a neat pile and passed the originals back across the table to Bea. 'Okay, that's the paperwork out of the way. I'll show you round the bar and introduce you to the others.' He rose from his seat and straightened his tie.

By the time Cal had given Bea her full induction it was like the scent of amber and honeysuckle was embedded in his olfactory system, not to mention the effect it was having on other parts of his body. Physically, something about this woman made his blood rush. Personality wise, he wasn't sold; she was overly breezy. But that was fine because it made it easier to ignore the subtle advances she threw his way. *Focus on the fact that her personality is annoying, not the fact that her legs are long and her neck is slender and completely kissable.*

As the evening morphed into night, customers were flowing into the bar like fast-moving treacle, although it was still light outside on account of the long, light summer evenings Scotland enjoyed. Throughout the shift, Cal served drinks, kept his attention on the floor and, in the name of monitoring her welfare and performance, glanced frequently towards Bea.

What he saw impressed him. Besides the fact that she would occasionally take a little longer do things, due to her unfamiliarity with the bar layout, she appeared entirely comfortable at Butler's. She could pull a perfect pint; there hadn't been a single cocktail for which she'd had to look up the ingredients nor a customer she didn't greet warmly. And many of them – particularly the male clientele – returned that warmth. Cal would need to monitor them; he couldn't have his bar staff being harassed or made uncomfortable.

'How're you getting on?' Cal inquired when Bea was between customers.

'I'm having a great time.' She flashed a wide grin and blew her hair off her forehead. 'Hot and busy, but it's great. I love the atmosphere. Everyone is so friendly.'

'Aye.' Cal glared at a customer who was ogling Bea. 'They can be. But don't take any crap from anyone, okay?'

'Oh, I never do,' said Bea. 'I know exactly how to deal with a tough customer, don't you worry.'

'I'll try not to.' Cal didn't need any more worries, seeing as he was already concerned with the fact that, on top of her physical attributes, he found this woman's competence behind his bar intoxicatingly and distractingly attractive. And that, since he was her boss, he really should not.

Chapter Thirteen

Bea had meant it when she told Cal how much she was enjoying her first shift at Butler's. Since quitting bartending in the spring, at Josh's behest, she'd missed it. Protestations to Josh that it was what she was familiar with, that the hours allowed her to get on with her writing, and that the tips were good, were countered with the argument that he could support her so she'd have all the time she needed to write.

In many ways, this was ideal for Bea as writing was her first love, but it didn't take long for the subtle sideswipes to come from Josh about how exhausting it was being the main bread-winner. As far as Bea could see, he wasn't working any harder than before she'd given up her job; he just liked to wield power over her. With the benefit of hindsight, Bea could see that he'd been manipulating her, although that insight wasn't enough to make the legacy of inadequacy subside fully.

An additional positive of being back behind a bar and earning her own money came from working so closely in the presence of the beautiful Cal Butler. Bea hadn't expected the owner of a successful bar to be serving customers himself, but

Cal liked to muck in with the rest of the staff. A small part of Bea – the part affected by Josh – wondered if he might be a bit of a control freak.

'Do you always work bar on a Saturday night?' she asked at the end of the shift, as they tidied up.

'Aye, of course,' he'd said, shrugging as if it were a strange question. 'It's my bar. If I hadn't wanted to work bar on a Saturday night, I'd have set up a cheese shop.'

'A cheese shop?'

'Or whatever. That's just an example. Point is, I'm not in the habit of hiding in the back office while my staff toil out front.'

'I wish some of my previous bosses were like you.' Bea meant in terms of work ethic, although she was aware of the other interpretation of her words. Not that it mattered. A little flirting couldn't do any harm, could it? Loosen the tension a little.

'Speaking of working, best get on and get things cleaned up.' Cal directed Bea's attention to the empty glasses scattered across the tables. 'Don't want to be here all night.'

'No, of course not.' *Surely, we could chat and clear at the same time but for all his team spirit, he doesn't want to talk to me. Have I done something wrong?*

'Do you live near the bar?' Bea decided to keep making an effort. She'd get through to this guy, eventually.

'I've a flat upstairs,' Cal said. 'But I mainly live in a cottage out of town.'

Well, he'd answered her question, although it sounded like he hadn't wanted to impart the information. And he hadn't asked her anything in return. *I guess he already knows where I'm living, since he's seen my résumé. But he could have asked if I've settled in okay, or how I'm enjoying Edinburgh.*

'Oh, how lovely to have a flat upstairs. So you can flop into bed as soon as work is over?' Bea could have sworn he stiffened slightly. Maybe he'd interpreted this as flirting and it made him uncomfortable, although she was simply being friendly. There was no need for him to assume that she was suggesting they flop into bed together.

'Yep, it's pretty handy. But I prefer to get out of town.'

'What's your cottage like?' Bea was genuinely interested.

'Not much to describe. It's small, but it's home. Would you mind giving those tables a wipe please? I'll do the ones over here.'

'Sure.'

Cal passed Bea a cloth and their fingers touched momentarily. She glanced up at him and the briefest of electrical storms crackled overhead. But the skies were clear outside. This was something between her and Cal only, not experienced by the rest of the city. His eyes flickered for a moment, before he rubbed the back of his neck and looked away as if nothing had occurred.

'Thanks,' he said.

Okay, that definitely wasn't a one sided thing. But he's ignoring it, trying to keep me at arm's length. Either that or he's not very friendly.

But Bea had seen Cal be friendly enough to all the customers. No, something else was going on. *Oh well, I'm here to write a book. So, if he's going to be frosty then so be it. It wouldn't be an interesting book if the hero and heroine fell into bed together without a bit of tension, would it?*

Bea wiped the tables. Hopefully time would warm things between her and Cal. And it would be good for her to flirt a little with a guy after all the years of her personality being trodden into the ground by Josh. Just gentle flirting, though. There was no need to play the pushy femme fatale now she was here with Cal and the fizz between them was established. Softly would do it. If something happened, then great. If it didn't, then she would still have met a hot Scotsman to give her writing inspiration. And the most wonderful thing about this whole experience was that she was thousands of miles from home and whatever was ahead of her, it would be like it wasn't real. It would be pure holiday escapism – like one of her stories.

Chapter Fourteen

After the busy night and all Bea's talk of flopping into bed, Cal realised he wasn't in the mood for the drive back to the cottage. He'd miss his Sunday morning surf but could make up for it on Monday. So, after ensuring that Bea and Kitty had taxis home, he locked up the bar, headed to the flat upstairs and poured himself a bedtime dram.

Thoughts of the evening filtered through Cal's mind as he decompressed. The bar was abuzz with customers, some regulars and many Edinburgh Festival revellers. At this time of year the population of Edinburgh doubled in size with all the visitors to the largest arts festival in the world. Without Zack, the evening had threatened to be a disaster, but Bea had easily slotted in and found her feet. She'd served as many customers as Cal or Kitty – give or take a few. She hadn't once complained about being tired, and she'd gone to change the barrel without hesitation when one of the ales ran out. She was warm and friendly and ... well, she was stunning. Cal inhaled. He could still smell her scent in his nostrils. How, in amongst the bar smells of beer and hundreds of people had that endured?

In the stillness, Cal could hear echoes of Bea's laughter as she shared passing jokes with customers. She had a way about her that could make patrons feel special and noticed, and that kept them coming back. She'd tried that on him as they were cleaning up afterwards. Questions about where he lived and what his cottage was like. Cal was stand-offish with her; he knew that. He couldn't bring himself to let his guard down. First off, he was her boss, so it was unprofessional to divulge too much. But there were other reasons too. He didn't want to let a woman in. Couldn't. It was like a reflex since Elisabetta, not to mention some who'd come before. Best to be alone for a while. Especially when so much other stuff was happening.

Cal checked his personal emails. There was an email from his brother Jamie entitled *Dad's 60th*. A reminder to organise the alcohol for his father's birthday the following month. Each year, Amanda Butler hosted a big birthday bash at their home in Kinshore for her husband. His children took their part in planning the event. Jamie was based in Kinshore so, along with Nate and Sean who also lived there, he took charge of most of the logistics. Cal with his links to breweries usually arranged for all the alcohol to be delivered.

Cal replied to the email thanking Jamie, checked a few other messages, sipped his whisky, leaned back on the couch and exhaled. When he inhaled again, he could still smell amber and honeysuckle. As he closed his eyes, she was right there, in her Butler's uniform, his surname on her ample breast. Smiling at him. Laughing warmly. Then she was dancing her nails with their perfect French manicure over the buttons on her shirt and flicking each of them out of their resting place.

For a moment, Cal considered fighting these thoughts, but why bother? He was alone in his flat and there was a difference between having the woman here and having thoughts about her. He continued to let imaginary Bea unbutton her shirt, glimpses of the lace of her bra appearing now. Her creamy cleavage right there before him. Cal sighed and felt himself loosen and harden at the same time. *Damn!* He hadn't wanted this to happen. Not even thoughts of her. But she was too much to ignore. *They're just thoughts. And you're hard as a rock now, so there's no going back.* Bea's bra was off. She'd undone it herself and her bounteous breasts were pointing upwards, perfectly rounded nipples calling out to be sucked. He did so, moving his hand downwards, unbuttoning her jeans and reaching into her panties to find the soft wetness hidden within.

It was too much. He didn't need to experience any more of Bea's imaginary body. Cal unbuttoned his own fly. He had to release the tension somehow and if he wasn't going to let himself have this woman in real life then he could at least indulge in his imagination.

Chapter Fifteen

The taxi, paid for by Cal, dropped Bea back at her flat after 2 a.m. Despite the hour, she was wide awake. The adrenaline from the shift was still coursing through her veins and she needed time to wind down before she could sleep. A few yoga stretches and some deep breathing would do it.

But yoga and deep breathing had nothing on the memory of one smouldering Scottish bar owner who Bea couldn't stop thinking about. Fantasising about. He smelt lovely; that lime and cedarwood smell she'd first noticed in the coffee shop had lingered all evening behind the bar. It intoxicated her when she was close to him. That combined with meeting those emerald eyes and imagining them locked onto her as he lay on top of her naked, had made it difficult for Bea to recalibrate and focus on the job.

In her attempts to dissipate some of the tension created by an evening in the proximity of Cal Butler, Bea moved to writing. If she put her fantasies down into words while they were fresh and almost tangible, it would free her body of the thoughts. Right?

Who was she kidding? Bea tapped away on her laptop for over an hour, the rough unpolished prose capturing the evening's experiences, the things she noticed about Cal, the way he moved, his energy, the cut of his jaw, the timbre of his voice, how she imagined being in bed with him. The words flowed onto the page, but by the time Bea had finished writing, she found that she'd been so long with imaginary naked Cal Butler – or Hal Hunter – that she had worked herself into an intense state of arousal. There was only one way to unwind.

Bea undressed and stepped into the shower, needing to clean off after the hot, sweaty shift at the bar. And while the water cascaded down over her breasts and onto her already soaking sex, she reached down, shut the world out and imagined it was Cal Butler whose hand, whose mouth even, was on her most intimate parts and bringing her to resounding peaks of sexual pleasure.

Chapter Sixteen

At 11 a.m., Bea climbed out of bed and showered again. Cal had asked if she would work today from four. But first, writing.

Her best intentions notwithstanding, the coffee shop was getting a little boring, and Bea needed to keep things varied, otherwise her writing became stale. She wondered if she could write at the bar. One of those little booths would be ideal. She could even steal glimpses at Cal as she wrote. It wasn't something she'd want to do all the time as she needed space from her workplace, but once could be fun.

Bea arrived at Butler's two hours before her shift and asked Cal if he minded her sitting there to write.

'Um, sure.' He scanned the room, as if wondering why she would want to write in a bar. 'If you don't mind the noise. It's not the quietest time of year. Or the most romantic.' He smiled.

Bea returned the warmth. *He remembers the genre of my writing. How sweet.*

'I'd say you could work in my office,' Cal added. 'But I kind of have a few things I need to be getting on with.'

'Oh, I wouldn't expect to work in your office, but thank you for the thought.'

Bea settled into the booth. Writing in Cal's office would have been wonderful. The scent of him and other reminders of him lingering in the air. Little emblems of who he was. Enveloped by the essence of the man. She could write a scene out of the intoxicating idea of that.

Less than an hour passed, and Bea was blocking out most of the surrounding customer hubbub when a conversation at the bar drew her attention. There was a petite blonde woman, dressed in tight pink jeans and a white blouse and carrying a giant Dior handbag, talking to Kitty.

'Is he here?' the woman was demanding to know.

Kitty, normally warm and amiable, was standing stiffly beside the bar hatch.

'Is who here?'

'Oh, come on, Katy...'

'It's Kitty.'

'Kitty. Well, I presume he's in the office, so I'll go through myself then.' The woman made to lift the bar hatch, but Kitty pushed it down.

'You can't come through here,' she said, palms pressed firmly on the surface. 'It's employees only.'

'Well, I think you know who I am, and you know I've been through there before.' The woman tried to push up the hatch from her side.

'Rules are rules,' said Kitty. 'It's more than my job is worth to...'

'If you're going to be like that, I'll phone him. The woman pulled her phone out of her bag, muttered something incomprehensible and tapped busily on the screen. Moments later, Cal emerged from the office, the enraged expression on his face making the one he wore when meeting Bea for the first time look friendly.

'What's going on?' he asked.

'Well, I came to talk,' said the blonde, 'but this jobsworth here wouldn't let me through to your office.'

Kitty shrugged and moved away from the hatch. 'I'm just doing my job.'

'No, that's fine, Kitty. Thanks. You did the right thing. Carry on with whatever you were doing.' Cal sighed, then lowered his voice so it was difficult for Bea to hear from inside the booth, but from his lip movements, he seemed to be saying, 'Why now?' to the woman. She, not having the same concern for privacy, did not lower her voice and Bea could hear everything.

'You'd like to talk about this in front of the entire bar? If you want the conversation to be online by this evening then go ahead, ask me that here. Otherwise...'

'Jeez,' Cal growled. 'Come through then.' He raised the bar hatch and, face as dark as the brooding Edinburgh skyline, led the woman out of the main bar and through to, presumably, his office where Bea was no longer privy to their conversation.

Bea sidled up to the bar to talk to Kitty. 'Are you okay?' she asked. 'And who on earth was that?'

'Oh, I'm fine,' said Kitty. 'It's nothing I haven't dealt with before. But I can't stand that woman.'

'She's certainly a little, um...'

'High maintenance?' Kitty spoke quietly so as not to sound off in front of the customers.

'Well, I suppose you could say that, yes.' Bea didn't want to pry about who the woman was. If Kitty were to volunteer the information, that would be fine, but she wouldn't press her, although she was insanely curious as to whether this was Cal's girlfriend.

'No idea what he saw in her,' said Kitty, again quietly. 'He deserves so much better than Elisabetta Angelsey.' She shook her head. 'Anyway, you'll be lucky enough not to even know who that is, coming from America.'

Bea laughed. 'You're right. I have absolutely no idea. Is she famous or something?'

'Kind of, but also no. She's mainly a dumb socialite. Best not to know any more.' Kitty glanced around the bar. 'Anyway, I should get on, there's loads to do. You're on at four, yeah?'

'I am,' said Bea. 'But I can start earlier if you like. Looks like you could do with some help.'

'Totally up to you,' said Kitty. 'I'll owe you one if you do.'

Bea grabbed her things from the booth and went through to the staff area to change into her work clothes. On the way, she passed Cal's office, but the thick walnut door blocked any sounds from inside. *Probably just as well,* Bea thought. *I'm keen to find out about Cal Butler but I wouldn't want to do that by eavesdropping on his private conversations.*

Chapter Seventeen

Oh, great, thought Cal. *My newest member of staff witnessing the wonder that is Elisabetta, on her second day on the job.* Not exactly the way to impress your employees. Although why it mattered what they thought of his personal life, Cal wasn't sure. He wasn't especially bothered what Kitty's or Zack's opinion was of his relationship with Elisabetta. He'd kept it to himself, never talked about it, and that was it.

But something was bothering him today about Elisabetta turning up like this at the same time as Bea arriving early for her shift. What was it? That she would think he brought relationship baggage to work? That he'd appeared ruffled and out of control? That Bea thought he associated with demanding and vacuous women? Probably all those things. Bea should see him as the consummate professional, her in-control boss, and now it looked like he let his private and personal lives mix, like some sort of curdled cocktail. One that, instead of giving you a good buzz, made you queasy and never want to go near it again.

Elisabetta appearing unexpectedly irked him. He'd called

her numerous times and she hadn't returned any of his calls. But now she chose to pop up at his workplace. If she wanted to air her laundry in *her* workplace – the internet – that was her choice, but he liked to keep his personal life out of the bar.

'What're you doing here?' Cal asked after he'd closed his office door and was certain nobody else could hear. Elisabetta was sitting on the chesterfield; he was leaning against his desk facing her.

'I think you know why,' Elisabetta said pointedly. 'I'm sure you've seen the messages I've tagged you in.'

'I've seen them.'

'And you didn't think to reply?'

'Sorry, I didn't realise that by tagging me in something that the entire world can read, it counts as a personal message. Were you expecting a response on your timeline or maybe a Tik Tok? I called you, Betta. So many times. I prefer to communicate using this.' Cal pointed to his mouth.

'There's no need to get sarcastic, Cal.' Elisabetta sounded a little choked; Cal was sure she was faking it. 'Although it always was one of your strongest points.'

'Aye, well, I can't help it when I'm placed in some of the most ridiculous scenarios. So, are you going to tell me what's going on?' Cal refused to say the word 'baby'. Elisabetta would need to be the first to say it. She'd been able to say it to the universe via the internet so far.

'I'm having a baby,' Elisabetta finally said.

Cal restrained himself from the impulse to feign surprise. More sarcasm would not help this situation. Playing the game the right way was important for getting straight answers. After all, keeping quiet on social media had led to Elisabetta being forced to come here to see him in person for his reaction.

'I'm aware,' Cal said cooly.

'And you might be the father.'

'Might? Okay.' This was news. Elisabetta was playing it as

if she knew exactly who the father was but didn't want to reveal it to the public so she could string along all potential dads as long as possible. But could it be that she didn't know herself?

'Yes, well, Cal, you need to understand that when we broke up – when you broke it off – I was heartbroken. And I did momentarily turn to someone else to help pick up the pieces.'

'Right.' Cal refrained from commenting that being so heartbroken shouldn't have meant forgetting to ask the guy to wear protection.

'And the dates...' Elisabetta continued. 'Well, I'm 80 per cent sure the baby is yours, but it could also be Tobermory's and—'

'Tobermory! You slept with a guy called Tobermory?'
'Yes.'
'Is he named after the whisky or the womble?'
'After the place, Cal. It's a family name.'
'Okay. Just checking.'
'What difference does his name make? There's a new life coming into the world. All that matters is that it's loved.'

'Aye, I know that. So you're here to let me know in person that I may or may not be the father of a baby that you already announced on social media and that I've already worked out may or may not be mine. What is this visit designed to add to the equation?'

'Are you actually being this heartless?'

Cal shook his head in disbelief. He would never make her see she'd gone about this all the wrong way.

'So you'll be having a paternity test?' he asked.
'Um, yes, although...'
'I'll pay for it, Betta. We need to sort this.'
'I've already told you, I'm 80 per cent sure.'
Cal was seething at what was happening. Elisabetta could

easily take a paternity test to determine who the father of the baby was, but if she could string the whole thing out as long as possible then that would be her preference. 'That's not enough,' he said. 'If we can find out for 100 per cent now, then let's do it. Then I can support you.'

'I mean, it's probably more like 85 per cent.' Elisabetta took her phone, opened an app and held the screen towards Cal. 'You see, we had sex on this date.' She pointed to a coloured grid Cal could barely make head nor tail of. 'And then we broke up and I slept with Tobermory a day or so later, but I think I'd already ovulated by that point.'

Cal glanced briefly at the bamboozling calendar of chaos before turning to the bigger issue. 'Why are you logging the dates you have sex? Why do you have this app? Were you trying to get pregnant?'

Elisabetta was silent, but she didn't need to say anything. That Cal was right was written all over her face.

'I wasn't exactly trying to get pregnant, but I figured that I may as well track things since I was in a committed relationship. I was always faithful to you, Cal.'

'And I was to you, but that doesn't make it okay that you came off the pill without my knowing. You came off the pill, right? That's the only way this kid could be mine. Why are you dangling this in front of me but refusing to take a test to find out?'

'I don't want anything invasive, and what if it's twins? You can't do those tests if its twins.'

'What? Is it twins?' Cal was flabbergasted at the route this conversation was taking.

'Not that I know of, but you never know. There could be one hiding behind the other.' Elisabetta was twisting things any way she could.

'I think we're done here for now.' Cal stood and walked to the door.

'Please, Cal.'

'I don't honestly know what else I can do here, Betta. I will pay for the best paternity test money can buy. If the baby is mine, I will help and support you. But you want me to dangle on a string for another six months. I'm not coming shopping with you for Moses baskets or going to antenatal classes so you can post about it online.'

'You'd make a great dad, Cal.'

Cal exhaled. 'Don't.' He knew Elisabetta was trying to twist things and appeal to his softer side. He would make a good dad – and he hoped that one day he would become a father – but this was blatant manipulation. Cal didn't even know why she was so keen for them to stay a couple, anyway. Besides physical lust, it was an empty relationship. Sure, they'd gone to parties and dined at some of the finest restaurants, but they'd had no connection.

'Okay, I won't say any more.' Elisabetta shrugged. 'But the baby is yours, I'm sure of it.'

'Eighty per cent,' Cal reminded her as he opened the door. 'You're only eighty per cent sure.' Then he was distracted by a flash of red. Bea coming out of the staff changing room. *Damn!*

'I'm sorry we couldn't resolve anything,' he said to Elisabetta, maybe trying a little too forcedly to give their conversation the cover of a business meeting. 'Perhaps if you go away and analyse those figures again, then we can talk further.'

But Elisabetta was no fool. She spotted Bea, too, clocked that Cal was putting on a front and remarked to him that she wasn't one of his business deals. Bea then disappeared back into the bathroom and Cal was left wishing he could sink into a giant bottle of whisky and drink the lot.

Chapter Eighteen

Bea was conscious she had, inadvertently, found herself privy to a Cal-centred drama that she shouldn't be witnessing. She wished to respect his privacy, so she waited several minutes before emerging from the bathroom.

But whatever was going on between Cal and that woman was intense, and Bea couldn't help but be curious. Kitty had mentioned the woman's name was Elisabetta Angelsey, and that she was a socialite. A quick Google search and Bea could probably piece some things together. She reached for her phone from the pocket of her jeans and tapped into the search bar. But then guilt swept in. It was wrong to google her boss's personal life, especially as she was at work. Even doing it in her own time seemed a betrayal to Cal, who was a fair employer. Plus, why would she need to do that? Unless she liked him. And she didn't like him, did she? She wasn't here to 'like like' a man. She was here to research for her novel. Googling wasn't necessary because she wasn't doing background checks for a relationship. Bea slid her phone back into her pocket and headed out to the bar. Despite the momentary setback, she was still early for her shift.

Cal was out front when Bea arrived. He acted as if nothing had happened.

'Hi, Bea, thanks for helping Kitty out. It's much appreciated.'

'Not a problem at all.' She flashed a smile and bounced on her heels. 'Happy to help.'

Cal shot her a half-hearted smile that was possibly meant to be friendlier, then headed back through to his office.

'I feel for him,' Kitty said.

'What? Why?' Bea suspected this had something to do with Elisabetta's visit and that Kitty was about to be rather indiscreet. She wasn't sure she wanted to hear, although at the same time she did.

'Just getting potentially tied to that woman for the rest of his life, you know. Sorry, I shouldn't say anything. It grinds my gears, that's all. Cal's such a great guy, but Elisabetta is giving him the run-around. She should tell him if the baby is his so he can get on with his life.'

'Baby?' *Cal's having a baby with this woman?* Bea grasped onto the beer tap. Oh, my goodness! No wonder he wasn't interested in her flirting. He had bigger things on his mind. A blend of hopelessness and redundancy washed over her, similar to when she discovered Avery was pregnant. 'Cal and the blonde lady are having a baby?' she asked Kitty, aware that her voice sounded robotic and meek.

'Not sure, but probably.' Kitty's face took on a sheepishness. 'But I've said too much already. Just know he's not normally as distant as he has been, but he's got a lot on his mind. He'll appreciate you starting your shift early. Anyway, best get on.' Kitty turned to a customer.

Bea thought again about the baby bombshell and how it made her weak limbed. Why? She'd known Cal for about five minutes. They had a boss–employee relationship, and she was on a temporary trip to gather writing material. This should be ample riches for her novel, plus she'd been thrown another plot line: the hero has a secret love child with his ex-lover potentially stymieing his relations with the heroine. Bea should focus on that aspect rather than the part that gave her the sensation of a rug under her feet being gently tugged at. So, that in mind, she put on her best bartender's face, attended to the customers and tried not to give her worries breathing space.

The following Saturday, Bea noticed a dark-haired man with warm hazel eyes trying to catch her attention from the other side of the bar. Five minutes later, she took an order from him for two beers, and when the man passed her the money for the drinks, he slipped a folded piece of paper into her hand.

She waited until he'd walked away before unfolding it.

Would love to take you out for a drink sometime. Call me! Craig. Then he'd written his number.

That's cute. Bea got hit on a lot in the bars she'd worked in, and this one was no exception, but they weren't often as sweet as to give her a polite note.

Bea located Craig over the other side of the room. He was distributing drinks at a table where his male friends were sitting. As if he knew she was watching, he turned back, caught her eye and shot a smile across the space. Bea gave him a little nod. He was cute. Nowhere near as electrifyingly hot as Cal Butler but definitely cute. And he was more relaxed than Cal. She slipped the note into her back pocket, tried not to break into a grin, and carried on with her shift.

Chapter Nineteen

One Friday afternoon a few weeks later, Cal's sisters, Eilidh and Cara turned up at the bar.

'Two fish and chips and the biggest bottle of champagne, please.' Cara was reverberating with excitement. 'We're celebrating!'

Cara got excited about a lot of things and would drink champagne because she'd had a good day or a because she'd had a bad day, but to Cal this seemed different.'

'What are we celebrating?' he asked. 'You're ultra-pepped about something.'

'Only Cara getting a role in a movie starring the one and only Jackson bloody McGregor.' Eilidh put her arm around her sister and beamed with pride, before apologising. 'Sorry, Car, that wasn't my news to tell.'

'Hey, my news is your news.' Cara leaned into her sister with affection. 'And that is the news!'

'Are you serious?' Cal knew she was. Cara was dedicated beyond measure to her acting career, and it was only a matter of time before it paid off. 'That's a cracking result.' He placed a bottle of the best champagne he stocked onto the bar. 'Tell me more. What's the movie? What's your role? When do you start filming?'

Cara glanced around. 'Well, I'm sworn to secrecy on all those things, so I can't talk about them in a public place like this, but I can tell you that filming begins next year and that it might involve a bit of kissing.'

'Bloody awesome, Car.' Cal popped the cork and poured the bubbling liquid into two glasses. 'We are so proud of you. You deserve this.'

'Thank you! I can't believe it. I know I work hard, but two years on a Scottish soap then a lead role in a Hollywood movie, albeit one filming in Scotland. That doesn't happen.'

'It happened because you're amazing,' said Eilidh. 'But be prepared for an insane amount of scrutiny if you're in a Jackson McGregor film.'

'Meh. Scrutiny, schmutiny.' Cara giggled into her drink. 'Nothing I can't cope with.'

Cal couldn't help but wonder what that level of scrutiny might do, not only to his sister but to the rest of the family. Cara was an immense talent, and he always knew she was going to go far, but what implications could this have? Cara's past, before she'd been adopted along with her triplets Eilidh and Nate, was a troubled one. What dirt might the media try to dig up? He fiercely wanted to protect her – his whole family – from that, at the same time as celebrating her success.

'You drinking with us?' Cara scanned the bar for a glass for Cal to drink from. 'Toast to your favourite sister?'

'Aye, but a soft drink as I'm working.'

'Can you not take the night off and get one of your *people* to cover?' Cara giggled again, probably because she knew Cal didn't refer to his staff as his *people*.

'We can have a drink next week. I'll cook you dinner. Unless you're out for lunch with Jackson McGregor to get on top of your lines.'

'Shhh!' Cara feigned outrage at the volume of Cal's voice. 'No, I'm not doing that for another eighteen months.'

Cara and Eilidh ate their fish and chips, drank champagne and talked non-stop while Cal worked and chatted to them during lulls at the bar. They mentioned continuing the celebrations elsewhere in town and Cal suggested they stay at Butler's. He preferred his sisters to be where he knew they were safe, but they wanted to go on a city adventure, so he proposed they get a lift home with him later or stay over in the upstairs flat.

'Okay, thanks, big bro,' said Eilidh. 'But where will you sleep?'

'Och, I'll——'

'Cal?' Eilidh waved at her brother. 'Where will you sleep? Earth to Cal.'

But Cal was gone from that conversation. His gaze was glued to the door of the bar where Bea – all curves and billowing red hair – was entering in the manner of a model striding down a runway. My God! Each time he saw her, she emptied his lungs of more breath.

'Evening, boss,' Bea chimed, as she approached the bar.

'Hey, Bea. How are you this evening?' Cal tried his best in front of his sisters to not appear utterly beguiled by Bea.

'Great! I got so caught up in some street theatre out there that I nearly forgot I was on my way to work.'

'Yes, that can happen.' Cal chuckled.

'Hey.' Cara waved at Bea. She waited a beat for Cal to make introductions, but when he didn't get in fast enough, she did it herself. 'We're Cal's *weird sisters*. Well, that's what he calls us. I'm Cara and this is Eilidh.'

Cal couldn't help but be amused. He would bet that Kitty had told Cara about the attractive woman working in the bar and now Cara had met her she wanted to see if she was girl-friend material for her brother.

'Weird sisters, huh? I'm charmed. Does that make Cal Macbeth?'

'They do try to tell me what my future holds.' Cal was impressed at Bea's response to Macbeth's witches reference. 'But I tend to ignore it and do my own thing.'

'He *doesn't* want to be king of the family company.' Eilidh spoke pointedly of Cal's reluctance to work for BDL.

'Ah, I see.' Bea laughed. 'Well, he does run a good ship here. Anyway, it's lovely to meet you, but I'm a little late so I'd best get ready for my shift.'

As soon as Bea disappeared to put her bag in her locker, what Cal would have put money on happening, happened.

'Oh my goodness!' Cara put her glass down on the bar.

'Oh my goodness what?' Cal knew exactly what she was getting at but pretended not to.

'She is stunning,' said Eilidh.

'And you guys have chemistry!'

'Aye, she's not bad,' said Cal, knowing fine well he was making a massive understatement.

Eilidh and Cara both burst out laughing.

'What?'

'Cal, come on, she's gorgeous and you know it.' Cara stared at the door Bea had gone through as if to check she wasn't coming back yet. 'Spill, please. What's going on?'

'And the more you deny it, the more you give away, by the way,' Eilidh added.

'Nothing is going on.' Cal was sure his face was burning up with guilt, even though technically he wasn't lying when he said nothing was going on.

'Okay, but would you like for there to be something going on?' Cara asked.

'Look,' Cal almost spluttered. 'Bea is a brilliant bartender.'

Damn right. She mixes drinks with aplomb, moves from the optics to the till as if she's floating on air, charms every customer she serves, and is genuinely happy the entire time. 'But that's it.' He was about to say that Bea wasn't his type: too confident, flirtatious, and full of ditsy affectation, but that was his old opinion of her, formed when he first met her under quite strange circumstances. In the coffee shop, she had reminded him of Elisabetta: of the nonsense he'd idiotically fallen for because his ego had sucked him in to imagining he was some sort of hero as she contrived things like getting her heels trapped in between paving slabs and dropping her handbag and half its contents in front of him – even several months into their relationship. He'd jumped to conclusions about Bea and judged her by those same criteria. But he could see now she was a different mettle of woman entirely. Bea was hard-working, down to earth and genuinely charming.

'I'm not buying that that's it.' Cara shook her head. 'Nuh-uh.'

'Me neither,' said Eilidh. 'We were getting singed from the sparks over here.'

Cal sighed. 'Okay, there might be a bit of chemistry or something between me and her, but we won't be going there.'

'Why not?' Eilidh leaned in.

'Well, for one, I'm her boss.'

'And for two?'

Cal rolled his eyes. 'For two, I'm staying away from women for a bit.' *Indefinitely – even hard-working bartenders – until all this baby stuff is sorted out, and I know how things are with Dad. I can resist temptation until Bea goes home. I can keep things on a friendly but professional level with her.*

'Hmm.' Cara and Eilidh knew Cal was stubborn and wouldn't admit anything more, but he could tell they were sceptical and unconvinced.

'Mark the words of your weird sisters,' said Cara as she and

Eilidh were putting their jackets on to leave. 'You and Bea would be good together. Don't be a Martian, Cal.'

Eilidh and Cal laughed together at this. 'Do you mean a martyr?' he said. 'And should you be having any more drinks? I think you should go home and get to bed.'

'Aye, that's the one,' said Cara, pointedly draining her glass. 'If you like her, then stop being a Martian ... a martyr and forget you're her boss. Life's too short.'

'She might have a point,' said Eilidh.

'Okay, thanks weirdos. Look, have a good night and stay safe.' Cal hugged his sisters goodbye. He loved them dearly, but he wasn't about to take advice from them on his love life. He could manage fine using his own radar to guide him. And his own radar said to keep things with Bea purely professional.

Chapter Twenty

1.05 a.m. the following day. Bea watched as Cal locked the door behind the last customer and allowed herself a sigh of relief. An empty bar at last. Not to mention alone with the boss for the first time since he'd hired her three weeks ago.

Cal, too, let out a huge breath and loosened his tie and collar. 'What a night,' he said. 'I've never seen the bar so busy.'

'I know. I wasn't sure we would ever get through that crowd.' Bea considered that Cal was even more sexy now than twelve hours ago when his crumpled white shirt with its rolled-up sleeves was crisp and fresh. 'It was six deep at one point. I hope it won't lead to bad reviews about serving time.'

'I think we'll be fine.' A rare smile drifted onto Cal's face. 'You've developed quite a fan base.'

Bea hoped this sideways compliment meant Cal was softening a little. She dipped her toe into the waters of flirtation. 'I told you, people will queue up for miles for my Manhattans.'

'Aye, it'll be your Manhattans, right enough.' Cal retorted without missing a beat. Then he grinned, grabbed a beer from the fridge and took a seat in front of the bar.

Oh, I like this Cal. Give me more.

But then Cal's voice dropped a semi-tone and he was back to serious. And disappointing. 'Listen, Bea, you put in the graft of Kitty, Zack and yourself combined tonight, so why don't you head off now. I'll clean up here.'

'Oh, no!' Bea's reaction to manual labour was so reflexive that she surprised herself. 'No way am I letting you clear all this up alone. You'll be here until opening tomorrow.'

Cal's eyebrows shot up. 'You enjoy cleaning?' He raised his beer to his lips.

'Well, I have hobbies that are further up the list. But cleaning's not so bad. Plus, I can't have you do all the work. You're exhausted.'

Cal swallowed a large gulp of beer and stared at Bea for a little longer than usual. There was something in that stare. What was it? Admiration? Surprise? Had he never had a bartender willing to clean? Or was it deeper than that? Women who didn't consider his needs, maybe?

'Okay, well I appreciate the help,' he said. 'More beauty sleep for me, I guess.'

'Not that you need it.' *Fuck, why did I say that? Who is this woman that this man is bringing out?*

Bea's words may have surprised even her, but they were also genuine flattery. Cal, however, did not appear comfortable. He rested his beer on the bar, cleared his throat awkwardly and grabbing a damp cloth said, 'I'll get the tables. You do behind the bar.'

'Sure,' Bea agreed. Dammit, even subtle compliments were too much for Cal Butler. She hadn't been doing her confident flirtee act, but something had flipped his 'off' switch.

For a short time, they worked in silence, Cal bringing glasses to the bar and wiping the cleared tables, Bea loading the dishwasher and mopping the floor. Occasionally she stole a glance at him, glimpsed his strong, tanned forearm as he purposefully swept the cloth over the tables, imagined the flex and tense of athletic shoulders inside his shirt. Did he know she was watching him? Was he playing the same game of look and look away and they kept missing each other? She certainly had that same feeling as in the coffee shop of his intense eyes on her. Cleaning had never been sexier. And the less they talked, the more the sexual tension swirled around the space, rising to the same level as when they were serving earlier. But then, mere inches existed between them. Now Cal was halfway across the floor holding a damp cloth and the thread of sexual promise was as taut as when he'd brushed against her at the optics or as he'd leaned over her to get a glass from the shelf and she'd inhaled the scent of fresh lime and cedarwood mixed with his own sweet skin and felt his warm breath on her neck.

After a time, Cal returned to the bar and plonked down on the stool again. The relief of having finished work seeming to soften him up a bit. It was that or the beer.

'So,' he said, 'Now I've seen up close what you can do, I have to ask, where exactly did you learn to work a bar the way you do?'

Bea continued emptying the dishwasher and resisted the temptation to remind Cal that he had her résumé. To be fair to him, if he'd been paying as much attention as she had to business matters in that interview, then he probably hadn't paid it much heed.

'I worked bar throughout college,' she said. 'I should have been studying literature but making Manhattans paid more than reading Jane Austen.'

Cal's face was steely and unreadable apart from his eyes, which flickered with interest. 'So, that's where the romance writing comes from?'

'Well, I guess so, although I'm no Jane Austen, and defi-nitely racier.'

Now the eyebrows rose, working in tandem with the eyes

to betray his interest. 'Ah, it's like that, is it? I'd love to read some of your writing.'

Bea nearly dropped a glass. 'Really?' None of the guys she'd dated had been remotely interested in her writing. This spike of curiosity sent an unexpected thrill through her. Unless Cal was joking.

But his voice bore no levity. 'Yes, really. Then I can decide which you should be making a living from: Manhattans or writing.'

Okay, this is too good not to latch onto. 'I'm not sure about my writing,' – Bea's voice bounced with joy – 'but I'll happily show you my Manhattans.' Then she realised that this euphemism would probably send Cal scuttling for the cleaning cloth again.

But Cal simply raised one of those dynamic eyebrows and let out a wry smile before nodding. 'Okay, deal,' he said. 'But I like mine with Scotch.'

Bea finished combining the Scotch, vermouth and bitters, then topped the drinks with a maraschino cherry before pushing them across the bar, one to Cal and one next to an empty bar stool. She then came round the front of the bar and took a seat facing Cal, watching him as he tried his drink.

The corners of Cal's lips lifted a fraction as he put the drink down. 'That is perfect,' he said. 'I can conclude that your Manhattans are definitely one reason people are flocking to the bar to see you.'

'Thank you.' Bea sipped her own cocktail.

'We should make this cocktail of the week, next week, if you're prepared to make lots of them.'

'That is such an honour. I'd love to.'

Cal sipped his drink again and flashed such an expression of warmth her way that Bea's stomach flipped a little.

'So,' he said, 'The bar trade definitely needs you, but what about your writing?'

'Oh.' Bea nervously raised her glass again to cover her face. 'What about it?'

'Well, I don't know, what have you written? Where can I read your books? You said you had come here to write so have you written much since you got here?'

'So many questions.' Cal hadn't asked Bea much in the time they'd known each other. Even her job interview was formal and to the point with little chit chat around the edges. So these questions astounded and delighted her. He appeared genuinely interested in her writing. Something that Josh hadn't been. Not that Cal was a future boyfriend or anything, but he was a man. He was definitely a man.

'I've written ten books. They are all available online. I can write down the names if you are interested in reading them, although I expect you probably aren't so interested that you'd—'

'Why not? Why would I not want to read them?'

'Well, because they are romance novels and, well, I don't know you all that well, but I am guessing that you don't read much romance.'

'Are you saying I'm not romantic?'

'Not at all – just that most guys aren't into reading romance.'

'So you're saying I'm like most guys then?'

'Oh, no, um...'

'It's okay, I'm kidding.' Cal's features softened a little. 'I'll admit that romance isn't my cup of tea, but – and this might surprise you – I have read quite a few romance novels. My mum is a huge fan and as a kid I would read from her collection.'

'Really?' Bea bit her lip, unsure if this was a joke. 'You read romance books as a kid. Why?'

'Hmm, well...' Cal swallowed back a mouthful of Manhattan and hesitated a moment. 'I'll admit that maybe I didn't read the entirety of any of her novels. Perhaps only selected scenes.'

'Ah! Okay.' Bea laughed. 'I get it now. Well, if you like those kinds of scenes then you might like my writing.'

'I'm sure I would. What's the name of one of your novels? Say, the one you're most proud of.'

'Oh, I don't know. That's a hard one. But I'd say I'm probably proudest of my first because it was the hardest to write. It's from my *Midtown Millionaires* series.'

'I see. So who are the Midtown Millionaires?' Cal shuffled forward on his seat.

'They're business owners: men who've made it in the business world but who have yet to find true love.'

'Is that what you get your kicks from then?'

'Get my kicks?'

'Sorry, I mean is that what you enjoy writing about. Businessmen who have yet to find true love. Surely you have to enjoy whatever you are writing.'

'Well, I love all my characters, especially the male ones. And you have to fall a little bit in love with them to make the reader do the same. As for businessmen with that missing piece... they do have a certain something.' Bea shrugged one shoulder noncommittally, wondering if Cal saw himself in this description.

He examined her with sage interest. 'I'd love to read some,' he said. 'Have you got any with you?'

Woah! This request threw Bea right across the room. Cal wanted to read her writing. My God. She didn't know what to do with this request. Tell him to go to the library? That was too dismissive. Tell him she'd order him a copy to be delivered to the bar. That would take too long. No, she had to find him something now. Strike while his interest was hot. 'Um...' She thought fast and reached into her pocket. 'I don't have any of the books with me, but I probably have some drafts on my phone.'

'Read some for me.' Cal spoke in that commanding Scottish burr that Bea was sure meant he always got what he wanted, from women at least.

'Are you sure? It might take me a bit of time to find anything suitable.'

'Aye, I'm sure. Why don't I make us another drink while you find a good bit to read. I can't promise it'll be as good as your Manhattan, but I will try.'

'Sounds like a deal.' Bea scrabbled through her phone for first the novel then a suitable scene to read, while Cal went behind the bar to mix his own version of the Manhattan.

'Okay, I think I've found something,' she said, as Cal brought round the deep red drinks and perched atop his bar stool again. 'I won't bore you for too long, but I think you'll like this scene. This one is set in Alabama and is from my Montgomery Millionaires series, the second series I wrote.'

'Brilliant. I'm ready when you are.' Cal's face was deadly serious. Bea wished she could ascertain whether he was interested in hearing her writing or if he was more attracted to the salacious aspect of it. In choosing which scene to read him, she'd gone for the latter, hoping she wasn't misreading the signs and making a monumental fool of herself in front of her boss. She was sure she saw a little something extra there behind those dazzling green irises. She parted her lips and stared at her phone. Then she looked back up at Cal.

'I'd like to say this is a rough draft but it's pretty much what went in the book, so if you don't like it...'

Cal remained silent and intently focused on her.

'I'll just read, shall I?'

'Aye.' He smiled and before she fell of her seat from the weight of the lust he invoked in her, Bea looked down at her phone again.

Jake swung the door of the summerhouse open and stormed in. He would make sure Holly Buchanan never made a fool of him like that again.

'Holly!' he called. 'I know you're here. It's Jake Dupree.'

'Oh, hi, Jake. I'm up here.' Holly's voice called innocent as peach pie from one of the upstairs rooms. Damn her! Making him climb the stairs to give her a piece of his mind and acting like nothing was wrong when she knew fine well she'd got him all riled up.

'Damn, you, Holly Buchanan. You sure like to make things difficult for a man, don't you?' Jake strode up the stairs two at a time. 'Now you listen to me. We need to set things straight about what happened today, so...'

Jake stopped in his tracks. Holly was standing in front of him in the frame of the bathroom door, naked but for a tiny towel wrapped around her. It covered a body which was soaking wet and covered in residual bubbles. Her hair was sodden and dripping onto her cleavage. Jake experienced a stiffening inside his pants.

'Now, what exactly could be so important, Jake Dupree, that a girl has to get out of the bath when she's soaking wet like this?' Holly asked.

'I was... I... Now you can't just do what you did this morning, Holly. Deep Bay is mine and you know it.'

Holly dropped her towel to the floor.

Bea glanced up at Cal. 'Do you want me to read more?' Cal's lips had fallen ever so slightly apart. 'Um... Are you kidding? You're stopping there? It sounded like it was getting good.'

'It kind of was, but I wasn't sure how many chapters you like to read in a day.'

'Well, I'm sure that wasn't a whole chapter so keep reading if you like. I'm still awake. In fact, I think you might say I'm becoming awaker.'

Bea liked this Cal, the version that was loosening up to her. She could see his wicked sense of humour filtering through the seriousness, like sunlight glimmering through the weave of a dark drape.

'I'm sure,' she said, teasingly, 'that you can imagine what happens next.'

'I've got a fair idea. Does she put her clothes on and they go for a picnic?'

Bea rocked with laughter. 'That's exactly what they do. How did you know?'

'I told you. I've read a lot of these types of books. Plus, I got a hunch. They both were hungry, I think.'

'Hmm, you'd be right.' She met Cal's gaze dead on and for several loaded moments, they were locked together in a magnetic forcefield. 'I think they are both starving,' she added.

Cal got it. Her meaning. He placed his drink on the bar, slid off his stool and stood looming above Bea but close enough to, no doubt, hear her heart thundering in anticipation. 'So,' he said, 'where can I find out what happens next?'

'Well, it's available at all good booksellers.'

Bea noted how her response caused brushstrokes of amusement to appear on Cal's otherwise intense expression. He touched her cheek, his palm warm and strong. 'Good,' he said. 'I'll buy it tomorrow.'

And now she could barely muster a response. She was being dragged along in a current of stupendously sexy and witty Scottish man cupping her face and pinpointing her with a look that carried a raft load of intentions, none of which were especially pure. 'Mmhm,' she said. Not that she wanted to talk. All she wanted to do was kiss Cal Butler. Or have Cal Butler kiss her.

Lucky then that Cal seemed to be thinking similar thoughts. Lucky then that at the moment she was thinking how much she wanted his lips on hers, Cal, with a direct focus driven by passionate intent, leaned down, pressed his mouth to Bea's and kissed her. And oh, how he kissed her. At first, he was soft, teasing, giving a taste of what was to come, then the hunger he'd alluded to moments earlier took over and Cal cranked the heat up, his mouth devouring Bea's, his strong palms cradling her face, drifting down to her waist, the small of her back, urging her up from her bar stool, sending the unequivocal message of how badly he needed her.

Bea needed this too, so much. She slid from her bar stool, standing to get closer to Cal, all the while kissing him back, responding to and equalling his hunger with her own, waltzing her tongue round his. His hands found their way to her face once more, before exploring her neck, then travelling to her back and pulling her to him so her breasts were pressed against that firm body pulsing with Scottish blood and heat and passion. Oh God! If this was how he kissed, the rest would be unbelievable.

Then, as if he'd been injected with a shot of adrenaline, Cal yanked away from the kiss; his hands dropping from Bea's face and plunging into his pockets, his expression suggesting immediate shock and regret.

'Fuck, I am so sorry, Bea.'

'Sorry?' Bea managed to splutter. 'Why?' *What on earth does he have to be sorry about? Definitely not his kissing technique, except to be sorry to all the other men out there because he put them in the corner the way he kissed.* Bea had experienced nothing like it. Tenderness combined with passion, a slow build to a crescendo of intensity. Though they hadn't quite got to that bit since Cal had backed off and now was throwing back his cocktail as if to wash away what had gone between them.

'Sorry,' he said, again. 'I'm your boss and that was wrong of me. I shouldn't be taking advantage of you like that.'

'Taking advantage of me? But I kissed you back.'

'Only because I kissed you first.' He met her gaze. 'It was unprofessional and I apologise.'

Bea shook her head as if to unblock her ears. If he'd tried to kiss her and she had rejected him, she could understand Cal calling himself out as unprofessional. But that kiss was between two consenting adults.

'I don't think there is any such thing as a professional kiss.' She tried to lighten the mood. 'Except if there were kissing championships, then you would have reached professional level.' Oh, she was waffling now and Cal was pushing in his bar stool and wiping non-existent dust from the bar. He'd moved on already.

'Look, Bea. You are a stunning woman and I think you probably know now how attractive I find you. But I never mix business with my personal life. It would only end in disaster. I'll get you a taxi.'

Wow! This sudden coolness shocked Bea and his words whipped her back to their first meeting in the coffee shop where he'd blasted her with his cool air of intolerance and acted like she was an idiot. She should have seen it then. Known his disposition was so diametrically opposed to her own and that he had the capacity to hurt her with his words. But she was also being cast back further, back to life with Josh where she didn't know where she stood from moment to moment and any attempts at affection were rebuffed. Both men had made her feel like a fool. Well, she wasn't having that any longer. She would not tolerate another Josh. As much as she liked Cal, this was never meant to be anything more than a trip to help her write and she didn't need a muse to help her do it. If Cal thought kissing her was a mistake, then so be it. He wouldn't get to kiss her again. She didn't need this after the time she'd had with Josh. So, as matter of fact as she could, Bea turned away from Cal and strode to the staff room to grab her purse from her locker and get out of here. She would walk away from the shame before it could strengthen its grip on her any further.

Chapter Twenty-One

Cal had fully intended not to flirt with Bea, but that had apparently been too difficult for him. He'd stupidly come in with that silly comment about her Manhattans, and when she'd complimented him, he'd got stage fright and walked away like an idiot, to clean. But because he was sure she was watching him, his blood had pumped harder. You could have cut the sexual tension in the room with a knife.

Thoughts were whirring in his mind. *Just talk to her about stuff: any stuff that isn't sex stuff.* He could barely even remember what they'd talked about because of that kiss. My God! That kiss! It was incredible. Bea knew exactly what she was doing, and boy did she do it well. It amazed Cal he'd had the willpower to pull back. But something had flashed across his mind. He was getting carried away again, putting his lust for a beautiful woman before any sense. Exactly what had got him into a mess with Elisabetta and he'd sworn he'd now avoid. And if Cal was good at anything, it was sticking to the promises he made himself.

While Bea was through the back getting her bag, Cal

picked up his phone to call her a taxi. His hands smelled of her perfume. *Fuck.* He was getting turned on again. He put the phone on speaker and poured a shot of whisky.

Bea emerged as Cal was hanging up the phone. 'Your taxi will be here shortly,' he said, wishing he didn't sound so matter-of-fact.

'Okay, thank you.' There was nothing about Bea's polite manner to suggest upset at what had happened. Cal half expected her to be frosty with him, but when her taxi arrived, she said, 'I'll see you next Saturday.' Then she let him unlock the door and watch her walk up the close to the safety of the Royal Mile, those beautiful curves accentuated under the Old Town lamplight.

Cal's instinct was to reach for another drink to douse his arousal. How on earth had he found it within himself to reject her? He raked his fingers through his hair. And had he made a colossal mistake? Should he have taken her to bed with him? Judging by the calibre of the taster session, it would have been mind-blowing.

Too late now. Once again, you'll have to use your imagination. Then Cal realised the pointlessness of refusing to take things further with Bea. She was going to be in his bedroom, anyway. She'd been there since he'd met her, seeping into his psyche. But it was too late now; she was in a taxi home and no way was he going to text and ask her to come back. The moment was gone and Cal had blown it spectacularly.

<h1 style="text-align:right">Chapter Twenty-Two</h1>

In the taxi, Bea sighed and pulled the piece of paper from her purse where she'd put it several weeks ago. She considered the handwriting. It was attractive: neat, yet complex enough to suggest an interesting character at the other end of the pen. Craig. She liked the sound of that name. It was solid and dependable. Cal was a solid name too, but Cal wasn't interested in her, so maybe she could have some fun with Craig instead. After all, she'd come to Scotland for fun.

The next morning Bea sat down to write with fresh creative material in her head. The kiss with Cal might have been a dead end in real life, but it was going in the novel, that was for sure. Except in the novel, it would lead somewhere. She wouldn't leave her heroine hanging out on a limb, like Cal had her

The inspiration of the kiss also led Bea to finish and publish to her website the 'Hal Hunter' short story she'd begun the day she'd met Cal. She put a quick post on her social media to let her fans know it was there, describing it as an apology gift for not being around much during her vacation, and a small taste of the novel to come, and said that she hoped they loved it.

The only problem about having such rich material to work with was that Bea got increasingly turned on by the thoughts in her head and the scenes going down on the page. She wanted kisses that weren't stopped short with apologies, hot skin against hers, lustful weeks of longing finally unleashed. Not for the first time since penning this story, Bea slipped her hand between her thighs and imagined an unbridled Cal Butler let loose on her body.

Oh, how she wished she had someone to help her unravel all her tension. A Scotsman. She picked up Craig's note sitting by her laptop. He'd been cute. Why not?

Less than an hour after she sent him a text, Craig replied saying how glad he was Bea had got in touch and would she like to go out for dinner. Bea agreed that would be lovely, and they arranged to dine midweek at a restaurant he recommended in nearby Bruntsfield.

The dinner went well. Craig picked Bea up in a taxi. He'd made an effort with his outfit and behaved like a gentleman. Bea enjoyed his company, and they chatted across a vista of topics accompanied by a delicious meal and well-chosen wine. After the meal, Craig walked Bea to her apartment where he gave her a kiss on the cheek, told her what a lovely time he'd had and asked if she'd like to meet for coffee the following week. She agreed and Craig said he'd be in touch.

On paper, it was all perfect. The man was good-looking, well dressed, smelled good, had impeccable manners and wasn't lacking in the conversation or humour department. He told Bea several times throughout the meal how stunning she was, and she could honestly compliment him back. But they had zero chemistry. No knowing intensity as their eyes met and refused to unlock. The sex would no doubt be decent, but decent was all it would be.

Bea sighed as she got into bed, still thinking about the faultless yet lacklustre date. Before this trip she wouldn't have considered sparking-off-the-grid-electricity a prerequisite for being with a man. But now her standards had soared, and she knew exactly why. Cal Butler. Since meeting Cal, something had changed. And quite frankly it was annoying because it was impeding her ability to enjoy herself. *Damn Cal Butler and his total hotness.*

Still, Craig could be a good choice. He's not bothered if I'm only in town for a short while and said it would be an honour to spend a bit of time with me. He's a hot Scotsman, and that's what I wanted. I don't want my hero to be a complete carbon copy of one person, after all.

So, for the rest of the week, Bea toiled on her novel and tried to replace any thoughts of Cal with those of Craig. She was successful in one out of two of those endeavours.

On Saturday, Bea got ready and headed to Butler's for her shift. It would be the first time she'd seen Cal since their kiss a week previous, although she'd seen him plenty in her mind and kissed him many more times, despite her attempts to keep focused on work and to think only of Craig.

'Evening.' Cal was the model of professionalism when Bea arrived at the bar. 'How are you?'

'I'm good thanks.' She wasn't about to say, *Oh, I'm great apart from the fact that I've been tortured all week by thoughts of you ravishing me in kisses and tearing my clothes off.*

'That's good,' said Cal. 'But listen, I don't know if you'll be fine once I tell you what I'm about to.'

What's this? Myriad possibilities flew round Bea's mind. *Is he about to apologise again for last week? Admit he made a mistake. Or is he going to say he can't go on having me as an employee because he's finding it hard to shake off thoughts of me in his bed? That would be even better than an apology. He'd no longer be my boss and wouldn't have to worry about professional boundaries.*

'I'm afraid it's just you and me tonight,' Cal revealed. 'Kitty fell and twisted her ankle on the way in and I can't get anyone else. To say I'm annoyed is an understatement, but there's nothing I can do about it. Except apologise to you. It's going to be a full-on night.'

That's it? Bea thought. *A busy night on the bar with Cal Butler. Doesn't sound bad at all. There might be some awkwardness after last week, but we'll probably be so busy that it won't be noticeable.*

'Not a problem at all.' Bea spoke perkily. 'I'd rather be busy.'

'I'll make sure you're well compensated.'

Bea imagined the perfect compensation: Cal wrapped around her, naked, huskily divulging his deepest desires into her ear in that rich Scottish timbre. She nearly said, 'I look forward to it,' but stopped herself in time and issued her body with a strict reminder that Cal was her boss and not interested in such shenanigans. More was the pity.

Chapter Twenty-Three

Cal was holding it together. He'd spent the week since his kiss with Bea congratulating himself on his professionalism and for doing the right thing by stopping things from going any further. Telling himself that this was why he'd come so far in the business world, because he knew that muddling his personal life into his professional life made for a dangerous cocktail.

But as soon as he saw Bea, Cal realised it would be a tough night. And not only on account of Kitty's absence, but because watching Bea walk through the door of the bar, fresh as a spring morning in a silk blouse, the early evening light catching her porcelain skin and making it more luminous than ever, he was struck sideways by how much he still desired her. Out of sight was almost out of mind, if you put your mind to it, but when this woman was in his sight she did nothing but take over his mind. At her mere presence, sweat prickled at the back of Cal's neck. And when she stepped behind the bar, her intoxicating, spicy floral scent made his body ache in places that were entirely inconvenient when working.

Bea seemed fine, though. She was acting as if nothing had

happened. 'Okay, boss, let's do this thing,' she said, before approaching her first customer of the evening. Cal knew this meant that she was assuming the role of employee and recognising him as her employer. That was good; he liked being a boss, enjoyed being in charge. He wasn't a dictator, but he'd built the company up from scratch and believed that acknowledgement of his being at the helm was fair recompense for all the hard work he'd put in over the years. However, none other of his employees addressed him as 'boss'. Just Bea. And it drove him to distraction. Instead of perfectly delineating the professional boundaries, it blurred them by stirring his longing for her even more. Yes, he was her boss. Yes, he was in charge. And he wanted to be in charge of all of her.

Serving together was like an intricate dance. It wasn't the first time Cal and Bea had worked the bar alone together, but it was the first time since their kiss and that memory lingered like the scent of an exotic trailing plant. If the memory were a dance, it was one where they both kept getting the moves wrong as their hands kept meeting or overlapping throughout the evening. Bea moved to the till at the same time as Cal, brushed his knuckles as they both went to serve the same customer. And Cal was perplexed as to why he'd done this, but when he'd noticed that Bea had something caught in her hair, he told her and then reached to retrieve it at the same time as she had.

'Sorry,' he said before turning back to serve the customers, some of whom were watching intently at the obvious chemistry being played out in front of them by the two bartenders.

'Not a problem, boss.' Bea appeared to be far more in control of her reaction to said boss than he to her.

Since the bar was heaving with customers, Cal tried to focus on the crowds. Security on the door could take control of rowdy behaviour, but, as people jostled to get served, there could be things happening that the bouncers might not see.

Tonight, thankfully, the patrons behaved themselves. It meant Cal had time to notice Bea leaning over the bar talking to a male customer. There was something about it that caught his attention. It was normal to lean in to hear what someone wanted to drink, but this interaction was more intimate: the prolonged focus on each other, the almost touching, the fact that when Cal trained his ear he heard the words, 'Deleted, number, phone'. *Who is this guy?*

The question burned at Cal as he continued to work. The man hadn't ordered a drink. Instead, he and Bea had exchanged a few more words and he'd said, 'See you next week.'

'Friend of yours?' Cal asked, after the man had left.

'What? Oh, that's Craig,' Bea said breezily. 'He and I went for dinner during the week. He lost my number, so he was popping in to let me know.'

'I see.' Cal kept his response short, but thoughts were darting round his brain. *Bea went for dinner with this Craig guy? Who is he? How does she know him? He clearly likes her since he's come into the bar to get her number.* Although Cal wasn't buying the losing the number act. The guy was marking his territory. Did Bea like him? From the way she'd leaned her ear close towards his it was his guess that she did.

Cal poured drinks with less care than usual. He got a couple of orders wrong and even made Bea jump when he pushed the till drawer in with too much vigour.

'You okay, boss?' she asked.

'I'm fine, aye. You know, you don't have to keep calling me boss. Cal is fine.' Suddenly Cal loathed the boss–employee divide between him and Bea. *There's no such partition between her and Craig and he's taking her to dinner. And who knows where else?*

'Okay, Cal it is,' Bea said. 'You okay, Cal?' This was even more intimate, and Cal's gut lurched as the boss–employee interaction took on a new dynamic. *She's asking how I am? How do I even answer that? Don't suppose she wants to hear that I hate the idea of her with other men?*

'Aye. Let's get rid of these customers, shall we?' Cal nodded to the crowd on the other side of the bar. Ordinarily he didn't mind a busy bar and thrived on the relentlessness of it, but tonight, after the appearance of Craig, he wanted them all to go away. He wanted to be alone with Bea. Needed to be alone with her. He'd made a huge mistake turning her down after their kiss, and he had to know if there was any going back from it.

Chapter Twenty-Four

'So, you're dating?' Cal asked once the bar was closed, and they were cleaning up.

'Well,' said Bea. 'Craig took me to dinner.'

'You have a good time?'

Bea couldn't work out if Cal was being an interested employer or curious for other reasons. She briskly tidied away clean glasses. 'It was lovely, thanks.'

'Right.' Cal swept a cloth across the bar with some force. 'That's good then.'

'Yes, it was.'

'And does he intend to show you any more of Edinburgh?'

Bea hadn't kissed Craig, never mind slept with him, but Cal didn't need to know that. She shrugged. 'I think we may have coffee next week, although I'm not entirely sure of his intentions regarding showing me things.' There was a double meaning in this and she fully intended there to be. Why not make Cal sweat a little?

'Right. Well, make sure he's treats you properly. I wouldn't trust half of the punters that come in here. You deserve to be treated well, Bea.'

'You think so?'

'Aye, I do.'

Bea folded her arms. 'You're right, Cal. But remind me. Why is it that I deserve good treatment?' If Cal was changing his mind about last week, then he was as culpable as the next guy of messing her around and he wasn't getting anywhere near her without earning it.

As if reading her thoughts, a spark appeared in Cal's eyes and for a moment he contemplated Bea in silence. Then without another word, he moved round to her side of the bar – mere feet from her – and spoke in that deep Scottish burr that set Bea seriously off balance.

'Because you are bloody amazing, that's why. Every punter in this place finds you breathtaking. That Craig guy doesn't know how lucky he is.'

'Oh yeah?' Bea almost drawled her words, 'I've encountered a few guys who haven't known how lucky they are.'

Cal glanced at the floor, then swiftly back up to Bea. That electricity was there again, like a flickering cord of static pulled between them.

'I think we both know I'm one of those guys, don't we?' he admitted.

Bea almost laughed at this unexpected frankness. 'Well, I didn't like to be the one to say, but...'

'No, it's fair enough. So, how much do you like Craig?'

'I like him.' Bea fiddled with one of the beer tap nozzles. 'He's nice.'

'Nice.' Cal nodded. 'Okay. Well, I can be *nice*. But do you feel *this* with him?'

'Feel what?' Bea met Cal's gaze dead on. She knew exactly what he was talking about, but she wanted him to explain his meaning. He wasn't getting to wherever has was driving to without a few stoplights on the way.

'This.' Cal waved at the space between their two bodies.

'The energy that's here when we stand next to each other. Do you get *this* with him? Because I've never experienced it with another woman in my life'

'Um.' At Cal's disarming candour, Bea loosened her hold on the beer tap. If what she thought was on the cards was on the cards, she might need both her hands.

'No. I don't feel *this* when I am with him,' she said, meeting his honesty dead on with her own. 'Only with you.'

Cal gave another curt nod but said nothing more. *Is that it? Was all he wanted ego-boosting affirmation that I like him more than I do Craig? I should have kept my mouth shut.*

'I'll cash up.' Bea opened the register, ready to get out of this toxic place.

Cal, standing on the other side, pushed the drawer closed with the same force as earlier and took a step towards her.

'Cash up later.' He fixed her with a look she'd seen a million times before yet had never seen in her life.

Bea blinked, pinned to the spot by the magnetism of Cal's presence. 'If you're sure.' She knew unequivocally that he was: the intent in his stare, the way his lips had fallen slightly apart. Everything about Cal emanated lust.

'I'm sure. Bea, I made a mistake last week after our kiss. I'm man enough to admit that. I should never have said that was the end for us.'

Man enough to admit he was wrong. This apology was filling Bea's cup in so many ways. God, she wanted Cal to kiss her, and somewhere from within, she heard emerge a whispered 'Okay'.

'I'm sorry,' Cal murmured, cupping her face, his touch warm and confident against her skin, eyes almost drunk with sincerity. 'Honestly, it's just the beginning.'

Bea's breath caught in her windpipe. This was huge. This was what she wanted. Really wanted. But thoughts of Craig flashed across her mind. She was at an intersection and she knew it: one where a split-second decision was in the offing. Cal held her face and her future in his hands. If she was going to tell him she chose Craig, now would be the time. Now, before this Cal flame that was flickering in front of her ignited into a full on blaze.

'Can you forgive me?' Cal's breath was a warm whisper on Bea's face, intermingling with her own. They were so close now.

Can I? Can I forgive him for stopping our desire in its tracks? For pulling me in then pushing me away, and now pulling me in once more, like a torturous game of cat and mouse. What's to say he won't do it again? Especially if I make it too easy for him. But what will I be missing out on if I let my head make the decision here? What if Cal is serious now and is ready to give properly what I had a taste of last week? What if he feels all that I feel and made a misguided choice? Then it would be foolish to let this go to even the score. Bea had mere seconds to decide what to do. She examined his face but could see nothing but seriousness in his inquiring gaze as he waited for her answer.

'I suppose I could go some way to forgiving you,' she whispered at last.

Cal took his signal from this and touched his lips tenderly to Bea's. Oh, it was hopeless. There was no way in the world she could walk away from this now. No way. Thoughts of Craig had evaporated in the heat of the air between her and Cal.

She kissed him back, soft, teasing flutters at first, to match his own. Then consideration of apologies or thoughts of other people were obliterated. Cal kissed with a passion that scorched away his cool exterior. There was fire and whisky and burning desire in his mouth. He gave what Bea desperately needed, what he desperately needed in return.

The kiss intensified; Cal pushed into Bea, his tongue hot,

finding hers, the force of his want inching her back towards the glowing optics. Bea returned his passion with every fragment of her existence. This was everything.

A glass crashed to the floor.

'Shit.'

'Don't worry about it,' Cal said huskily, overtaken by animalistic need; broken glasses were not on his agenda. 'The cleaner can get it.'

'The cleaner?'

His hungry lips hovered, waiting, eager for this conversation to be over, but somehow enjoying its implications. 'Aye. In the morning.'

'You have a cleaner?'

'Mmm, did I not mention it?'

A smile of realisation crept onto Bea's face as Cal's twinkling emerald eyes drifted up to meet hers. There was a definite shimmering of guilt in there. She tilted her head, flicked her tongue across her top lip and eyeballed him. 'No, as a matter of fact, you didn't.'

'Do you mind that it slipped my mind?' He was biting back lascivious amusement.

How could she mind when he looked at her like that? So confident already that he'd got away with it. 'I can think of ways my time might have been better spent,' she said. 'But...'

Once more, Cal pressed a firm and resolute kiss against Bea's mouth, granting her exhilaration she hadn't known existed until she arrived in Scotland and met this man. Arousal surged into parts of her body it had never reached before. Who cared about a little white lie when this was happening? This firm body – the one she'd dreamed about for weeks, smelled from too far away, scrawled down thoughts about in a haze of fantasy – was separated from hers only by a thin cotton shirt and pants which were failing in the most spectacular way possible to veil the effect she had on him. Bea inhaled the delicious, warm male scent of Cal. The lime, the cedar, the need. It was too much. She drove her palms into his muscular back, trying to bring him closer to her, to become one with him. The heat from the fevered skin underneath was volcanic.

'Oh, Cal, I want you so much.'

'I want you too,' Cal growled, 'but this isn't the place for me to show you how much. Come with me.' And to Bea's surprise, he reached out and tugged her away from the bar, through the back room to his office.

In the office, her hand still enclosed in his firm grasp, Cal navigated around the desk towards the chesterfield that stretched along the side wall. Settling onto it, he leaned back, directed a determined yet encouraging look Bea's way, and drew her closer. Bea dropped and straddled his lap. His hardness was underneath her now, so close to her own pulsing arousal.

'You're so beautiful,' Cal murmured, freeing Bea's hair from its clip and passing his fingers through the long red waves.

Her senses melted. Beautiful. Not 'hot' or 'sexy' which she'd heard many times. Beautiful. There was something deeper, more enduring, about the word Cal had chosen.

'So are you,' she murmured.

'Thank you.' Cal spoke distractedly, his attention diverted by Bea's chest, where the word Butler's was intricately stitched onto her shirt. He ran his thumb across the fabric, tracing the embroidery and circling when he found her nipple.

Bea gasped.

Then, buttons were flying across the room and Bea was sitting astride Cal, her top half covered in only a lace bra, erect nipples pointing through the delicate black fabric.

'I'll get you another one of these.' Cal cast aside the shirt he'd yanked open and gazed at the uncovered treasure. Bea inched her breasts forward, needing his touch desperately.

Eyes glazed, Cal reached round to unclasp Bea's bra, his other hand holding her face as he kissed her hungrily again. Passion, tenderness and skill. Bea thrilled. Josh would have fumbled about whilst remarking how 'fucking hot' she was and saying things like 'Oh wow, baby, need to see those titties'. But Cal needed no assistance, allowing every molecule of Bea's body to submit to the sensations he was provoking in her.

She was perfect. Just perfect. Enormous breasts with immaculate dusky nipples and feminine hips that fit magnificently into the curve of his palms. The essence of his perfect woman. Cal took one of those sumptuous breasts, sucked on the nipple and hardened even more as Bea whimpered with pleasure. Oh, how glad he was that he'd made this move tonight, that he'd stopped letting his work-ethic conscience turn him into some sort of soft-hearted, indecisive monk. This was a goddess of a woman, clearly on the same page as him, whose body had taunted him for so long: these curves, this creamy décolletage that heaved as she breathed. And he'd wasted that time trying to resist. No more.

As Cal whipped his tongue across Bea's nipple, the other between his thumb and finger again, she moaned deeply and he let out a groan of appreciation. This hadn't happened with Elisabetta; she'd been greedy and, truth be told, Cal had found her cries of pleasure selfish. But this woman was different. Cal could tell from the heat in Bea's kisses that she gave as much as she took. It was as if their bodies were entirely in sync with one another.

Cal could feast on Bea's beautiful breasts all day, but he needed more. There was more of this flawless body underneath her clothes and he wanted badly to see it. He travelled his touch down the peachy skin of her stomach. She was sublime. Just the right level of toned. Not too hard, not too soft. The slightest running of his fingers above the waistband of her skinny jeans and he heard her sigh gently.

'Take your shirt off. I want to see you,' Bea commanded hazily.

Cal obliged, carefully unfastening the first few buttons, before tearing the rest of the shirt over his head. Bea inhaled in what he presumed was pleasure. He brought her to him, so her soft breasts pressed against his chest, and kissed her deeply.

'You are perfect,' Bea murmured between kisses. 'The perfect Scotsman.' She stroked her hands down the front of his chest. 'Oh, my God, you're so hot and hard!'

Cal roused at these words. At a woman calling him perfect, even if he knew he was far from it. He was definitely hard, though, although he knew Bea was referring to his torso rather than anything else. Hungrily, he sucked on her breast again before dragging his mouth away to deliver teasing kisses down her pillowy curves towards the waist of her jeans.

'Oh, Cal. Please. I need this. I need you.'

'Don't worry. You're going to get me.' Cal flicked open Bea's jeans button and pulled down the zip, revealing the virginal white of her panties. As he reached in and traced his fingers across the sheer fabric from the base of her soft mound, the tightness in his jeans intensified.

'Oh!' Bea whimpered.

'You like that, huh?'

'Dammit, yes. Please don't stop.'

'I'll need you out of these jeans then.'

* * *

Bea stood up from the chesterfield so she was no longer straddling Cal. He inched forward to the edge of the couch and urged her jeans down over those hallowed hips. She stepped up to let him take each leg past her ankles before casting them aside. Now her panties were level with Cal's face. He leaned his head to her and planted soft kisses through the fabric. The skin was so sensitive to the touch. Bea urged her sex forward. She needed this man so badly, with his flip-your-heart emerald eyes, kisses to ruin her, and now this mesmerising body.

'Come here.' Cal was staring up at her now, pulling her hips down towards him again. Bea straddled his lap again, the ache between her legs intensifying.

Cal sunk his tongue into her mouth and danced it with her own, at the same time brushing lightly across the underwear at her most sensitive area. She adored that he placed such importance on kisses as part of the whole experience. It was so much more intimate this way – so much more arousing.

Speaking of which, Bea knew how wet she was already, just from light touching through the white cotton of her panties. What would she be like when Cal met her flesh, or when she finally saw the full extent what was already evident through his clothing? It wasn't long before she found out. Cal tugged Bea's panties to the side to reveal her soaking sex, delved a finger into her folds, the others on her breast manipulating her nipple. Capitulating to his touch, her head fell back and she pressed down into his hand. Pleasure surged everywhere; she needed him inside her. That was the only way to quell this.

'Cal, I have to see you.' Bea reached for his jeans to undo them. Meeting his eyes for a moment, she saw them rich with need.

'I'm so hard for you, Bea,' he said. 'I want you so much.'

He wasn't lying; she knew that. She could feel the hardness

he talked of, insistent through the fabric of his jeans. What she hadn't been prepared for was how magnificent he would be when she pulled him free from his boxers.

'Oh, Cal,' was all she managed to say.

Cal smiled and Bea very nearly melted. Then he pulled her down to kiss her again, and she wondered if she would ever be whole again.

Chapter Twenty-Six

Everything about Bea was intensifying Cal's erection. Her soft skin, the lingering scent of her perfume, the glistening arousal between her legs. Not to mention the delight that spread across her face when she pulled down his boxers. Cal wanted nothing more than to ride Bea into orgasmic abandonment and was glad his physique would be part of the package. But when she encased his cock in her warm grip, he knew they were on a time sensitive journey.

'Oh, Jesus,' Cal growled. 'I need you now, Bea.'

Without saying a word, Bea rose up and removed her panties. Cal watched this awe inspiring woman in front of him, now naked from top to toe. She was no longer touching him, but he groaned from witnessing her fully unveiled. She was unbelievable. The voluminous breasts, cascading down to the slender waist and infinitely kissable stomach. And now this. The most perfect sex he'd ever seen with the neatest triangle of hair sitting above the sensual heat into which he soon would sink.

Cal grappled around the side table for his wallet, fumbled for a condom and somehow got to the stage of sliding it down his shaft. He couldn't remember the last time an erection felt in need of such urgent release. Thinking of Bea when he was alone came close, but the real thing was unsurpassable.

'You ready?' he asked.

'Do I feel ready?' Bea blinked down at him, her eyelashes laden with lust.

Cal pressed his fingers into her wetness. 'So ready,' he said his tones so low they were almost hoarse.

'I am. Please, Cal. I need you now.'

Bea surprised herself with the intensity of her craving for Cal. Never had she heard herself admit she needed a man in such a way. But she was too far gone to be set back by shame or self-consciousness. If sex could be this good, then it was to be embraced, not shied away from. She would have Cal Butler. She wanted him and she deserved him.

'Lie down.' Cal motioned to the couch.

Bea did as he bid. The surface was soft, the cool touch of the leather momentarily pulling her out of her haze. But then Cal's scorching body was resplendent over her and there was nothing else she could think of but him. For a moment, their eyes met and something unspoken yet monumental passed between them. A need, an understanding, a colossal desire that overrode everything. A desire that had to be listened to.

As Cal's tip nudged against Bea, their pleasure converged in mutual gasps. He lowered himself to her, biceps rippling and claimed her mouth with another kiss. Caught her off guard because before she knew it, Bea was being filled like she had never been filled before. A masculine thickness sending rippling shockwaves of pleasure through her sex and radiating throughout her whole being.

'Oh, Cal. Oh, my God.'

'Fuck, Bea, you feel incredible.' Cal's jaw tightened. And

just as Bea thought she had all of him, he pushed in deeper, closing his eyes as if to concentrate on feeling her. With impunity, she drank in the angular planes of his face, the coarse stubble that drove her wild, the subtle tension only an intimate partner would see. When he brought himself back into the room, he locked onto her with those insanely green eyes and said, 'I'm going to make you come, Bea.'

Bea's hips reflexively arched upwards. There was no doubt that she would come, but Cal's insistence on it happening just about sent her right there and then. As if his length and thickness had not been enough, his promise made her swell and grip onto him tighter as he moved deep within her – quickly at first before slowly pulling back and teasingly entering her again.

'Please, Cal. More. I need all of you now.'

Cal thrust hard into Bea, and she thought she might split apart. This was a man who knew exactly how to use what he had to arouse a woman. He was eviscerating everything she thought she knew about sex, eviscerating her. She reached down to touch herself. But a strong hand met her there.

'I've got this.' Cal spread Bea's arousal across her throbbing heart, giving to her whilst taking what he needed. How did he do it? Lose himself but remember her. She had no idea, and no brainpower to think about it because a storm was building within her. Bea arched her body, her breasts surging upwards, her sex demanding more of Cal – every inch of him – until it all rose to a crescendo and her muscles were clenching and contracting in endless euphoric waves and his name was ringing on the air in what must be her voice. Amidst this, Cal's own climax came hurtling in and her fluttering continued as he hardened to a rock and roared with a primal ferocity borne of so much longing and repressed desire finally being allowed to escape his tormented body.

Chapter Twenty-Seven

The sex was mind-blowing, and it wasn't just Bea's physical attractiveness that made it so. Cal had never shared chemistry with anyone like he shared with Bea. This woman obliterated all his self-control. Not only that, but she gave as much as she took. The only question remaining was why he had held out for so long; it now seemed like the most ridiculous decision ever.

'That was amazing.' He gazed down at Bea's radiant face.

She glowed back at him. 'It was. We were.'

He thought he must be glowing too. 'Question is,' he said, venturing where he knew it was necessary to go. 'Can we do it again?'

'What? Now?'

'Well, maybe not right now, but, say, in five minutes?' Cal kissed her softly and smiled to show he was joking, although he was pretty sure he could go again in five minutes with this goddess. He pulled himself up, grabbed a blanket from a chair and wrapped it round them both. 'I mean it, though. That was great and I don't think one dose of you will be enough for me.'

Bea laughed at the compliment. 'It was like the most fantastic medicine ever,' she said.

'You're here in Scotland for how long?'

'Another two months.'

He thought for a moment, then said, 'Look, Edinburgh is a fantastic city. There's so much to see and do here. But what better culture than some time with this Scotsman here?' Cal's delivery was deadpan, but Bea seemed to appreciate the humour and the intrigued tilt of her head suggested she was keen for him to continue talking. 'I know your time here is limited,' he went on. 'So, I don't want to put pressure on you to spend you break with me, and I don't want it to sound like some kind of sordid arrangement, but I think that was too good to not do again. And, well, I think we could have a lot of fun.' Cal knew he was doing the opposite of what he said he'd do – avoid women until things were off his mind – but how could he close the box now he'd seen what was inside?

It was difficult to gauge Bea's feelings about this request. She didn't respond straight away. In fact, for a moment, she gazed downward and Cal wondered if he'd said the wrong thing. Thrown the ultimate insult at her, maybe? Was she going to look up and he'd see her eyes full of rage, or worse, heartbreak? Or was he giving himself too much credit for the effect he had on a woman?

In what was probably only seconds, but felt like minutes to Cal, Bea met him face on. 'You may have a point,' she said. 'I came here to get over a nasty break-up and, to be honest, I think a couple of months of no-strings physical fun might be exactly what I need.'

Oh wow! Cal couldn't quite believe this. 'No strings. You're sure? You're not, I don't know, in a difficult place after your break-up?' Cal had never heard a woman offer no strings in such a way before. It was like he was being lured into a trap. He also wanted to make sure Bea wasn't emotionally fragile and making a foolish decision. The last thing he wanted was to hurt her.

'I believe I'm of sound mind,' Bea said. 'Break-ups are never easy, but I don't see why no strings would be a problem.'

'Hmm.' It wouldn't be right to question her any further, so Cal said, 'Well, I think you're a woman who knows her own mind so I'm not doubting you. As long as you're sure?'

Bea nodded. 'I'm sure. Truly. This is the tonic I need. Although...' She glanced at the chesterfield. Cal clocked exactly what she was getting at.

'I have a bed,' he said. 'In fact, I have several. I can keep things varied. Don't want you going home with the impression that Scottish men are boring lovers. At least not this one.'

Bea laughed. 'I haven't got that impression so far,' she said. 'I may even write a feature for the tourist board about how highly I recommend taking a Scottish lover.'

'Hmm, please don't do that.' That comment reminded Cal how much he wanted to keep his private life exceptionally private. He might not be an A-list celebrity, but he was known in the Scottish business world and, more specifically, Edinburgh, and word got around about these sorts of things. Cal liked his reputation to be twenty-four carat business, not to mention the fact that his father wasn't keen on having the Butler name tarnished by his son's escapades with what he referred to as 'flibbertigibbets', Elisabetta being a prime example.

Bea appeared a little taken aback. 'Oh, okay. I wasn't serious, but sure, I won't do that.' 'You don't like being flattered?'

'Ach, I can do flattery, if it's sincere. I'm just not a fan of being written about.'

'I see. Have you been written about before?'

'Kind of. I'd rather not talk about it to be honest.'

'Okay. Well, we'll keep it solely between us. Two months of fun, then bye bye.' Bea sapphire eyes shimmered.

Two months, then bye bye. This bothered Cal a little. *Why? She's giving exactly what you want. Don't you want her to want the same thing?*

'Sure, two months then we say goodbye, having given each other some amazing memories. I'm glad you approached me in the coffee shop that day, Bea. And that you persevered with getting a job here. You've enhanced the place.' Cal stopped. He was gushing too much. It wasn't his style, wasn't the style of a 'two months, then bye bye' guy. But he couldn't help it. Things were so much better since Bea came into his life … into the business's life. And a happy bar manager made for a successful bar. Yep, however you looked at it, it all made great business sense.

Chapter Twenty-Eight

A warm glow spread across Bea's face as she thought about what had happened between her and Cal. The sex was incredible. She had never known anything like it. Never known a man to set her body on fire like he had. But no strings? *Who was the person that made you say those words? Who was it that agreed to heat herself with the fire but keep it under control and not let the flames spread?* Bea didn't know that woman, but she did know that she liked her. Strings were Bea's default setting when it came to men so it would be something else to let herself go. Abandon herself to that body, those kisses, more orgasms. Many more. Now she would have Cal on tap for the rest of her working-vacation. There was a potent chemistry between them. It was perfect. Perfect for her well-being, to give her some time where she could switch off and only be focused on being in physical heaven with a Scotsman, perfect for giving her mind a break from thinking of Josh, and perfect to help stoke the fires of her writing. She was proud of herself for the decisions she'd made which had led her to this point. For taking control of her life.

Cal was such a different lover than Bea had known. Josh

was below average in bed but had constantly wanted his ego plumped to confirm that he was superb, wanted her to tell him how much she enjoyed sex with him; he believed he could offer women the pinnacle in lovemaking. Cal, on the other hand, didn't need his ego plumping at all, and delivered the goods. He wanted to please Bea and gained as much from her enjoyment as she did herself.

Can I do all this without falling for him? It was a tricky question, but probably she could. Cal was hot and sexy as hell, but personality wise he wasn't what she needed. *He's too closed off, too aloof, maybe even moody.* Bea needed more of a free spirit. Sure, Cal had raved about the sex, but she didn't suppose he was especially effusive with emotions, and after Josh, Bea needed kindness and openness.

There was also the issue of Cal probably becoming a father soon. He wouldn't have any interest in a new woman in his life when he'd have a little baby to shower love upon, especially in the early stages. And even if Bea never experienced anything stronger than lust for Cal, she didn't want to risk stirring up feelings of being second best. She didn't want to witness her lover cooing over his child and recoil in inadequacy, the way Josh had made her feel. When she was ready for a new relationship, Bea wanted to be that man's number one priority, to be his everything, to have a baby together. Was that selfish? She didn't think so. After what she went through with Josh, Bea deserved to be wholly loved. Cal Butler may not be the man to do it, but she could still appreciate him in other ways. And, ultimately, she had come here to write, and find the old carefree Bea again, and both those were apparently happening.

'So,' Cal said. 'Will you come and stay over tomorrow night? At the cottage at Belhaven. Besides the full pleasure package, I can offer you a selection of whiskies before bed, a hot shower and breakfast in the morning. Plus, neither of us is working on Monday so we can spend the day together. I'll take you surfing.'

Bea did a double take. 'Surfing? In Scotland?'

'Sure. Didn't you know we surf here?'

'But it's so cold.'

'Cold, pah! You Americans.'

'Oh, it's like that is it? Us Americans!'

'Ha ha. Yes, it is. You can't let a bit of cold stand in the way of living your life. We have some of the best waves for surfing and the beaches are near empty most of the time because, like you, most Scottish people are scared of the cold water. I have wetsuits and I'll teach you all you need to know. Then, afterwards, I'll enjoy peeling it off and seeing what's underneath.'

Bea chuckled. 'Well, when you put it like that, it sounds kind of tempting. And, to be honest, you had me at full pleasure package.'

Cal stood up and held his hands out for Bea. 'I'm looking forward to this,' he said as she joined him on her feet. 'I'm going to make sure you have an amazing time in Scotland that you never forget.'

'Well, I've already one episode in my memory bank, but I am definitely excited about adding more.'

'I'll pick you up at six then?' He pulled her to him and kissed her and a rushing river of anticipation rushed through Bea at the times that lay ahead with this gorgeous man who was holding her so confidently in his arms.

Chapter Twenty-Nine

As he'd promised, Cal arrived promptly at Bea's apartment at 6 pm on Sunday. As soon as she had determined via the intercom that it was him, Bea grabbed her small overnight bag and made her way down the stairs. She didn't want Cal to see where she was living, even if it was only temporary. She bet he hadn't ever lived in accommodation as bad as hers.

As she reached the front door, Bea's phone beeped with a message from Craig.

Just checking you're sure? Thought we could have a good time together.

Yes, absolutely she was sure. She'd called things off with Craig in a phone call that morning. It didn't sit well being with Cal and still having someone else in the wings, and Craig was never going to work out, not after last night's experience.

Cal was waiting outside the main door at ground level, wearing jeans and a blue button-down shirt and looking fresh and handsome in the low evening light. He kissed Bea gently, and she got a waft of his delicious cedarwood and lime scent.

'You look beautiful this evening,' he said.

'Thank you. You're very eye-catching yourself.'

'I try my best.' Cal reached for her bag. 'I'd have come up and got that for you.'

'Oh, it's nothing,' she replied. 'Not even heavy.'

'So, it's about an hour's drive,' Cal explained as he pulled away from the apartment. 'Hope you don't mind having to talk to me for that time.'

'On the contrary. I can't wait.'

'I would suggest you read to me, but knowing what's in your books, I'm not sure I could be trusted to concentrate on the road.'

'That is very flattering.' Bea glowed at the compliment. 'And I'm a big believer in road safety so let's stick to safe topics. Until we get to your house, at least.'

Cal smiled. The knee-weakening effect was something that probably cost Hollywood studios thousands in make-up and strategic lighting to create, and Cal just had it naturally. She would be sorry to have to leave that face behind, but what was the point fast-forwarding when they'd just begun their adventure together?

'So why do you live so far from the bar?' she asked. 'Far for Scotland that is. You must enjoy driving.'

'It's not that I enjoy driving as much as I need to have somewhere to get away from it all. I grew up in a village called Kinshore on the Kintyre Peninsula and I crave the country quiet to help recharge my batteries, you know? The bar can get intense and I love that, but I need the flip side too.'

'I understand,' said Bea. 'I grew up in a small town, too.'

'You did?'

'Yeah. New York City is an amazing place to live, but sometimes I need to go home to unwind and take my foot off the accelerator. So I can appreciate NYC when I'm back there.'

'Yes, exactly,' said Cal. 'I couldn't be Edinburgh Cal without Belhaven Cal. But too much village living and I'd go stir crazy. I need a break where old ladies don't chat over scones and tea about the fact that they saw you posting a letter that morning.' He chuckled.

'Are you something of a local celebrity, then?' Bea asked, then thought she saw something shift in Cal's face at this question. But if it bothered him he didn't reveal anything further.

'I'm definitely no celebrity. Although, I think maybe a few of the pensioners might have a bit of a crush on me. Dorothy Mackay asked me out on a date last week.'

'She did?'

'Aye, I went into her house to change a lightbulb and she asked if she could take me for tea and cake.'

'Are you sure it wasn't to say thank you for your handiwork?'

'Well maybe, but you weren't there, Bea. You didn't see the glint in her eye. She'd have me; I know she would.'

Cal's humour warmed Bea like gentle Scottish sunshine. There was a sweet and funny man underneath the cool exterior and spending time with him would be most enjoyable.

'And what was it like growing up on the Kintyre Peninsula?' she asked. 'It must have been idyllic.'

'Well, it's not all picture postcard, but it had its plusses. Again, there are places to surf, which me and my siblings love. And there's a ton of whisky. And, of course, some of my family.'

'Some?'

'Cara and Eilidh live down here, just a few houses along from me. Niall is in Australia and Sean and Nate are in Kinshore, as is my brother Jamie who works for the family business. Dad's the CEO, Jamie's the Chief Operating Officer.'

'You didn't want to work for the family business?'

'You ask a lot of questions, don't you?'

Maybe she was asking too much. She and Cal were meant to have a no-strings arrangement. Perhaps they shouldn't learn so much about each other's lives. He didn't appear to want to talk too much about his family, beyond the basics.

'Oh, sorry. You're right, I do. I think it might be an occupational hazard.'

'Of being a bartender? Mine is that I can tell what people's favourite drink is within five minutes of meeting them.'

'I meant writer but, wait, you can do that?'

'Yeah, I mean it took less time with you. Thirty seconds in and I knew you were an almond mocha drinker.'

'Ah! You're joking.'

'Well, I am about that, but, no, I meant I can tell what alcoholic drink someone likes. I knew you were a Manhattan woman, both literally and metaphorically.'

'You did? Why is that?'

'You're rich and decadent. Bold. And you struck me as a woman who isn't afraid of her whisky.'

'Oh, you're good,' said Bea. 'I'm not afraid of whisky. Although, I will admit to not knowing nearly enough about Scotch. Perhaps you could teach me.'

'Absolutely.' Cal's face lit up. 'I've a cellar full of inspiration and education. I did grow up pretty much bathing in the stuff, after all.'

After a while on the main road, Cal turned off onto a minor road leading to a small village signposted as Belhaven. A few minutes later he pulled up next to a stone cottage that must command exceptional views of the bay. It was stunning and Bea almost tumbled out of the car so she could absorb her surroundings.

'Welcome to my home.' Cal admired his house as if he had built it himself, the radiant joy in his face highlighted by golden evening sunlight.

Bea threw her hand to her heart. 'Oh my goodness, it's stunning,' she said. The wide bay was a deep teal blue with white-crested waves folding into the shore. Out in the background sat an enormous rock.

'That's the Bass Rock,' Cal explained. 'There's a castle and a lighthouse on it, as well as about 150,000 gannets.'

'Wow!' Bea scanned the coastline. There was barely a soul around, save a few lone dog walkers and one surfer catching the last of the evening waves.

'I don't suppose he has to worry about sharks at dusk,' she remarked.

Cal looked a little surprised that Bea knew the danger times for surfers when it came to sharks. She just smiled.

'Aye,' he said. 'It might be bollock-cold but it's extremely unlikely we'll meet anything more dangerous than the swell itself out there.'

'It's impressive swell,' said Bea. 'I never knew Scotland had such excellent surfing conditions. Although, it is "bollock-cold" for sure.' She rubbed her arms, encased only in a silk blouse.

Cal touched her arm for a moment. 'Come on, let's go inside. Can't have you getting a chill.' He grabbed Bea's bag from the boot of the car and led her to his home.

Through the door, Bea marvelled at Cal's cottage. The low raftered ceilings, the open fireplace, the large stove which sat under a window with breathtaking views across the bay. It was traditional, homely and characterful.

'Just like me,' Cal said, playfully when Bea shared these thoughts with him.

Bea noticed the table in the dining area of the open-plan lounge was set for a meal. There were placemats, cutlery and even empty wine glasses. Cal caught her staring.

'I was going to throw something together for dinner,' he

said. 'But I've had a different idea. How do you feel about fish and chips on the beach?'

'That sounds delightful,' Bea chirped. *It sounds even more perfect than dining indoors. For someone who isn't trying to pursue a romantic relationship, he's making quite an effort. If only all guys were like this.*

Chapter Thirty

Things were going well with Bea, Cal thought. The chat on the drive over was interesting and effortless, although he'd been keen to avoid too much talk of his family as all roads invariably led back to his father. Chat about his dad's illness when he was still trying to assimilate it was like swimming in the dark. The last thing Cal wanted was to start struggling with his incipient grief in front of Bea who was here for a bit of fun. Generally, though, he was at ease in her company. There were no awkward gaps in the conversation, and she understood when he was joking. Often his deadpan delivery confused people, so it was great that she was on his wavelength.

That they liked each other's company was a plus. Of course, for the type of relations they were going to be having it didn't strictly matter too much, but Cal couldn't go to bed with a woman without having some kind of communication with her. You had to talk, right? He was by no means a hopeless romantic, but he valued getting to know someone a bit before sleeping with them.

This all said, as soon as Cal took Bea into his cottage and

watched her clock the table setting, he saw how ridiculous the romantic meal idea was. What had he been thinking? It was over the top, even if he'd only been planning to rustle up a quick risotto.

So, in those moments of panic Cal changed their dinner plans and opted for fish and chips on the beach. It would be a brilliant way to show Bea the bay but with a low-key meal, so she didn't think he was coming on too 'Romeo'. He'd make sure they took a nice bottle of wine with them so his status as drinks connoisseur was intact.

Cal was grateful for Bea's ebullience and enthusiasm for his idea. Her effervescence had irked him at first but was great at pasting over any discomfort. Underneath it all, she could be feeling awkward, but for now he would take at face value that she was excited about dinner.

They walked to the local fish and chip shop where Cal ordered each of them a fish supper, explaining to Bea this was a Scottish name for fish and chips. Her curiosity and interest in something as trivial as this pleased him, particularly when she started asking what other Scottish idiosyncrasies he could teach her.

'I'll have a think,' Cal said. 'The only thing that comes to mind is that, contrary to myth, nobody in Scotland says "Och aye the noo" or eats deep fried Mars Bars. If you could spread the word on those, that would be great.'

Bea laughed and agreed that she would tell everyone she knew.

On the beach, they ate sitting sat on a small blanket Cal had brought from the car. He poured Bea a glass of chilled white wine and considered this might also be a bit too romantic, but he wasn't about to stand up and suggest that they get down to what they both knew was on the menu for afters. The best thing was to keep to general chat and not get too involved. It would be hard; he was curious about Bea, wanted to know more, to find out what made her tick, to keep making her laugh.

After they had finished eating, Bea was sitting cross-legged on the chequered blanket, holding a glass of Chablis, and staring out to sea, entirely entranced. Cal examined her face, hoping she wouldn't mind. Her pale skin was luminescent in the evening sunlight, the red hair that fell around her ears wisping lightly in the breeze; her neck long and graceful like a swan. How he wanted to crane in and inhale her scent. Then he would take her to him in an embrace and make passionate love to her on the sand and... *Wait! What?* Cal caught himself on this thought. What was he doing, thinking about 'making passionate love' to this woman? *Get it together, Butler.*

'Sorry?' Bea turned to him. Cal started in shock. Had he said that out loud?

'Oh, nothing. I often mumble to myself when I'm out here, because usually I'm alone. Forgot I wasn't.'

'Charming.' Bea sipped her wine and he couldn't work out if she was amused or not.

'No, no, it's a compliment,' he insisted. 'Means I'm comfortable in your company.'

'We've come a long way since the first day we met, hey?' Okay, she wasn't pissed off at him; that was good. 'I think maybe you hated my company that day.'

'Hate is not a word I like to use, but let's just say I wasn't entirely charmed. Although I appreciated certain aspects of you.'

'You did? And what might those be?' There was a glint in Bea's expression.

Cal shifted closer to her on the blanket. He tilted her chin, raising her face slightly to the dimming evening sun. 'Well, there was this for a start,' he said. 'This face, these beautiful blue eyes, this perfect skin ... these.' He traced his thumb along Bea's lips and they parted slightly at his touch. She met his gaze, and they became hypnotically entranced, silent, breathing the other in.

'Your face,' Bea said, finally. 'It's mesmerising. I know you were grumpy at me for skipping in the line that day, but I saw a gleam in these emerald eyes that lit me up somehow. And your voice.'

'My voice?'

'Yes.'

'What? This voice?' Cal affected a deeper timbre.

'Yes, even that "pretend Cal" voice. I could listen to it all day, whether it's ticking me off for jumping the line or telling me to take my clothes off. Your Scottish tones get me here.' Bea placed her fist on her heart. 'And other places too.' She smiled softly.

'So, if I were to whisper in your ear,' Cal asked, 'could I make you do anything I wanted?'

'You could probably do that anyway,' she said. 'But please, whisper all the same.'

Cal leaned towards Bea's neck again, reeling gently from the soft honeysuckle scent. 'Bea Gracie,' he whispered, 'I'd like to take you home, take your clothes off and do unspeakable things to you.'

For a moment, Bea's eyes fell shut, and Cal could swear he saw something rush through her. When she opened them again, her lids were low and her pout seemed pinker, fuller somehow. She gazed at him dreamily, trancelike, before dropping her sights to his mouth. Taking his signal from this, Cal leaned towards her perfect face, gathered those peach cheeks in his hands, and did what was easily becoming one of his favourite things in the world – kissed Bea.

Chapter Thirty-One

The late summer sun dipped and the temperature cooled considerably, a light breeze adding an extra layer of chill to the sea air. The cold North Sea crashed into the shore, but Bea barely noticed any of it. The kiss with Cal was consuming almost every fibre of her being. She wanted to be aware of each moment; her senses concentrated on all the detail. His strong hands caressing her skin as their mouths pressed hungrily together; the ridges of his muscular arms that ignited something ancient within her; his masculine scent pervading her senses and intermingling with the sweet natural aroma of his skin; the light glance of his rough stubble on her face.

Cal pulled back and Bea found she was now holding his face, both of them breathing yet barely. His jaw was powerful under her gentle touch and she liked the way his chin bristled in her palms as he spoke.

'I think we have to go home now or risk getting arrested for public indecency.'

'Does this mean I have to stop kissing you?' Bea nuzzled her face into Cal's neck. He smelled divine: the citrus and cedarwood had crawled into bed with the warm undertones of his skin and morphed into a unique and dangerously delicious Cal Butler scent.

'Only briefly. It's about three minutes to the house, then I'm all yours.' The vibrations from his voice made her skin tingle.

'Mmm, okay, if we have to.'

'It's for the greater good.' Cal stood up. 'Let's clear up and get going.' He reached out out for Bea and she rose to meet him on the blanket. Then he brought her to him again and ravished her with more kisses.

'I don't know about the greater good, but this feels pretty damned nice,' Bea murmured.

'Aye, but I think old Dorothy might keel over with shock before her eighty-fifth birthday if she spots me doing all the things I want to do to you on this blanket. Right, come on. Jings, woman, I never knew such poor willpower until I met you.'

Bea's skin prickled at these words, at knowing this man found it as hard to resist her as she did him. She had never been one for sex in public places but if Cal had tried, she didn't doubt that they would have made love on the picnic blanket on the freezing Scottish beach, regardless of who might have seen.

As Bea watched Cal's capable hands unlock the door of the cottage, she imagined them all over her body again. In the porch, they slipped off their shoes, then as soon as they were behind closed doors, Cal dropped the bag and blanket and wrapped his arms round Bea. Now there would be no holding back, no restrictions.

'Come here, Ms Gracie, and let me at you.' He placed his delectable lips on hers once more. 'Mmm, you might need warmed up.' Bea's goose bumped arms were encased only in a thin cardigan.

'I'm freezing,' she agreed. 'You're like a furnace, though.' Through his shirt, Cal's firm and febrile body was, despite the temperate weather, pumping heat. Another excuse to get close to him.

'I'm fairly hot-blooded. And it takes a lot for a Scotsman to get cold. But come on, let's get your temperature rising.' Cal reached out for Bea's hands and took the stairs backwards, melting her with the need in his eyes. It was like he relished the anticipation. Bea had no idea how he could handle the torment of going backwards when she was struggling to move fast enough the right way round.

The bedroom was larger than Bea expected, for a cottage of this humble size, and commanded views out to sea, similar to those of the kitchen.

'Look at that view.' She was transfixed. The sun had dipped down to the horizon, and the sky was a vibrant palette of apricots, pinks and purples.

'Yeah, it's spectacular. But never mind that view. What about this one?' Cal did a circular motion around his face, making Bea laugh.

'This view blows that one out of the water,' she said.

'Yeah, likewise. Waves are nice and all that, but I'm more interested in you. So, if I promise to warm you up, can I take this off?' He held her cardigan at her shoulder blades ready to peel it from her body.

Bea was never going to do anything but nod to this. Cal gently pulled the garment down her arms and cast it onto a chair.

'And this?' He traced along the V of her blouse above her cleavage, skimming her décolletage as he approached the top button. She made a hum of consent. He would drive her wild if he undressed her at this pace. But, as Cal slowly undid the buttons on the blouse, as if reading her thoughts, he made an admission.

'Just so you know, I'm driving myself crazy here.'

'You're driving me crazy too.'

'I just want to appreciate you.' The blouse joined the cardigan and Bea was in only her bra and jeans now. Her nipples stiffened as Cal's sensual gaze roamed over her.

'What about you?' she said. 'I want to appreciate you too.' Her hands gravitated to the buttons of his shirt and she began slowly revealing the frame of a god which hid beneath. She knew he was watching her intently and was close enough to feel the increasing appreciation in his pants.

Once Cal's shirt was on the floor, Bea visually devoured him, from the angular jut of his clavicles to the faultless sculpture of his abs. He was perfect. But before she had time to admire any further, his solid palm was on her back, encouraging her to him then unhooking her bra. Her nipples grazed firm, fevered skin. Moments passed. She could hardly bear it – the heat surging through her from just the tips of her breasts meeting this man's body.

Cal evidently couldn't bear it either. Seconds later, his mouth claimed Bea's, hot and ravenous. The urgency burned in the room as intense as the amber sunset outside.

They fell to the bed, denim, naked skin and need. Cal crawled up Bea's body then hovered over her, propping himself up on his strapping arms and gazing at her unveiled breasts.

'These are fucking incredible.'

'You don't think they're too big?' Bea had at many points in her life been self-conscious of her ample chest size.

But Cal was adamant. 'Absolutely, definitely not,' he said, before gravitating to one nipple and sucking it with zeal as if to assure her of his approval. He shifted to move himself up her body and Bea felt the force of his erection once again.

'Oh, Cal, that is so good,' she said breathlessly. Then he flicked his tongue across the tip and she could form no words, only thousands of mini exhales, until she had no choice but to breathe in again.

Just as Bea didn't think she could take the intensity any more, Cal travelled down and down, kissing her stomach all the way to the waistband of her jeans, one hand still indulging her breast as he went. When he reached the sensitive skin above the top button, Bea spoke. 'You don't even have to ask'.

Cal smiled and with a deft flick, the button was free and the zipper descending. He stood at the foot of the bed and peeled the jeans from her legs. She knew her arousal was visible through the white fabric of her panties.

Sure enough, he didn't miss it.

'Oh jeez.' Gently Cal coaxed her knees apart and caressed the damp fabric. 'You're soaking.'

'I know,' Bea shuddered.

He teased her some more by continuing his caresses. She needed no more than this light stimulation. Anything more would have been too much. Whimpering, she closed her eyes. He took the waistband of the panties between his teeth and pulled. The anticipation was almost unbearable. 'Oh, Cal. Please don't stop.' Bea's cries punctured the air.

'I haven't even started yet.' He edged her underwear over her knees and across her ankles. 'Fuck! Look at you.'

Bea was now fully naked in front of her boss, although the employer–employee dynamic had long been obliterated. Nevertheless, something about it sent a shot through her, like whisky on fire. There had been a barrier of something akin to ice between them and now here they were, pulsating with longing for each other. Having Cal finally let go and admit how much he wanted her was what set things going and Bea was so glad he'd realised that they had too much chemistry to ignore. Now there would be no protestations that he had to keep a professional distance.

Cal nudged Bea's knees apart a little further so she was

fully exposed to him. For a moment or two, he gazed in a trance. Then he reached for the buttons on his own jeans and removed them. Was he going to penetrate her already? Bea wondered. Although she was aching for him, she knew that as soon as he was inside her, the road to climax would be a short one and she wanted to prolong this experience as much as possible.

'Don't worry,' Cal affirmed, as if reading her mind. 'I'm just getting more comfortable.' Bea relaxed. She could see the impressive bulge jutting through his boxers. It couldn't be comfortable having to encase that within the confines of denim jeans. 'I don't want this to be over yet and once we start, I don't think we'll be on the go for long.' He climbed onto the bed and kneeled between Bea's legs. He was so close. She ached. And when he talked about being together in the way he did, in his rich like-honeyed-Scotch accent, it made her desperate for him.

'Please, Cal, I can't bear it. I need you to touch me.'

That wish was his command and Cal teased across Bea's soft wetness. With volume that ordinarily she'd be self-conscious about, Bea cried out and he continued tantalising her soft undulations, looking like he couldn't quite believe this was real.

'Bea, you are perfect. Every inch of you. You turn me on so much.'

Bea could barely speak to return the compliment and Cal appeared to relish that she was so lost in bliss at his hand. She met his desirous gaze and her heart leapt. He was so utterly gorgeous it was almost unbearable. Then, staring into her eyes, Cal plunged his fingers deep into Bea's sex and she was powerless to do anything but beg him for more. Without hesitation, Cal circled his thumb whilst his fingers moved through her heat. She had wanted him inside her as she came, but that chance was gone. Her climax was approaching, and the window for saying no was gone.

'I'm going to come, Cal. If you...' She was trying to say that if he wanted inside her and feel her orgasm then he had better do it fast. But Cal appeared intent on letting Bea soar to her pinnacle by the skill of his hand alone. So she watched him watch the promise of an orgasm circling up from her depths. It was so intimate, and in that moment Bea wanted, more than anything, for him to see her climax. She didn't have long to wait as this thought was the trigger that sent her spiralling into paradise and her eyes fell closed, her head tipped back and Cal's name rang from her lips, her euphoric cries ringing in synchronicity with each rich and vibrant pulsation in her sex.

Chapter Thirty-Two

Cal loved watching Bea come at his touch. The quivering as her sex shuddered with its climax, intensified his erection a thousandfold. She was real, this woman. Honest, grounded and full of heart. Cal had always prided himself on being genuine in life and in bed, and now here was a woman who was the same. She was a little self-conscious about her body, and that made her more human, which he loved. She enjoyed sex; she wasn't faking it on any level and, more pertinently, she enjoyed sex with him, although, they hadn't got to the penetration part yet. But they would. Cal needed to be inside Bea, and he was in no doubt that he could make her come again, so she would enjoy herself as much as he was.

Bea was basking in the afterglow, her lids drowsy, her nipples pert from the chill in the air. Cal roamed his gaze down her body, from the full breasts, to the curve of her womanly hips – those hips that wiggled and teased him as she walked – then to the convex dip that led to everything he so badly desired. He needed this woman so much.

To his surprise, as he was imagining entering her, Bea sat

up on the bed. She leaned over and kissed him softly on the lips.

'Thank you,' she said. 'You know how to satisfy a woman.'

'There wasn't a dull moment for me either. It looked intense.'

'Oh, it was. And I want more. But first, I want to see you come.'

'Oh aye?'

'Oh, aye.' Bea reached down to the waistband of Cal's boxers he was still very much erect and ran her fingertip across the skin inside. Cal groaned. 'Oh, Bea.' He wasn't sure how long he could last.

Bea inched the boxers down over Cal's hips and let his cock burst free, this partial release taunting with the promise of full abandonment. He watched as she marvelled at what she had uncovered. Delight surged through him, knowing Bea liked his body. But when she poised her mouth over him, Cal spoke firmly.

'No,' he said.

'No?'

'I do want it, but if you do that now, I'll come in seconds. Lie back down.'

Bea did as he asked. Cal reached over to the bedside cabinet and grabbed the condom he'd laid there earlier. He ran it down over his length then moved over Bea.

'I want you to enjoy this as much as me,' he said. 'I'll make sure you do.'

The vision of sensuality that was Bea's face at his promise and the way she subtly raised her hips in response meant Cal could wait no longer. He guided himself into her. She was so soft and soaking from her earlier climax that he heard an unfamiliar primal sound emerge from his throat.

'Shit, you feel so good. You're so wet. And hot.'

Bea's eyes had glazed over, as if rock hard Cal inside her

had brought her back round to the beginning again. 'You like that?' he asked.

'Oh, Cal, I've never felt anything like this.'

'Me neither.' He thrust deeper into Bea, his senses attuned with precision to everything her body told him: the resonance of her moans, the minor shift on her face from pleasure to something else altogether. Then, he sunk in and found the spot fathoms within her that was going to take her to a place of no return. She bucked up and dug her nails into his back. That was it. Bea was done for. Cal was done for. He surged deep – so deep – until her muscles were contracting in rapid pulsations around his cock. His job was complete in carrying her onto the wave of her second climax and, at last, Cal released into Bea, his thunderous roar reverberating around the house and through the walls and out onto the ocean where it met his precious waves in force and intensity.

Chapter Thirty-Three

'I think you should stay a couple more days,' Cal murmured as he curved his body round Bea's, atop the bedcovers.

Bea's mouth and soul lifted upwards, as much at the sensation of his powerful arms as his words. 'I'd love to, but what about the bar? Don't you need to be there?'

'I think I might have to call in a favour from someone. I wouldn't normally but this is an emergency.'

Bea laughed. 'An emergency?'

Cal was deadpan as ever. 'Aye, a serious one. You're going to be leaving this country soon and if I don't get as much of you as possible before then, I might sexually dehydrate.'

Bea's laughter intensified, and she turned to face Cal. 'Sexually dehydrate! I would never have thought the first day I met you that you could be so funny. In fact, I will admit to not seeing you as much more than a pretty face – a kind of grumpy pretty face – but you have depths.'

Cal arched his eyebrow in amusement. 'Oh, I have depths, do I? Nice of you to notice.'

Bea nodded. It was true. When she'd first met Cal, she'd

immediately sensed chemistry between them, which she'd thought was purely sexual. But the more time she spent with this man, the more she saw of the person underneath the gruff exterior. He was passionate, attentive, and he had a wicked sense of humour. In fact, it made Bea question what exactly sexual chemistry was. Had that sexual compatibility encompassed something else? Had her body instinctively known that she could have much more than a physical connection with this man? That they could click on a personal level, too?

'Well, you have to admit that you don't give much away,' she said.

'Hmm, okay, you have a point.' Cal draped his arm around Bea and pulled her closer. 'But I'll tell you something, there's not many people are invited to this cottage and get to spend forty-eight hours up and personal with me.'

Bea suspected she was hearing the truth. Cal Butler seemed a very private person. So why had he let her in? Did he solely want to bed her and let her go? Or was he feeling this something that she was? Were they letting themselves in for trouble by spending this time together?

Oh, stop overthinking it. You know it's short-term thing. He's said it himself. Sure, he's invited you to his cottage, but that's because he's a gentleman and not the type to invite you over for a couple of hours then call you a cab. Remember, you're an author doing research and getting plenty of material whilst having a very nice time indeed, and this is nothing more than a bridging experience between your break-up with Josh and whoever comes next when you go back home. You need to be tougher, Bea.

'You okay?' Cal gazed questioningly at her. 'If you don't want to stay longer, just say and I can drive you home.' His expression was serious and Bea knew his concern that she might not be having a good time was genuine. She drifted her fingers over the rough stubble of his cheek.

'Three things,' she said. 'I am having a fantastic time, I do not need to go home, and what are we doing tomorrow?'

Cal laughed and a tension that Bea hadn't noticed in his body disappeared. 'Well,' he inched himself even closer until they were touching intimately again, 'in case you have forgotten, we are going surfing. You all right with that?'

'Um...'

'I can get you a wetsuit so you don't have to worry about the cold.'

'Okay, so the only thing to worry about is me showing you up with my surfing skills?'

A huge grin spread across Cal's face before he appeared to think better of it. 'You know, I assumed that you can't surf, but that is totally wrong of me. Can you surf?'

'Maybe.' Bea attempted an enigmatic smile.

'I can't wait to find out. But you know what's important before getting out in the water is a proper warm-up. So, be prepared for that first thing.'

Bea laughed, and Cal stopped her merriment with a kiss. 'I don't know why you're laughing.' He was as droll as ever. 'A warm-up is an important thing.'

'Oh, I know.' She skimmed her touch down Cal's ripped back. 'I can't wait to wake up tomorrow and get started on the impressive swell out there. But I think we should probably do a practice run on your other impressive swell, right now. If that's okay with you?'

The room rang with Cal's laughter. 'That is more than okay with me,' he said, his agreement rich and deep, like coffee laced with a mature malt. 'More than okay.'

Chapter Thirty-Four

Bea fell asleep first and Cal lay awake marvelling at this amazing woman he'd invited into his home. He hadn't been lying when he said that was something he didn't normally do. But Bea was only around for a short while, so it was pointless grabbing an evening here and there. They had to make the most of the time they had. It didn't mean he was making a commitment to her. And even if he liked her a little more than physically, what did it matter? She was going back to the US soon, so he'd need to get over it. Plus, he was serious when he'd said he wasn't getting into any more relationships until the baby drama was over.

The baby drama. Oh God! Cal didn't want to think about that; the sex that had potentially brought a new life into being was nothing compared to what he'd just experienced with Bea. He'd been walking around blind, accepting half-hearted because he thought that was as good as it got. Thank goodness Bea was so provocative in the coffee shop that day. Even if they could never have a future, he knew now not to settle for anything less than astounding.

The moonlight cast Bea's long red waves in a warm

glowing balm and Cal reached out to touch them. *What if I never meet anyone as incredible as her? What if I don't want to?*

He pulled away, rolled onto his back and closed his eyes. He needed to switch off these pointless thoughts so he could get to sleep.

The next morning, Cal awoke before Bea and lay watching her in the morning light streaming through the windows. Last night, they'd fallen asleep without shutting the curtains. She was perfect, tendrils of luscious scarlet cascading across the pillow, the soft swell of her breasts rising where the covers stopped. Cal wanted to reach down and cup those, let her stir, a light buzz of sexual arousal bringing her round from whatever dreams she was enjoying, then let his hand move lower, caressing and stimulating her until that shimmering buzz was all-encompassing rhapsody. He couldn't wait to see her come again.

There was an intensity in the room, in his thoughts, nudging at Cal. He'd noticed the beginnings of it last night, and it was here again now but louder in the morning light. There was something about just watching Bea. Not only did he want to reach down and touch her, he wanted to hold her, to pull her to him and feel her next to him as if they were one. *These are dangerous thoughts. Hopefully, getting in the fresh morning surf will help clear the heid.*

Cal threw on some boxers and went downstairs to make a light breakfast. They'd need some energy before their surf, then they could feast on whatever they wanted, food and otherwise. There was only one hitch to getting into the cool morning waters and that was getting Bea a wetsuit. This meant texting his sister, Cara, to ask if he could borrow her spare. But Cal didn't want to text Cara because then Cara would want to know why Cal needed the wetsuit and would no doubt insist on bringing it round, which would inevitably lead to her seeing what was happening between him and Bea.

Maybe, if he timed it right, he could pop out to meet Cara on the road while Bea was in the shower. Not that he wanted to hide Bea from his family. He just didn't need any more questions about his personal life than the baby situation had already caused. He sent his sister a text.

Less than ten minutes later there was a knock at the front door. Cal knew before he even opened it who it was. Exactly what he hadn't wanted to happen. He should have gone to Cara's unannounced.

'Morning, Sis.' Cal raked his hand through his hair and tried to look pleased since she was effectively doing him a favour.

'Morning. I thought I'd save you the bother of coming round and... Oh, hello again.'

'What?' Cal turned to see that Bea was standing in the kitchen wearing a pair of his sweatpants and a t-shirt from the chair in the bedroom, a look which, despite its casualness, sent flames of desire through him. How could one woman be so sexy first thing in the morning, in his own clothes no less?

'Morning, Cara!' Bea said, brightly, approaching the door.

'Hi again, Bea, isn't it?' Cara was exuberant with friendliness, although Cal knew that she'd be lining up a thousand questions in her brain and he fully expected MI5 style interrogation at some stage in the next five seconds. 'So nice to see you again. I brought this wetsuit for you. It doesn't fit me, so you're welcome to keep it.'

'Oh, that's incredibly kind of you,' Bea said, with faultless politeness. 'Thank you. I can't wait to go surfing.'

'Aye, thanks, Cara,' said Cal. 'You didn't have to come over. I'd have come and got it off you.'

'No problem. I was taking Freddo for a walk, anyway.' Cara motioned to the small white West Highland terrier at her feet.

Bea leaned down to ruffle the dog's fur. 'Oh, he's

gorgeous.' Freddo took to her, panting in delight. Something warmed in Cal that she was so friendly to animals.

'He likes you.' Cara looked up at Cal with a face full of annoying knowingness. Had she clocked the way he was gawping at Bea? Dammit. He loved his sister, but she didn't miss a trick.

'And I like him.' Bea stroked the dog's ears. Cara grinned at Cal, deciding to focus on the alternative meaning to this statement, and forced a smile back that said, yes, I know exactly what you're thinking but we're not having this conversation any time soon.

'Okay, well thanks, Cara.' Cal moved the door a fraction towards his sister. 'I'll bring back the wetsuit during the week.'

'Honestly,' she said. 'You're welcome to keep it.'

'Thank you. That's very kind of you.' Bea stood up again. 'But I'm heading back to the States in a couple of months.'

'Oh, what a shame.' Cara's face fell as if she were genuinely saddened by this. He could see her visually trying to nudge him, as if she wanted him to tell Bea not to go, that she could stay with him, which he would never say because that wasn't what they'd agreed and wasn't what Bea wanted. And if he was going to say it, it wouldn't have been in front of his sister.

'Aye well, why live here when you could live in New York?' Cal wondered if a hint of grievance came through in his words. He hadn't meant them to sound that way. Was he jealous of New York because it would soon get this wonderful woman back and he'd be on his own again?

'You should show her some of Scotland before she goes back,' Cara declared.

'Aye, Cara, thanks. I'm on it. That's why she's here. We're going surfing, remember?' Cal was lightly hinting that he'd like to get on with the morning pursuit they had planned. This conversation was irritating him slightly, as well as eating into time he should be spending with Bea.

'In fact,' said Cara. 'You should come to the party for our dad. She should come to Dad's party, Cal.'

Cal couldn't believe Cara had said this, although, if truth be told, it was typical her. His father's party was a personal family-and-close-friends affair at a sensitive time. He knew that Cara knew this, but that she would be so proud of their dad that she would want it to be a celebration for everyone to attend. Although, he suspected something else. Cara knew her brother inside out and she'd have been able to tell from the way he glanced at Bea that he was well on his way to being smitten. If she saw an opportunity to expedite Cal settling down with someone, then she'd take it, whether that person lived in Edinburgh or three thousand miles away in New York City. Cara meant well; it was just that that she was ridiculously tactless. He had to be grateful that she hadn't mentioned the baby this morning.

'I don't know if Cal's told you—' Cara began.

'Cara!' Cal spoke firmly to his sister. 'Thank you for the wetsuit. We both appreciate it, but...'

Cara's face flooded with some understanding. 'No problem, I understand,' she said. 'I'm getting ahead of myself. They doled out all the family reserve out for the firstborn.' She winked at Bea. Cal bit his lip. If he'd been trying to retain any family mystique, his sister could put paid to those plans in an instant.

'Sorry about that,' he said to Bea after he'd closed the door. 'My sister can be quite ... interfering.'

'I thought she was charming,' said Bea. 'Just like her big brother.'

This was enough to loosen the knot of frustration that Cara had created in Cal's gut. It hadn't helped that all the things she'd suggested were thoughts that had already run through his mind, including the possibility of Bea coming to his father's party. But it had felt like too much. It could be dressed up as showing her the best that Scotland has to offer: an insight into Scottish family life that the average tourist would never experience. But it could also come across as too full on, as if he were imagining himself as her boyfriend, taking her to meet his family for the first time. Bea wasn't that sort of woman. No-strings lovers didn't come to family gatherings. And she didn't have an expression of expectation on her face, which suggested she wasn't bothered about being invited.

Cal enveloped Bea in his arms. 'Well, thank you very much,' he said, roused by mere seconds of her closeness to her. 'You are a sight to behold in my clothes.' He murmured into her neck, 'But I will have to ask you to take them off,' and skimmed along the neckline of his shirt where Bea's cleavage was visible.

'Oh, that's right,' said Bea. 'I've got a wetsuit to put on.'

Cal loved this woman's cheeky wit: how she could know exactly what he was thinking but subvert his words to make them mean something else, all in the name of teasing him. A product of that lively mind he'd previously interpreted as making her high maintenance when she was simply vibrant and alive. And boy did she bring him alive. A hundred per cent vital, from his brain to his toes and one other exceptionally vital place in between.

Chapter Thirty-Five

Removing Cal's clothes from her own body under the flimsy premise of putting on a wetsuit, Bea took her time, making sure she had his full attention as she slowly and deliberately released each button from its buttonhole. Fortunately, the blinds were still closed, so she didn't have to worry about being seen by anyone on the street outside.

Bea could quite easily have worn something of her own when she'd awoken this morning, but the lack of Cal in the bed beside her had made her crave his presence, a longing that had caught her off guard. This was the first overnight they had spent together, and already the bed was empty without him. She'd pressed her nose into his pillow. It smelt of Cal, and Bea's sex fluttered, but something in her heart too. *What is going on with you? You must be lightheaded from not enough sleep.* It didn't escape her notice that as she glanced to the chair by the window for something to wear to breakfast, she was gravitating towards Cal's clothes. And as she slipped his shirt over her head and pulled on his sweatpants, that fluttering happened again.

The fluttering was turning to a throbbing now as Bea slowly revealed herself to Cal, his sights intent on her, rich with lust but something else too. Admiration, maybe? *Well, I suppose most men would admire a woman who stripped for them in their lounge.*

Bea reached the last button, and the shirt fell open to reveal her bare breasts. Cal stood fixed to the spot, drinking her in. Passion flared resoundingly in Bea's sex as she watched him watching her. That he was getting pleasure from her body made her blood rush. Her nipples hardened. She tweaked one of them. Cal's eyes widened and a quick glance to his boxers told Bea how aroused he was already.

'You like this?' she asked, knowing full well what the answer was.

'Aye,' Cal said lowly. 'You have the most beautiful breasts ever. Keep touching them for me.'

Bea wet one of her fingers with her tongue, then placed it back on her nipple, moving in circular motions. She tilted her head back a little and let out a whimper. There was no faking going on here. This was turning her on in the most magnificent way possible.

'Oh, baby,' said Cal, and Bea's sex fluttered again. Calling her baby was intimate, somehow. 'Keep touching yourself. Tell me how it feels.'

'It's so good,' Bea whispered. 'I'm imagining it's your tongue.' She caressed both nipples. 'Oh, Cal,' she moaned, 'it's so fucking good.'

'Show me more,' Cal demanded. 'I want to see all of you.'

Bea stepped out of the sweatpants. She'd been nude when she put them on, so she was now fully exposed to Cal.

'Oh, shit.' Cal's eyes were clamped now on Bea's sex. 'You are even more stunning every time I see you like this.' There was no denying he desperately wanted to touch her but was holding back. Bea could understand; the anticipation was incredible, which meant that when they finally took each other, it would be even better. She delicately trailed her touch from her nipple down her stomach to graze across her soft pubic hair where she lingered, waiting for a command from Cal. She didn't have to wait long.

'Touch yourself for me, Bea,' he said. 'Make yourself wet.'

'I'm already wet looking at you. But I'm going to get wetter.' Bea plunged her finger into her slick heat and stimulated herself, her moans growing in amplification.

Cal pulled off his boxers to reveal his magnificent morning erection and manipulated his cock. 'Oh, Bea.'

Bea whimpered as she watched him masturbate, urging herself towards him with potent need.

'You need me, don't you?' he said.

'I need you so much.' From the strain on his face, the hunger was mutual. She glanced around the room before coming to rest on the kitchen table.

Knowing instinctively what she was thinking, Cal said, 'Sit on the table; I have to get a condom.'

As Cal ran to get protection, Bea hitched herself up onto the table. Moments later, Cal returned, drenched in lust at the sight of her ready for him, put the condom on and in one sweeping motion they were as one. Deep in her soaking heat, he steadied the back of her neck with his hand – plunging so far into her that it was like he was invading her soul. Where last night they had both wanted to prolong things as long as possible, this morning they had a desperate urgency about taking each other's bodies, as if they needed both to grab as much as possible from the other, to take their kicks while the kicks were still there for the taking.

Watching Cal steer himself in and out of her, Bea swelled impossibly until she could swell no more and soon her orgasm was crashing over her again and again and again. As her climactic pulsations gripped Cal's thick manhood, his erection hardened beyond belief and she watched, encapsulated in pure ecstasy as he threw his head back and let go a tremendous bellow, his climax finally overtaking him, body and soul and everything in between.

Chapter Thirty-Six

Wetsuits finally on, Cal and Bea grabbed their boards and made their way down to the beach. It was still early and save for a few more dog walkers than last night, the beach was again a vast expanse of emptiness.

Bea watched Cal stride towards the water, so strong and confident. She could tell it was his passion. And the man she had spent the night with was passionate about a lot of things: his business, which he put so much effort into, his family, who she could tell he cared deeply about just by the way he was with Cara, his staff, and treating others fairly. Not to mention surfing and herself. The way he made sure that she gained sexual satisfaction first showed he could put himself before others. And now he wanted to spend his time sharing his beloved waves with her. It was a delight having Cal revealed to her minute by minute. Bea watched in wonder as he threw himself under an incoming crasher, then rose again, hair slick with seawater. He was so damned sexy.

'It's fresh!' Bea remarked as she waded into the water to hip level.

'It's not the warmest, but once you're in and moving around you acclimatise, and all you have to worry about is where your next hit is coming from.'

Bea thought this sounded like her experience with Cal so far. Where was her next hit coming from? She plunged under the water too, then came up gasping in quick breaths. 'Oh! Scottish water is co-o-old!'

Cal grinned. 'Yep. Do you need me to show you what to do? Or have you done this all before? We never quite got to the bottom of that, and I think you might be about to show me up.'

'You know.' Bea shot Cal an indecipherable look. 'I'll give this one a go on my own.' She jumped on her board and paddled, ducking under and embracing the rush each time an exhilarating Scottish wave came crashing over her head.

* * *

She could surf. Boy, could she surf. Cal stared open jawed from his board as Bea rode the previous wave and he waited for the next one to come in. She cut a magnificent figure out there on the powerful blue. He could imagine a photo of her surfing a wave at dusk, those beautiful curves silhouetted against the teal and grey backdrop. He would hang something like that on his wall. Have it as a screensaver on his phone. *What the…?* He was losing it for this woman. She was invading his mind, his body, his everything. And unlike the Cal he knew, he wasn't trying to fight it at all.

The swell of the next wave surged up and Cal swung his board round and paddled. Soon, the wave was peaking under him and he was jumping up and riding it into the shore to meet Bea who was getting ready to paddle back out to do it all again.

'I had an inkling,' he said when they were both hip deep in

water again. 'Looks like I was right. You can surf. And you're bloody good.'

Bea laughed, spilling over with sea air and exhilaration. 'I never quite got round to telling you that I grew up in California. Learned when I was a kid. I love it.'

Cal shook his head in amazement. Could this woman be any more perfect? He wanted to bring her into an embrace, reach round and pull down the zip of her wetsuit, fall into the water with the waves roaring above them as they devoured each other's bodies in the surf. But he knew that could never happen. Amongst other reasons, Scottish water was barely warm enough to surf in; nobody would be stupid enough attempt to have sex in it. A kiss, however, was a different thing.

'You were sensational out there,' he said. 'I'm really impressed.' Holding onto his board, he brought her to him and kissed her, a salty yet warm kiss made of layers of desire and a new understanding. Bea kissed him back with equal energy, the softness and heat of her mouth countered by the cold of the water surrounding them.

Cal opened his eyes and met her head on. Those sapphire eyes were sparkling under wet lashes, her face was make-up free, fresh and flawless. She was a natural beauty and a natural soul who belonged in the ocean as much as she belonged behind a bar. And she was with him. It felt good – to know that for the next few weeks Bea was his woman to kiss, make love to and marvel at. But at the back of Cal's mind a question was niggling at him. *How on earth am I going to let her go and meet someone else quite this amazing? There can't possibly be another package like this out there.*

* * *

Bea adored the exhilaration of the morning surf. It was some time since she'd been on a board and she had no idea how

156

easily her muscle memory would kick in. Hence, she hadn't wanted to tell Cal that she could surf. But it all came back as easily as riding a bike and she was entirely at home in the Scottish water, not even noticing the chill of the waves after a while. Another place she was at home was in Cal's presence. She'd admit it was a bit of a bonus surprising him with her surfing abilities, seeing him so bright with joy that she shared his love for the ocean. And even more of a rush when he pulled her to him in the surf and kissed her hotly. She was pretty sure she was the luckiest girl in the world at that moment in time.

As Cal kissed her, Bea kept one hand on her surfboard and ran the other through his wet hair, trying hard to savour every sensation. This wasn't going to last for long. Soon she would have to go home, and she wanted to appreciate the short time with this wonderful man. But the more Bea focused on enjoying the moment, the more something niggled that she couldn't ignore. Just as the waves tried to pull away Bea's board, something was tugging at her heart. Something Cal-shaped. Could she ride the wave she and he had said they would ride together? Could she make it to shore, enjoying the energy under her as she went, feeling the rhythm of the ocean below her feet and taking in the surroundings? Or was she going to wobble, fall and get pulled under by the current? She wasn't sure, but with this beautiful man's lips on her own, in their own island of warmth while the waters rushed around them, she was helpless to say no.

Chapter Thirty-Seven

Cal and Bea surfed for another hour or so, until they came to an unspoken agreement that they were starving and needed to grab an early lunch.

'Hungry work, eh?' Cal was making sandwiches at the kitchen table, his wetsuit pulled down to reveal his perfectly sculpted abdominals and surfer's arms. Bea was sitting on the other side of the table with a big bath towel wrapped around her.

'Mmm,' she said, making no efforts to hide what she was humming in appreciation of.

Cal laughed, recognising her thoughts. 'You're insatiable, woman. Can't a man make some sandwiches without being ogled at?'

'I'm afraid if you will make sandwiches dressed like that and looking like you do, then you're going to get ogled.' Bea took a bite of the large salad bloomer Cal had passed to her.

'Well, maybe I need to put my t-shirt on then.' Cal spoke in his usual deadpan style, but laced with irony. 'So I can concentrate on sandwich making without feeling objectified.' Bea could see he was trying and failing to keep a straight face.

'I don't think there's any need to go that far,' she countered. 'In fact, I think a large part of how good this sandwich tastes is because you made it with your top off.'

'You do? Hmm, maybe there is something in that. Maybe I should serve drinks like this too.'

'Hmm, no.' Bea shook her head. 'This view is only for me.'

Cal tensed. He stared at Bea for moments that felt like hours, whilst holding a knife in mid-air, and seemingly forgetting to blink. *Dammit. That sounded so possessive and wrong. He's going to remind me now that this is a casual thing and we can see whomever else we want and that I've no right to claim his body as only mine. I sound like a jealous girlfriend.*

'You want this view to only be for you?' Cal asked finally, the air loaded with his words.

'Um...' *Is this a trick question?* Bea wasn't sure how to answer. Oh, why had she made that silly comment and got backed into a corner like this? Whatever she said now could be wrong. If she said yes, she wanted the view of his body to be only for her, then she risked coming across as possessive and having sunk in deeper than he had. If she said that she didn't then he would wonder why she had made the remark in the first place.

'Because that's fine with me,' said Cal. 'On one condition.' He put down the knife and moved round to Bea's side of the table where soon his breath was warm on her skin. 'That this' – he untied the top of Bea's towel, scooped both her breasts into his palms and softly kissed her neck – 'is only for my view.'

Bea gasped but managed to squeeze out some words. 'Oh... Mmm... Deal.'

'Good. That was an easy agreement.' Cal kissed her neck again, lingering for a moment before tying her towel back together and going back to his side of the table. He sat down and recommenced eating his sandwich, but not without giving her a playful glance that said, *that was fun*. Bea's insides turned to mush.

So, they were both on the same page, in the respect that they wanted one another's bodies to be exclusive. That was fine. It relieved Bea that Cal wouldn't be seeing any other women while she was in town. But something about it didn't set her at ease at all. The arrangement was purely physical. Cal grabbing her breasts so possessively had shown her that. It was wonderful, as ever, to have him touch her, but she wished he wanted more than her body. She only had herself to blame, though. If she hadn't been so lasciviously gaping at his chest then he wouldn't have taken her lustful lead.

She sighed inwardly as she watched Cal across the table. Sitting together, eating lunch like this was the most natural thing in the world. She was so comfortable with him. Yet, in that comfort lurked danger, particularly as she'd been here less than twenty-four hours. Maybe she shouldn't stay any longer.

Oh, come on, you said you could handle a no-strings fling. You've had a hot Scotsman fall into your lap. If you told any of your readers you'd walked away from that they would tell you that you were nuts. Be like one of those characters that can do this thing; be like that girl from the coffee shop; she could do it. But Bea also knew that the characters in her novels could never do no strings without falling for each other. It was a trademark trope of the genre.

'You're a million miles away,' said Cal. 'Is it the sandwich or my dreamy abs?'

Bea laughed, letting his humour pull her out of her stupor. 'It's a bit of both,' she said. 'I was dreaming of eating my sandwich off your washboard stomach.'

Now it was Cal's turn to laugh, his features spreading into generous warmth. 'Sounds like one of those hipster plating arrangements.'

Bea relaxed somewhat. He was amazing company. She didn't want to walk away and spend her evenings in her gloomy tenement flat when the vibrant colours of Cal were being revealed to her.

There was a knock at the door of the cottage.

'I should cover up.' Bea rushed to grab the sweatpants and t-shirt still on the chair from earlier. Cal searched for the first thing he could find to cover his top half and went for the door in a bizarre wetsuit/apron combination.

'Oh, afternoon, Dorothy.' At the door was a grey-haired older lady dressed in beige slacks, a loose floral top and comfortable shoes.

'Hello, Callum, dear,' she said. 'I'm sorry to bother you, but I have a dripping tap and it's awfully irritating and I wonder if you wouldn't mind...'

'Coming to fix it? Absolutely no bother at all.' Cal shot the woman a winning smile. 'I'll come over when I've cleared away lunch.'

'That'd be lovely, Son, thank you. Oh...' Dorothy was about to turn away when, keen-eyed, she spotted Bea sitting at the kitchen table. 'Sorry, I didn't realise you had company.'

'Sorry, Dorothy,' Cal began. 'This is—'

'Elisabetta, is it?' Dorothy asked, with not such spectacular vision after all. 'How are you, dear?'

Cal tensed. 'Um, no. This is Bea. I'm not with Elisabetta anymore.'

'Congratulations, dear,' said Dorothy, either not hearing or not listening to Cal. 'I heard from Callum's sister that you're expecting his baby. I'm so happy for you. I always thought you were a lovely couple.'

Bea reeled. It was like someone had doused her in icy water then punched her round the head. How could a little old lady say something that hurt so much? Bea had to suppress every instinct in her body telling her to run upstairs, throw her belongings into her bags and get as far away from here as possible. This woman had mistaken her for Cal's ex and unwittingly smacked her in the face with a huge reminder that another woman was likely expecting his baby. And a huge reminder that her ex left her for a woman expecting his baby. Cal would be a father soon and it had nothing to do with her. She wasn't part of Cal's future, and she wasn't part of his future as a parent.

What on earth have I done?

The answer to that was that she'd come to Scotland to write, to focus on her novel and make something of herself, to prove that she could be successful all on her own. She'd let herself get involved with Cal because it was no strings, convincing herself she was a cool modern woman who could have fun with a guy and use him as inspiration for her writing without falling for him. But she'd ended up getting way more inspired than she ever should have done. This reminder of his life without her, of how things would go on once she had left the country was a cold, sharp blast of reality. *Who were you kidding? You should never have needed to be with Cal to feel inspired. You're a writer, you should have an imagination. Finding a muse and going to bed with him is fanciful nonsense to try to distract you from the hurt of breaking up with Josh. All you need to do now is get on with the business of writing your book.*

Bea didn't hear the rest of the conversation Cal was having with Dorothy because she was thinking all these thoughts and the action on around her was like a fuzzy dream sequence. But she jumped out of her daze when she heard Cal shut the cottage door.

'I'm so sorry about that,' he said. 'She's blind as a coot.'

'It's fine.' Bea gripped the side of the chair.

'She didn't know you weren't Elisabetta. And I feel bad

because that was no way for you to find out about the um... "maybe baby" situation.'

'The maybe baby?' Bea had to pretend she didn't know because Cal didn't know that she did.

'My ex is pregnant,' Cal said. 'But she won't confirm or deny whether it's mine. She's a little bit difficult. Hey, are you okay?' He touched Bea's shoulder and examined her with concern. 'You've gone pale.'

'I'm... um... fine,' Bea stammered. 'I just... I'm sorry, Cal. You know what. Maybe I shouldn't have come here.' Dealing with the raw reminder of Cal's impending fatherhood was bothering her. Way more than she realised it might, but she couldn't admit this because she would come across as jealous.

'Oh! I thought we were having a great time. We were having a great time. It's not the baby, is it? Believe me, Betta is a piece of work. I've told her I'll support her all the way if she can say it's mine. I'm not that other kind of a guy.'

'I know you're not. I've worked that out already.'

'Ah, okay. So, you're jealous cause Dorothy wants to spend some time with me?' Cal was joking but Bea didn't laugh, and he appeared to realise he'd overstepped the mark. 'Sorry,' he said. 'My comic timing is woeful.'

'Don't worry about it,' Bea said. 'Look, I think I might go for a walk on the beach. I'm a bit drowsy after lunch.'

Cal furrowed his brow. 'Okay, well, if that's what you want to do. I'll get showered and come with you.'

'No, please don't. I'd rather be alone.'

Bea went upstairs, grabbed her purse and changed back into her own clothes. She was getting out of here. There was bound to be a bus or something. There was no way she could have this out with Cal, admit to him that she was falling for him and was insecure of his baby with another woman – it sounded ridiculous – so she would have to do the cowardly thing and walk away. She'd leave her overnight bag. It didn't matter. All that mattered was getting away from the intensity of her feelings for Cal and the fact that he was on a different chapter, never mind page. Oh, how naïve she'd been.

Chapter Thirty-Eight

Bea glanced toward the main road. She had seen a bus stop on the way in and it couldn't be that far. A bus back to Edinburgh would give her the escape she needed, an escape that a walk on the beach would provide only in temporary measures.

As Bea turned right out of the front gate, she sensed someone watching her. Instinctively, she glanced towards the little cottage next to Cal's but no one was there. She shook off the sensation and headed up the street towards the main road.

The road out of the village was longer than Bea remembered. She passed a lot of houses she hadn't noticed on the way in, probably because she was so enthralled being with Cal. She saw a couple of people taking their dogs to the beach but dipped her head in case they knew Cal and might alert him to her whereabouts if he came looking for her.

The weather until now was clement: a light sea breeze, but also intermittent September sun to take the edge off the early autumnal chill. But the clouds that the sun was periodically disappearing behind had taken on a more sombre hue and Bea could see that the sky was shifting from blue to grey and the clouds were darkening by the second.

She shivered and hurried along the street. Where was the bus stop? Surely she hadn't passed it already. A blob of rain dropped onto her nose. Oh no. And another, this time on her shoulder. Then, with an impatience to have their way, the rain-drops tumbled down. Bea was wearing only jeans and a blouse and would get soaked. Time to jog.

By the time she reached the bus stop, Bea's clothes were soaking wet. *Please let the bus come along soon, because if I have to stand here for too long, I'll freeze and catch a chill.* As she was rubbing her arms to keep warm, she caught a glimpse of herself in the bus shelter. What a sight: her clothes were clinging to her in a hideous way, her hair was bedraggled from the earlier saltwater and her expression was miserable. She felt even worse. At least a bus was due soon and she could get out of here and back to some normality. That was, if they let her on, sea monster that she was.

'Bea!'

Bea spun round to see who was calling her name. It could only be one person. Nobody else knew her round here.

And right enough, standing on the other side of the main road was Cal. He had ditched the wetsuit and apron and was now wearing jeans and a black t-shirt that were drenched and clinging to every last sculpted piece of him. Bea stared. Even from across the street, his eyes seared into her soul. He was so beautiful it made her heart ache. But how she wished he would go away, that he wasn't heading across the road to the bus stop to stand right in front of her.

'Bea, what are you doing here? You're soaked through.' Cal reached out and touched her arm. His hand was warm, and she wanted him to wrap his whole body around her and heat her to the core. 'I thought you were going for a walk on the beach.'

Oh, why can't he see? Why do I need to spell out what's wrong? A thing I can never do.

But Bea couldn't lie either. Couldn't pretend she'd come a different route for a walk, got caught in the rain and taken refuge in the bus shelter. She didn't feel like pretending. So instead she said nothing. Stared at Cal until she couldn't stare at him anymore because concern combined with stupendous handsomeness was too much when you couldn't have it.

'Are you going to say anything?' Cal asked.

Bea found the mettle to let a few words escape her lips. 'How did you know to find me here?' she asked.

'Dorothy said she saw you heading up this way when I went round to fix her tap. You said you were going to the beach, so I thought maybe you'd got lost.'

'Yes,' she turned back to him. 'I got lost.' This was true. She had got lost. Very lost, but not in the way Cal assumed. She had got lost in her emotions for him. Lost in direction. Lost in love? She glanced along the road and saw the bus approaching.

'Well, it's lucky I found you,' said Cal.

For a split second, Bea allowed herself to indulge in a fantasy of those words meaning something else. Of Cal expressing how lucky they were to have met each other in this big old world. But he just meant finding her at the bus stop. And the bus was even closer now. She pressed the outside of her purse to check her wallet was inside.

As she did so, Cal gripped her arm, pulling her away from the road.

'Watch out,' he said. 'There's a massive puddle. You don't want to get soaked when the bus goes past.'

Guilt swiped at Bea as she realised what was happening. Cal thought the bus was driving by. He didn't suspect that she was planning to get on it. Looking straight at the oncoming vehicle, she stepped to the kerb, alerting the driver to pull in.

'Bea?'

As she found the courage to lift her eyes, Bea's voice constricted with emotion. 'Cal. I have had such a lovely time with you here, but I've overstayed my welcome and I need to go back to Edinburgh.' She was pretty sure that sounded like the lie that it was. And Cal's narrowed gaze told her she was on the money.

'Are you serious?'

'I am.'

'But why?' Cal asked. 'Please be honest with me. We were having a great time. Or were you not?'

'No, I was.' Bea glanced at the now open bus door, and the driver who was staring expectantly to see if either of them were getting on board. There were mere seconds to decide. But she could see Cal needed her to say something. It was almost like he knew the words but needed them to come from her. Did he know she was upset about the baby? It seemed obvious, she supposed, because of the timing with Dorothy, but he wouldn't know what had happened with Josh and how that crushing insignificance she had tried to escape was bearing down again. He couldn't possibly understand about her insecurities around motherhood and that they were wrapped up with her burgeoning feelings for him.

'Are youse getting on or not?' The bus driver looked at his watch.

'Could you give me one moment?' Bea's voice was trembling, her teeth were chattering. Couldn't the driver see how important this was? Wasn't he used to delays because of romantic crises?

As if silently reading her mind and agreeing to meet her halfway, the man shook his head and puffed out a loud sigh, but stayed put, rapping his fingers on the steering wheel.

Bea turned to Cal. She owed him an explanation, but how to do it without revealing that she was falling for him? How could she frame it? What could she tell him? It was impossible.

'Cal, I... Look...'

But Cal saved her from death by explanation. 'Bea, please don't go,' he implored. 'Or if you have to, for whatever reason, would you at least come back to the house, get your bag and get showered and warm. If, after that, you still want to go back to Edinburgh then I'll drive you, no questions asked, okay?'

Well, how could she say no to that? Yes, the bus was here, and the temptation was to get away immediately, but her belongings were at Cal's and she was freezing. And, to be fair, he was good to her. Bea sighed. She would bear the pain of being near him, caring as she did but not having it requited, for a few more hours. Tonight, she'd be back in her bed in her crummy apartment and things would be less intense.

'Sorry,' she mouthed to the bus driver, whom she could have sworn rolled his eyes before closing the doors and accelerating with an aggressive growl of the engine.

Thankfully, the decision had made one man happy. Cal was beaming, and Bea remarked to herself that she'd never seen such a luminescent smile on anyone's face. Certainly not his.

'You know, Dorothy was right,' he said.

'Dorothy was right about what?'

'You. You're stunning. And standing here soaked through with salt water in your hair, you are the most beautiful woman I've ever seen.'

'Dorothy said all that?'

Cal laughed. 'Dorothy said she could tell you were beautiful inside and out.'

'That was lovely of her to say. But I thought she couldn't see me.'

'She saw you from her window once she had her glasses on.'

'Oh, okay.'

'She's an excellent judge of character. She also said that you were a million times nicer than Elisabetta.'

Hearing these words, warmed Bea's heart. It was a wonderful sentiment, but how she wished that they were coming from Cal, rather than from a lady in her eighties who lived next door to him.

Chapter Thirty-Nine

Cal and Bea walked back to the cottage in silence. The rain had stopped, but the atmosphere was damp and gloomy, both meteorologically and metaphorically. For all of his happy exterior, Cal was struggling to work out where things had gone wrong. It was somewhere around Dorothy mistaking Bea for Elisabetta. *But why would that bother her? She's superior to Elisabetta in every way and has never come across as lacking in confidence. Plus, this is a short-term thing, so an unborn baby that may or may not be mine wouldn't be a problem. Would it?*

Cal gave Bea a towel and told her that a hot cup of tea would be waiting after her shower. He also invited her to take a bath, to warm up fully, but Bea said that a shower would be fine. She was keen not to prolong her stay. That stung. Cal had so been looking forward to cooking her dinner this evening and talking while they ate. He couldn't let her go back to Edinburgh – it wasn't time yet – so he decided that when Bea came back downstairs, he would try to convince to stay for a meal. He'd drive her home afterwards, but she needed to eat, and she may as well do so here.

While Bea was upstairs, Cal tried to busy himself in the kitchen, tidying away the lunch things and sorting out what he needed to get for dinner. It was difficult focusing on the task. The sound of the water running upstairs made him think how much he would love to be in the shower, too. He'd kiss Bea on that luscious rosebud mouth of hers and tell her that it would all be fine and that whatever had upset her, she could talk to him and they could work it out. He'd tenderly stroke her back while the water cascaded from the shower, pull her close and hold her until she knew she was safe. Jings! What were these strange feelings? Such a heady mix of sexual desire and tenderness.

When Bea appeared at the foot of the stairs, Cal swallowed so hard that his Adam's apple must be bursting out of his throat like he'd swallowed his heart. She was dressed in nothing more glamourous than tight black leggings and a peach-coloured sweatshirt; her damp hair was combed in a side parting and her face was make-up free, but he couldn't look away.

'Feeling better?' Cal placed a cup of tea on the coffee table.

'Warmer, at least.' Bea smoothed down her hair awkwardly before taking the tea.

'I've put the fire on, so sit by it until your hair dries, otherwise, you'll get cold again.' Cal motioned to the two-seater by the hearth. 'If I had a hairdryer, I'd offer you one.'

'Thanks.' Bea smiled, but it was a fraction of the wattage Cal had become accustomed to.

'Listen,' he said, sitting in the chair opposite her and resisting the impulse to lean over the coffee table and take her soft hands in his own. 'Do you want to talk about whatever's upsetting you? If I've done something wrong, tell me and I'm sure we can make it right.'

Bea bit a corner of her lip and shook her head gently.

'I don't need to talk about it. You haven't done anything.'

She lifted her tea and her face was obscured by the cup as she sipped.

Cal was unconvinced by Bea's insistence that all was fine, but what could he do if she wouldn't divulge her worries? He didn't want to push it. Best to put her at ease and maybe then she'd feel comfortable enough to open up.

'If you still want to head back to Edinburgh, I can take you,' he said. 'Although, I think you should stay for dinner first?

'I don't know.' For the first time since he'd met her, Cal could see reluctance flickering in Bea's eyes.' I think I've outstayed my welcome.'

'Are you serious? You've under-stayed your welcome as far as I'm concerned.'

A modicum of darkness lifted from Bea's features and Cal was encouraged.

'There's no pressure to stay for dinner,' he continued. 'But you've got to eat, and I've got a bunch of stuff in and I'm cooking anyway. It'll save you having to do it when you get back to your flat. What do you think?'

Bea regarded Cal so intently it was like she was reading his thoughts. And she was taking her time, as if reading the entire chapter of a book. The uncertainty was killing him. He desperately wanted her to stay; her presence in his cottage made it a warm comforting home, even at the times when the fire grate was bare.

Eventually she spoke. 'Okay,' she said. 'I'll stay for a bite to eat. Thank you.'

'You're most welcome.' The tension in Cal's chest released. He would cook Bea a spectacular dinner and show-case the best that Scotland had to offer in terms of food. Hopefully that would go some way to cheering her up.

Bea sat by the fire and drank her tea while Cal sorted dinner. He glanced at her from time to time. At first, she was staring into the flames but then she chose a book from his shelf and was reading and occasionally chuckling to herself. Eventually, when he decided the mood might be a little brighter, he threw a dishcloth over his shoulder and attempted some humour from the edge of the kitchen.

'Since you enjoyed your good old Scottish fish and chips, tonight I'm going to continue the theme and cook you some haggis.'

'You are?' Bea laid her book on her lap, clearly interested. There was sun peeking through her clouds now, a welcome return of the old spark.

Cal shrugged. 'I'm kidding. Haggis isn't the way to a lady's heart.' Was that a stupid thing to say? Haggis wasn't romantic but he wasn't trying to win her heart. She nearly had his, but he was loathe to intimidate her. Nevertheless, he continued 'But if you find heated sheep's guts endearing, I can nip out to the butchers and get some.'

To Cal's relief, Bea laughed.

'Maybe I'll have something else from the menu,' she remarked with a glimmer in her eye. Thankfully, she hadn't stopped to dwell on the heart comment and seemed to be returning to the old sparky Bea.

'There will be plenty of local delights to choose from. I want to show you the best of Scotland.' Cal held Bea's gaze, hoping to see warmth returning there.

But Bea looked down at her lap and mumbled, 'Oh, you've done more than enough already,' leading him to wonder if he was getting the brush off again.

* * *

Cal couldn't have been more different from Josh. Even in their early days of dating, Josh had never been as enthusiastic as Cal was about pleasing her. He'd never placed a bowl of anything down in front of her with the kind of zeal that Cal did as he served her up her starter, even announcing what it was as if she were a guest in his restaurant.

'Kilbrannan scallops with capers and a peanut and pistachio puree, Madam,' he said. He was trying to make up for earlier, despite not knowing what he was making up for. Bea's heart swelled at the effort he'd made. She had intended to go back to Edinburgh, but the suggestions Cal made – have a shower, sit by the fire, stay for dinner – were so enticing and comforting that she found it harder and harder to keep her resolve. She wanted to stay with him in the comfort of his cottage, know again the cleansing warmth of his shower, the heat by his fire, the nourishment of his cooking, and the protection of his arms. Oh, she longed to be in his arms. She knew she should go back to town. Staying would lead to more hurt, but as the initial blow of Dorothy's words wore off and Cal's charm seeped in again, Bea found herself less desperate to leave. She could try to forget about the baby and the associated insecurities for now.

'These are divine, Cal.' Bea took a scallop into her mouth and it melted away, the food helping in some ways with the forgetting. 'How did you get them so tender?'

Cal beamed. 'Butler magic, Madam. You may already have seen some of it in action.'

'I believe I have.' Bea couldn't help but glow like the aurora borealis as she met his gaze, and he returned the warmth. This was too lovely to back away from.

For the main course, Cal had prepared wild smoked halibut with chunky chips, a parsley sauce and horseradish cream potatoes. Was there anything this man didn't do well? A successful businessman, a surfer, man about the house, amazing in bed and now a cook extraordinaire. It made Bea sad that he would become someone else's. She had to enjoy this for what it was, but it was hard. She wanted to get up, walk to Cal's side of the table, wrap her arms around him, kiss him and thank him for the effort he had put in to making her experience so wonderful.

'You deserve it all.' He kept his eyes on her as he lifted a glass of water to his lips. 'You've enhanced my business and so much more. I don't know what I'm going to do when you're gone.'

So much more. What does that mean? Bea's heart leapt. But Cal didn't extrapolate, and she didn't dare ask in case she made a fool of herself by interpreting the wrong meaning of the statement.

'Ready for dessert?' Cal got up and lifted away Bea's empty plate.

'You made dessert too?'

'Well, I will admit that I cheated and bought some ready-made sticky toffee puddings. Although I am about to make a whisky sauce to go with them, if you've room for more.'

'I suppose it would be rude not to. And I have to find room for whisky sauce made by a Scotsman.'

'You do.' Cal winked. 'I'll grab a bottle of whisky from the cabinet.' He disappeared down the hall and into another room before returning with a bottle of Scotch. Or 'whisky', as they called it in Scotland.

'So, where did you learn to cook so well?' Bea asked.

'Thanks for the compliment. And I don't know if my cooking is that good. I've picked things up along the way: learned from recipe books, the internet, eating out at some fantastic places.'

'You should branch out into Butler's brasserie or something. Expand the family business even further.'

'Ha, yeah, maybe. Although, I think I'm busy enough with the bars.'

'Your family must be so proud of you.'

The warmth in Cal's expression dropped by a degree, and

Bea wanted to usher on dessert to warm things over. What had she said? Was his family a touchy subject? Did he not speak to them? Was there a big feud she'd alighted on? But she'd met his sister already, and she'd mentioned the party for their father. If there'd been a problem, surely Cara wouldn't have said anything. Then again, Cal was non-committal about whether or not he was going.

'My family is... Well, it's hard to make a family proud that already run the most successful whisky company in the country,' Cal said. 'But they value what I've done with my business, I think.'

Did Bea detect a hint of uncertainty in Cal's tone? There was something unconvincing about what he was saying, but she couldn't say what and she didn't want to press him further in case his shutters came down and she was left with coffee-shop Cal Butler: aloof and unamused. She needed to try to pull him out of whatever was dragging him down.

'Cara's lovely,' she said.

'Aye. She's a sweetheart.' Cal perked up a little at this. His sister wasn't a sore point, at least. 'I'm lucky to have her and Eilidh so close.'

'Do you hang out much?'

'Aye, we go for a drink or have dinner parties at each other's places. Cara's good company. Nosey as hell, but maybe actresses need to be. Luckily, Eilidh is a bit more sensible and balances things out. She's a teacher in Edinburgh.'

'And tell me about your other siblings.'

'Jamie, like I said before, works for the distillery as chief operating officer, Niall runs a surf school in Australia, Sean is a cooper who makes barrels for the company, and Nate is a vet at his own animal sanctuary. He's Cara and Eilidh's triplet brother.'

'Oh, triplets! That's amazing.'

'I know. And what's amazing is it's so rare for mixed sex

triplets which makes them even more special. My parents adopted them when I was a kid. I'm so glad they did because I can't imagine the family without them.'

'Gosh!' said Bea. 'Anyone who adopts is to be admired, but to adopt three children at once is something else.'

'Aye, my folks are something else.' Cal nodded and took a large drink of wine. Something about this topic was emotional for him, and Bea sensed that he didn't want to divulge anymore. Maybe he didn't want to get close by bringing her into his family fold, and although she would love to know more about them, she supposed it was probably for the best that she didn't.

Chapter Forty

With his vision on the darkening road to Edinburgh and Bea in the passenger seat beside him, Cal was thinking hard. But however he contemplated this situation, he couldn't justify what he wanted to do without sounding like he might be coming on too strong.

He wanted to ask Bea to his father's party.

Not only did he want to make the most of every moment with her, he wanted to make his father proud. To show him he could make a success of things, women being one. Despite Jimmy Butler going through the wringer for many years before getting together with Cal's mother, Cal was sure that his dad wondered why Cal was thirty-four and still hadn't met the right woman – one who didn't bring shame on the family name. Jimmy had never said as much but Cal owed it to his dad now to make him proud, no arguments.

He knew his parents would be proud of Bea. *I'm proud of her. I want to show her off – show that an incredible woman wants to spend time with me, leaving out the short-term fling bit; that doesn't matter.*

Before Cal knew it, the words were filling the space between him and Bea.

'Bea, I would like it very much if you would accompany me to my family's celebration next week.'

As soon as he said it, Cal knew he sounded like a boyfriend waiting in the wings. *But it's not wrong to like her company, is it? We're getting on well, and why can't two people who enjoy each other's company spend some time together? Also, it could be useful for her writing.*

'I'm sure you'd find it fun and it's a way for you to see the real Scotland,' he added. 'Meet a real Scottish family.' That was it. Make it sound like his chief objective was to help Bea with her novels. 'We'll stop off at places on the journey you might find inspiring for your books. There's some stunning scenery on the journey to Kintyre.'

Cal hadn't a clue what Bea was thinking, and a knot formed in his stomach as she took forever to respond. Because he was driving, he could only take the occasional glance at her. He tightened his grip on the steering wheel, then it went a little clammy, so he reached for the radio to add an upbeat soundtrack to what was becoming an awkward scene. But as his fingers reached the dial, Bea spoke.

'Are you sure your family won't mind me coming? I wouldn't be intruding, would I?'

Cal breathed out a gust of relief he hadn't realised he'd been holding in.

'Are you kidding? They'll be delighted to have you there. They should be grateful, in fact. And my brothers will probably hit on you cause they're idiots.'

'Charming.'

'Oh, no. That came out wrong.' Cal was a teenager again, blundering through communication with girls. 'I meant because they'd be hitting on someone who's with their brother, not because of anything to do with you. It'll shock me if they don't hit on you, to be honest. Any sane man would.'

'You recovered well from that.' Bea spoke in a deadpan style usually the reserve of Cal. He turned to glance at her and saw a twitch of a joy at the edge of her lips. *Thank goodness.*

'So,' he said, reaching out to touch her leg and hoping it wasn't too much after their earlier rift. 'You haven't said if you're coming or not.'

'I wasn't sure if you'd finished selling it to me.' The warm breeze Cal loved about Bea's voice was back.

'That wasn't a sales pitch, but to sway you, there will be ample food and your own personal guide for the duration of your stay. And did I mention the accommodation has views to die for? A beach on the doorstep, as much surfing and whisky as you like, and sex on tap. It'll be the perfect inspiration for your writing. Well, maybe not the sex bit – probably best not to write about that – but the rest.'

Bea laughed. 'Well, in that case, sign me up for the full package.'

Cal glanced at her for as long as he could without taking his eyes dangerously off the road. 'Really? Are you sure?'

'Yes, really and I'm sure. You had me at sex on tap.'

'Wait, that was the last thing I mentioned.'

'Well, the other stuff sounds wonderful, but that was what sold it to me.' Bea returned his leg touch gesture but with a tender squeeze. Cal caught a little wink from her and his heart somersaulted in his chest. *She's got me. She's well and truly got me. How did I let that happen? And how am I going to put all the pieces of the puzzle together when they don't quite fit?*

Chapter Forty-One

At 8 a.m. the following Friday, Bea was adding the finishing touches to her make-up. Lipstick in hand, she checked out of the flat window to see if Cal's car had arrived. All was quiet. Good, because she wasn't quite ready.

Minutes later, after a subtle swipe of Autumn Rose lip gloss, a spray of face mist and a few dabs of perfume on her pulse points, Bea was set for the mystery Scottish road trip Cal had insisted they go on, en route to his family's party. All she needed now was for the man himself to arrive. Bea imagined sitting in the passenger seat next to Cal, watching his hair caught by the sun. Then she remembered she wasn't in the States and that there would be no top-down in the crisp Scottish fall. She'd have to settle instead for the heat of his company.

As she was pacing around the flat, waiting for Cal, Bea's phone rang. It was Amira.

'Hey, babe,' she said. 'What's up?' It was the middle of the night in New York. Why would Amira be calling now, unless something was wrong?

'Hey, Bea.' Amira sounded choked, like she'd been crying.

'What? What is it? What's wrong?' Bea's nerves spiked. She'd hoped Amira might be calling her tipsy and excited, perhaps after meeting a cute guy on a night out, but this didn't sound right at all. 'Are you okay?'

'Yes, yes.' Amira sounded like she was trying her best to keep her voice calm. 'Oh, Bea, I'm such an idiot.'

'What? Ams, tell me what's happened. I presume no one has died?'

'No, no one has died. Apart from half my brain cells. I've been such a complete and utter dumbass. Oh, God. I'll explain. I was seeing this guy. It was going somewhere; I was sure of it. We were going to go on vacation over Christmas, to Puerto Rico.'

'Uh-huh,' said Bea, feeling ominous.

'So, he said he would book it all, but could he borrow my bank card to do so. He would pay me back as soon as he got paid. He said he was expecting a big payment from a job he did for someone.'

Oh no! Bea could see where this was going already. Amira was a wonderful friend but she could be awfully naïve.

'You gave him the card?'

'Yep, and tonight I walked home from Uptown because I had no money for an Uber because my whole account has been cleared out.'

'Oh no! Oh, Ams. I'm so sorry. Are you sure it was him and not a clerical error or something?'

'Well, considering he isn't answering his phone and is blanking my messages, despite them being read, then, yes, I'm pretty sure it was him. It's too much of a coincidence.'

'Oh, babes, I'm so sorry. You have to go to the police about this. And if there's anything I can do from this end, please let me know. Do you need some money?'

'Oh, Bea, I don't expect you to give me any money.'

'I know you don't, but you need money, right? He cleared you out. You to eat and get to work and pay your bills. I'll transfer you as much as I can this minute. Have you cancelled all the cards he has access to?'

'Yes, but, babe, you don't have to do that.'

'Yes, I do. Of course I do. You're my best friend and I love you. My rent is paid for this month and I've some put aside for the road trip I'm going on. I can afford to help you out. You need it more than I do.' Bea put the phone on speaker as she logged into her online banking.

'Please don't leave yourself short.' Amira sounded weak and too defeated to argue.

'I'll be fine.' Bea's bank balance wasn't exactly high, but she could spare enough to help her friend out. She clicked the send funds button and just as the money had gone through someone rapped at the door. That would be Cal. Damn! She'd wanted to catch him before he came up to the flat.

'Ams, listen, I'm going to have to go. My ride is here. But the money is sent and I'll check in with you as soon as I can, I promise.'

'Of course, thank you, honey. Thank you from the bottom of my heart. I'll pay you back as soon as I can. And I'm so sorry for being such a doofus.'

'You're not a doofus. It could happen to any of us. Remember, I love you.' Bea wished her friend goodbye and ended the call. Poor Amira. She loved to be in love and got carried away by the promise of romance.

Speaking of which, Bea flattened her palms down her hips and headed to the door. She opened it to see Cal, resplendent in morning freshness, sporting jeans and a crisp white t-shirt which encased the swell of his biceps perfectly (lucky for Bea that he didn't notice the cold) and made his emerald eyes sparkle even greener. The usual woody, lemony Cal scent wafted to Bea's senses and made her want to bury her face into his neck.

'Morning, M'lady.' Cal's smile was as warm as a California sunrise. 'I believe you've a trip to Kintyre booked. Can I help you with your bags?'

Bea laughed. 'I do and absolutely. I'll get my holdall from the bedroom.' But before she could tell Cal to hang on, he was moving past her into the flat.

'Oh, Cal, you don't have to... I can get it, it's not that heavy.'

But it was too late. Cal entered the bedroom. He stopped for a moment to take in his surroundings and light perspiration broke out on the side of Bea's nose. She saw the room from his perspective. The paintwork with scuff marks on it, the threadbare patches on the dirty carpet, the faded and grotesque artwork that she would never have chosen for a place of her own. Cal must wonder why on earth she lived here. Did he feel sorry for her that she had to, even for a temporary period?

But Cal's face didn't show any sign that he was thinking these things. In fact, he only commented on one aspect of the room.

'Nice bed.' He clocked Bea's bag on the floor. 'This it?'

'Um... yes,' Bea said. 'And the bed is pretty comfortable.'

'That's important,' said Cal, knowingly. He lifted Bea's compact but well-laden overnight bag, seemingly oblivious to its weight or Bea's concern over her accommodation. And for that she liked him that little bit more.

Half an hour later and they were coasting out of Edinburgh, over the gleaming Firth of Forth and into Fife from where Cal said they'd head into Perthshire then west to embark on his mystery itinerary. All he'd said was to pack for the same weather as Edinburgh – temperate yet sunny – but with a bathing suit, although he'd also said that was optional if

Bea was comfortable naked, and she'd tingled with anticipation. She was more than comfortable naked with Cal.

They stopped for lunch at a little farmhouse café – Cal said he'd earmarked it especially for her – where they dined on wholesome farmhouse broth with soft bread and Scottish butter followed by steaming rich coffee and a luscious chocolate brownie. It was all so comforting and homely and Bea reflected how thoughtful it was of Cal to bring her here. She also reflected that if he was going to continue to be this nice to her, she would have trouble keeping her feelings in check.

'Are you having a good time so far?' Cal drained the last of his coffee. 'Think you've seen anything that you can put into your writing?'

'I am having the best time ever.' Bea resisted the powerful urge to reach for his hand. That was something a girlfriend would do. 'I've seen so many things this morning that I can write about. Thank you for continuing to show me Scotland.'

'My pleasure. I want you to love it as much as I do.' He held Bea's gaze a fragment longer than usual before interrupting his own contemplation. 'I'll get the bill and we can head off.'

'Oh, let me.' Bea reached for her purse. 'It's the least I can do to thank you for showing me this place even exists.'

'No, my treat.' Cal's tone was non-negotiable, and he left the table before she had a chance to argue.

Bea bit into her lip and looked around at all the other patrons. To debate now would cause a scene. She would have to ensure that she paid for the next meal, and that he took the money she'd set aside for accommodation and gas. Having him pay for everything was not something she was okay with, irrespective of whether they were in a relationship or not. Bea never wanted to be accused of freeloading again.

They drove on through the Scottish countryside, zipping past fields dotted with cows, small stone farm-steadings, an endless curtain of foliage in shades of russet, gold and crimson dancing in the breeze. During a break in the trees, Bea gasped at the snow-capped peaks surging out of the landscape beyond. She had wondered if coming to Scotland at the tail end of summer was injudicious, but today in the warm apricot sunshine it felt like the best choice ever. And, even if the whole of Scotland was drenched in rain, nothing could erase the magnificence of the scenery on offer, including the man in the seat next to her.

Chapter Forty-Two

'Welcome to Glen Tummel Lodges, Mr and Mrs Butler.' The receptionist almost sang her greeting.

Cal suppressed a slight smile at this error but held back on correcting the woman. Wondering if Bea minded being assumed his wife, he turned and saw amusement glimmering at the edges of her perfectly pink lips. Clearly not. And had he imagined it, or did she slide her left hand behind her hips?

Mr and Mrs Butler it was.

The receptionist clocked Cal and Bea's shared look and adopted a little 'Isn't wedded bliss adorable?' expression which she held whilst clacking at the keyboard and entering Cal's card details to complete the booking. Cal was sure he sensed Bea stiffen at the sight of his credit card, but he suspected she wouldn't bring it up if trying to give the illusion of being married. And that was fine with him. Bea was of a different mettle to Elisabetta and the other women he'd been intimate with, and her offering to pay for her lunch today had cemented that idea in his mind.

The accommodation turned out to be as Cal had hoped.

Only a few footsteps from the loch's edge, separated by a small shingled beach, sat their lodge – a hot tub on the fenced deck overlooked the deep blue of the water. Inside was perfect, too: two spacious bedrooms with huge king-sized beds, an enormous bathroom with double monsoon shower and ample windows with copious natural light streaming in and affording views out to the cobalt loch and mountains beyond. The entire place smelt of wood and mountain air. And a complimentary bottle of vintage champagne and artisan chocolates sat on the dining table. Cal hoped Bea was as enamoured as he was.

It seemed they were on the same page.

'Oh, Cal, this is perfection.' Bea was spinning slowly and soaking in her surroundings as if she were a character in a fairy tale. She floated around the lounge, skimming her fingers over the surfaces before drifting into the main bedroom and bouncing on the bed next to where he'd put her bag. His own was in the other room: even if they were to share a bed, Cal thought that Bea might like some space to get changed and dressed in private. 'But I can't let you pay for this.' She stroked the lambswool blanket folded across the foot of the smooth cotton bedspread. 'It's too much.'

'Och away, woman.' Cal stood in the doorway drinking her in and thinking how luminous she looked in jeans, a light sweater and understated make-up. 'It's nothing.'

'It might be nothing to you, but it's not nothing to me.'

Bea was talking about money, but Cal let his mind flirt with the alternative meaning to that comment. This was feeling less like the nothing they both protested it was as each day passed. Of course, he wasn't about to admit that to Bea, not when she was here for a bit of fun before she went back to the States.

'Bea, I know you are fiercely independent, but would you please accept this as a gift from me?'

Bea sighed. 'I know you can afford this, Cal. I know how hard you work, but you don't have to prove anything to me.'

'I'm not trying to prove anything. I just want you to appreciate Scotland. This loch is one amazing part, but I don't expect you to pay for my choices.'

'Maybe you could have given me the choice?' Bea poured herself a glass of water from a bottle on the dresser.

'Of all the lochs? There's about thirty thousand to choose from...'

'Don't patronise me, Cal. You know what I mean.'

'I know. I'm sorry. I'm being flippant. But, Bea, I am more than happy to pay. I want to treat you, is that so wrong?' *Jeez, that was something a boyfriend would say.* 'Think of it as an employer reward,' Cal added, putting the thoughts 'employer' and 'treat' together in his head and coming up with nine. 'For being my best bartender, ever.'

Bea hit Cal with a stony expression he couldn't read, her sapphire eyes dark. This was hard work, exactly the sort of hard work he hadn't wanted. Maybe they should pack up and go back to Edinburgh. Tell the receptionist that the marriage wasn't working out.

'I don't want you doing all these things for me when I can't repay the favour,' she explained.

'You've already repaid the favour.' Cal cursed that his mouth was in drive before he'd considered where it was driving to. 'You're...' He shuffled his feet and rethought his words. 'It's like this. I pay for the lodge and you... what is it you Americans say? You bring it.'

'I bring it?' Bea folded her arms. 'That sounds all kinds of wrong, Cal.'

'Och, I didn't mean it that way.' He truly hadn't. All he'd been trying to say was that she was so amazing that he wanted to do something in return. It wasn't meant to sound sordid.

'Well, what did you mean? Because to be honest, what you said makes me feel extremely cheap.'

'Cheap? Oh, Bea, come on. How could anyone think that *you* are cheap? You're the most exquisite woman I've met in...' He didn't finish his sentence. She was the most exquisite woman he had ever met, but he couldn't say that out loud, could he? It sounded too intense.

'You have no idea, Cal.'

'No idea about what? You're right, I do have no idea. Please tell me, help me understand.'

Bea's eyes flared. She shook her head and brushed past him and out of the room. Cal followed her out onto the veranda where she leaned on the rail and stared out to the loch. How he wanted to hold her and show her she was safe, but it seemed that Bea had words she needed to let breathe.

'Bea? What is it?' Cal spoke as tenderly as he could to encourage her to open up. 'What have I no idea about?'

'It's not something you need concern yourself with.' There was a brittleness to Bea's voice but he knew it was from fear rather than wanting to drive him away.

'I don't think that's true,' he said. 'Whatever's upsetting you, it's affecting things between us.'

'Officially, there is no us,' Bea countered.

Cal was more than aware of this and it was bothering him. But how could he word a response to her without sounding possessive, or like he had the two of them labelled as a collective. 'Okay, well I know there's strictly no us,' he said. 'But it's affecting this trip, you having a nice time while we're here. You won't relax and let me pay for lunch or this place without being offended. Why?'

'It's hard to explain, Cal.' Bea gripped the veranda rail.

'I do understand that you want to pay your way,' Cal said. 'But there's no need to feel cheap because I'm paying for somewhere nice that I chose. It would be a dick move to make you pay for that.'

Bea turned to him and he could see the glistening of incipient tears. Oh, how he wanted to wipe them away, but he knew that first he had to listen, because if she was upset there would be no pasting over things on his part. She deserved to be one hundred per cent happy.

'I can't help hating you paying for me,' Bea said finally. 'Because for the past five years all I've done is feel cheap – because that's what one man did to me.'

Cal noticed Bea's face change as she opened up to him. Those precious eyes filled now with tears instead of light, the sweet lips that laughed so readily were quivering. The last thing he wanted was for her to have to relive any trauma, but he also needed to understand, to be able to make this better.

'I'm so sorry, Bea. Who was he? I'm presuming it's a he.'

'Yeah. My ex, J...'

'It's okay, you don't need to say his name.' Cal knew this might be difficult for her. For years, his mother referred to his biological father as 'him' or 'he'. 'But can I ask, did he...?' Cal didn't want to finish the sentence because it killed him to even suggest out loud that someone might have physically hurt Bea.

'No, he didn't.' Bea answered Cal's unfinished question. 'Only slowly wore me down with five years of emotional control: of forcing me to stay home and not work, but then withholding money from me and making me beg him if I needed any. When you put up with that, after a while you believe it yourself.'

Cal's head was spinning. It stung to hear about Bea going through what she'd described. He understood well that emotional abuse could be as harmful as physical. He'd been a young child when his biological father had done the same to his mother and he would forever wish that he'd done something to stop her pain, even though he'd only been a little boy.

All he'd been able to do was try to comfort his mum with words. The same was true now.

'I'm so sorry, Bea,' Cal said. 'The guy sounds like an absolute arse.'

'He was.'

'If you don't mind me asking, what happened in the end? Did you leave him?'

Bea choked on a laugh and Cal narrowed his gaze. He was pretty sure this wasn't funny and the laughter came from incredulousness or nerves.

'Would you believe it, that he left me?' she said, revealing the irony of the situation.

'Well, no, I wouldn't. What sort of muppet would leave you?'.

'Muppet.' Bea smiled tenderly. 'Yes, he is what you'd call a muppet, although that's an insult to Kermit and the like. And he's the sort of muppet who basically got a better offer, a trust fund baby who would support him.'

'Sounds pathetic.' Cal tensed, wondering if he should hold back on the judgements but knowing he couldn't. This sort of behaviour riled him too much. 'Sorry if you think that sounds sexist, but any guy who expects his girlfriend to support him, without a genuine, necessary reason, is a sorry excuse for a person as far as I'm concerned.'

'But is it okay the other way round?'

Cal took a deep breath but said nothing for a moment. He needed to get his words right on this one and show Bea that to him this meant more than she could know. 'One person taking advantage of any one person is not okay,' he said. 'But I know that's not what's happening here. You haven't come with me expecting anything, I can see that. And, if anything, I blame myself for the confusion between us.'

Bea scrutinised him and Cal wondered if he had said too much. He didn't want to talk about this, but something bigger was driving the compulsion. She'd opened up about a huge part of her life and he owed her an explanation.

'Bea, my dad – my biological dad – he wasn't the nicest of guys. The dad we are going to visit is my adoptive dad, my uncle actually. But to me, he's my real dad. You can't deny biology, but my birth father was a different man from me and from my adoptive dad. Different in so many ways.'

'Oh, I see. Did you know him well, your biological father?'

'Not really. He died when I was four. But well enough to get the measure of him. At the time, I looked up to him, wanted his approval for things, because what kid doesn't want to be loved back by their dad. But I learned over time that he wasn't all that. He was a liar and a drunk, to name but a few things. And I know my mum went through years of trauma counselling even after he died and she'd got together with my Uncle Jimmy. Over the years, he's shown what a real dad should be like and I've been lucky to have that. He's been like that mountain over there in terms of support to all of us. It takes some man to take on three children fathered by your awful brother, have another one and adopt three more.'

Bea's eyebrows almost hit her hairline at Cal's revelation. 'Wow, Cal, I never knew this about your family. I mean, I knew about the triplets, but not about everything else.'

'Of course you didn't. And I'm not telling you because I need sympathy or anything. I just want you to know that I've always been a bit fearful of turning out like my biological father, so I sometimes overcompensate and end up being an arse anyway.'

'Oh, Cal.' Bea leaned into him. 'You're not an ass. Or how you say it. Arrrse.' Bea tried to roll her 'r'.

'Well done. Well, I was putting my own agenda first and not considering how that might impact you. So for that I apologise.'

'You weren't to know,' said Bea. 'And I didn't know about

your family background. It sounds real complex and challenging.'

'It was, but I'm a big boy now and I'm lucky to have a dad like the one I do. A man who taught me the meaning of hard work and right from wrong. And there's probably something else you should know before we get to my folks'. Cal swallowed hard, the words he'd feared saying for what they might do to him, backing up in his throat. But he had to tell Bea; this was the time. 'My dad has recently been diagnosed with motor neurone disease, or ALS as you might know it. This is the first time I've seen him since he got the news.'

'Oh, Cal.' Bea grasped his hand. 'Oh my goodness! That's huge. I am so sorry.'

'Thanks.' Cal took a breath to steady himself. He'd said the words and the world was still turning. 'He's always been this total presence of a man, a force to be reckoned with. To see that diminish is going to be so strange.'

'I completely understand.' Bea comfortingly stroked Cal's strong fingers. 'I remember when my own father died; it was so hard watching him become smaller and smaller, although the spark of him was always there. I guess it will be the same for yours.'

'Aye,' Cal agreed. His character will always be solid, steely Jimmy Butler with a heart as wide and as deep as this loch.'

'That's exactly it And that will be what you remember, too.'

For a moment or two, Cal stared out at that very loch, lost in his own thoughts.

'Aye, I hope so,' he said. 'All I want is to be as good a man as he is and make him happy and proud of me before he goes.'

'You are a good man,' Bea assured him. 'And I'm sure he is bursting with pride about you. How could he not be?'

Cal shrugged. 'I don't know. I've never felt I measured up. After all, what's running a piddly wee bar compared to a distillery empire? He turned back to Bea, knowing he needed to stop now before his words pulled emotions from too deep within him. 'Anyway, we weren't meant to be talking about me. The original point was that I appreciate that I can't undo five years of whatever your ex has made you think; that would take a lot longer than we have together, but I think that to solve the money thing, how about from now on we go Dutch?'

Bea nodded. 'If that would be okay,' she said.

'But on one condition?

'Okay, what?'

'That tonight, you enjoy yourself with me.' Cal swept his arm towards the pebbled shore where the loch lapped gently and then back to the hot tub. 'Are we going to stand here and argue about money when we've all this to enjoy?'

'Um... well,' Bea conceded. 'You do have a point.'

'Yeah, I do.'

'Okay,' she said. 'It's a deal, about the going halves.'

'Great. Now can I make another suggestion?' Softly touching Bea's shoulder, Cal manoeuvred her to face him. She offered no resistance. 'I don't know about you,' he continued, tucking one of Bea's delicate red curls behind her ear, 'but I thought I'd start by getting naked and into that hot tub, and I wonder if you might join me?'

She glanced towards his hand, a twinkle in her expression, then shifted back to his gaze, her face solemn again.

'Hmmm,' she said. 'I thought that I might like to do something more wholesome. Say pick some pebbles on the beach. Before it gets dark, you know?'

Cal cocked his head to the side. 'Oh, really?'

'Yeah, I told my mom I'd bring her back some Scottish pebbles.'

'You did?' She was teasing him and he knew it, but he'd humour her. If she was willing to wait then he could too, although it would be bloody difficult. 'That's an interesting way to use up your luggage allowance but picking pebbles it is.' He separated himself from her before all the free will drained from his brain. 'I'll call reception and ask for a basket.'

Bea threw her head back and laughed, and Cal, thinking she was the most beautiful creature he'd ever seen, felt something even more potent and dangerous than sexual longing stir inside him.

Chapter Forty-Three

It had taken all the willpower Bea had to even temporarily forgo the chance to get into the hot tub with Cal, particularly as he'd mentioned he would start off naked. But she had her principles, and it would take her a little while to get used to the fact that he was treating her to all this. With the promise that they would go Dutch from now on, some of her worries were assuaged, but she needed time to let things sink in.

Josh had accused her – albeit subtly – so many times of being a freeloader that it was part of her psyche now. Cal had assured her that he didn't see her that way and that was important. It mattered for her self-respect, it mattered for her dignity. But did it matter for another reason? Was Cal's opinion of her integrity important because of her desire for something more sustainable?

For goodness' sake. Bea's inner critic piped up again. *You have to get it into your head that only thing sustainable about this will be the memories. And the words you put on the page. The rest will have to be throwaway because you are going back to the States: Cal knows it; you know it. This house was never built on anything but sand.*

Speaking of sand, this beach was not the softest underfoot... Oh yeah, she was on a beach.

Cal must have noticed Bea emerging from her daydream.

'So not only have you not picked a single pebble, but you haven't said one word to me either.' He was standing on the shoreline, eyes to match the backdrop of green mountains, the gentle sun sending shimmers to his dark blond hair, and in his hand was the basket he'd got from reception: a basket which now contained several pebbles.

'Where did...? Did you pick those?' Bea gaped at the basket.

'Aye. Lucky one of us is here to do what we said we would cause your mum is going to be disappointed otherwise.' He winked at her.

'Sorry,' Bea's heart bounced like a skimming stone at his gesture. 'I was miles away. Thanks for getting those. They're so pretty.' God, he was lovely. Few men could carry a Red Riding Hood basket full of pebbles and still be completely sexy.

'No bother,' Cal swung the basket gently. 'Want to talk about it?'

'The pebbles?'

'Beatrice! Come on now. You know I don't mean the pebbles.'

Bea whipped her eyes up from the basket to meet Cal's. His calling her by her full name sent unprecedented frisson right through her. Wow! Well, two could play at that game.

'You got me there, Call-um.' She savoured the word. It was rich around her tongue and she wanted to enjoy every syllable. And what fun in paralleling his gesture.

Cal raised an eyebrow. 'Are you getting cheeky, Mrs Butler?' He grinned as he referenced the receptionist's error from earlier.

Well, that was it. No one man was allowed to look as gorgeous as Cal Butler did, standing by a loch with a basket full of pebbles that he'd collected for her, then address her as if she were his wife. No such man was allowed to do that to Bea Gracie without being kissed hot on the mouth right this instant. She stepped towards him knowing that entering into this role-play was dangerous, but being powerless to resist.

'Is that going to be a problem, Mr Butler?'

Cal dropped the basket, came to meet her, and took her face in his hands.

'Not for me,' he said. 'No.'

Chapter Forty-Four

After they returned from early dinner at the main lodge, Cal lit the fire in the lounge and they relaxed on the sofa with a glass of whisky. Bea nestled in between his legs, reclining onto his warm chest. She sipped her drink, letting the rich alcohol settle in her mouth for a moment before allowing it to slip down her throat. Unadulterated Scottish decadence, making her woozy. Just like a certain Scotsman.

'What can you taste in the whisky?' Cal asked.

'Hmm, let me see.' Bea counted the flavours on her fingers. 'We've got Manuka honey. Orange peel. Maybe a hint of maraschino cherries?'

'You've got your whisky tasting game going on. I'm impressed.' Cal placed his drink on the side table, dipped his index finger into the glass and brought it to Bea's lips. 'How about this?'

Letting his finger rest on her bottom lip, Bea flicked her tongue across the thick pad. 'Hmm, I'd say sexy Scottish man soaked in the finest thirty-five-year-old Kintyre malt. Hints of west coast heather, stormy sea air and a unique Butler intensity inherited from many generations gone by.'

'Those are some tasting notes.' Cal burred in appreciation, clearly roused. He kissed her hair and lightly trailed his fingers across her neck. Instinctively, she reached up to meet him and for a moment they held onto each other, Bea listening to the beating heart of this Scotsman – as complex as the vintage malt warming her core – thump into her spine.

She guided him to her breasts, where he found her nipples through the fabric of her blouse and circled his thumbs around them. 'These taste perfect,' he said. 'I know that already. I really want to make some tasting notes for the rest of you. All the best places that is.' Cal let his words hang in the air.

Bea inhaled deeply and moulded herself further into his firm frame. His erection was insistent at the base of her back, a promise of what could be hers. What would be hers. A flickering pulsed in her sex at the thought of his mouth on her, at last. Just as she had dreamed.

'You thinking about that?'

'Yes.'

'Aye, me too. And it's making me hard as a rock.'

'And I'm thinking about tasting *you*,' Bea said. 'I bet you taste perfect.'

'Oh fuck, woman.' Cal shifted under Bea and the extent of his arousal was more than apparent. Deftly, he unbuttoned her blouse, reached inside her bra, his breath heavy on her neck. Bea arched to allow him to reach round and unclasp her bra. But before Cal returned to her breast, he sunk his fingers into his whisky glass again. With the amber nectar dripping from them, he moistened her beautiful, dusky nipples, softly, tenderly, deliberately. Driving Bea wild.

'I need these so badly, baby.' Cal, unable to take the torture any longer, inched himself out from under Bea, knelt between her legs and hovered his hungry mouth over the exposed breasts he was starving for. And as he made first touch with single malt on her perfect aureole, a primitive sound emerged from somewhere within him.

'Told you I liked my Manhattans with Scotch.'

'You did. What do I taste of?'

'You taste of spirit. And not just booze. Like the spirit of a real woman. I could drink a cask of you.' Cal whorled his tongue over her again. 'And there's a seriously hot Californian sunrise. And maraschino cherries straight from one of your Manhattans.' His emerald gaze, charged with intent, met her dead on. 'And now I'm going to find out about the rest of you.' He lifted her skirt and tugged down her panties. Bea inflamed like wildfire on heather at the exposure of her sex to this Celtic god.

Cal's mouth was on her, softly at first, as he teased around her lips, gently caressing the sensitive skin. Bea's whimpers guided him to as he kissed and explored every millimetre. No guidance or encouragement was needed. He took his fill, feasting on her hungrily, like a ravenous man devouring a buffet he might never see again.

'Oh, Cal. Please, please you're so damned good at this.' This thing he was doing was incredible and Bea needed it to go on forever.

'It's because you taste so damned good.' Cal pulsed her with his digits while his tongue ramped up the speedometer, hurtling her down the road before she knew she was even on the road. This whole thing was like swerving round a giant hairpin bend she hadn't seen coming at all. But Cal was the driver and he knew exactly what he was doing. And the sounds of appreciation coming from him, suggested that he was as much in the moment as she was.

'Come for me, Bea. Come with my mouth on you.'

Bea was powerless to resist. She would do for him what he

was doing for her, but for now all she could do was abandon control, buck forward with everything she had and let Cal Butler happen to her, until, like ripe apples from a shaken tree, his name was falling helplessly from her mouth, and she was grinding and burning into him. Hard. Desperate. Pleading.

'Oh God, Cal! Oh God! Please don't ever stop!'

But it had to end and, gradually, he released his touch and the incessant surges in Bea's core subsided. She sank down to bask in the afterglow, her face morphing into a blissful smile.

'That was outrageously good,' she murmured. 'Ten star Scottish hospitality. I'm surprised any tourists go home.'

'Ha.' Cal planted a kiss on her belly. 'Not everyone gets the ten star treatment, you know.'

'I hope not.' She reached and raked her hand through his hair. 'I want to do that for you too.' She truly did. Wanted to know – more than she ever expected she could want to – what her mouth round Cal Butler would be like.

'You don't have to return the favour,' he said.

Bea examined Cal's erection, potently visible through the fabric of his clothing. She climbed off the couch so he could lie back. 'I think you need me to,' she said. 'I think maybe you badly need some American hospitality, honey.'

Cal smiled, sunk his head back and nodded gently as she nudged herself between his legs. She could see how tortured with arousal he was and pressed her lips together in anticipation of helping him let it all go. She wanted to please him as he had pleased her. Give as he had given. But, also, she wanted to feel him harden round her lips, knowing that she had made him that way and listen to every last quaver of pleasure that came from him as she took him deep into her hot, sensual mouth.

What she hadn't expected as she did this was for Cal, in the midst of what appeared to be unprecedented sexual pleasure, to reach out and squeeze her hand. Tight. It was such a gesture of intimacy that Bea blazed with affection for all that she had found in this incredible Scotsman. And when he hardened to the point of no return and his climactic roar blended with the sound of her name on his lips, Bea felt her heart flap and flutter like the wings of Capercaillie beating in flight across the loch outside.

Chapter Forty-Five

They sat on the veranda with blankets wrapped round them, sipping whisky. The moonlight illuminated Bea's skin and dappled golden highlights onto her hair, unkempt from their lovemaking.

'You're so beautiful.' Cal tucked one of her strands of hair behind her ear.

She turned. 'Thank you. So are you.'

Cal kissed Bea and remarked how she still tasted so decadent. He could have stayed like this forever, next to this woman who was changing his life with each moment she was in it.

The following morning, Cal awoke early again. For a while, he lay curled round Bea, trying to commit the feeling of her naked skin touching his own to memory so he wouldn't forget it when it was over. When she was gone. Knowing it was fruitless and that memories could never replace the real thing, he gently prised himself from her and climbed out of bed.

It was a perfect crisp autumn morning with a soft golden sun lending a tender warmth. Cal stood on the veranda and inhaled the fresh loch air and the breathtaking view. God, he loved this country. Okay, it didn't have the glorious sunshine of America or the palm-fringed beaches of Australia but all the rain meant it was lush-green and in a season like autumn, it was stunning.

Cal's phone beeped with a message and the name Elisabetta flashed onto the screen. He didn't want to read it but there might be a problem with the baby so he figured he'd better.

Hey. Didn't know about your dad's party. Hope you have a brilliant time. Wish the family well from me.

Cal frowned. There was something odd about this message. Of course Elisabetta knew about the party. It happened every year and he'd talked about this one for some time. But why was she mentioning it now? Was she making a point about not being invited? Why on earth would they have invited her? As for 'the family', why not 'your family'? She talked as if they were her family too. It was so hard to tell if the message was sarcastic or not. There weren't any emojis, such as hearts or even kisses to suggest sincerity, and Elisabetta was a big fan of emojis. Something about the message worried him. But he knew he had a tendency towards cynicism, and one thing he was learning from being with Bea was to be a little less bleak and more positive. It was just a message from someone who knew and liked his family (even if they weren't massive fans of hers) wishing one of them well.

Thumbs moving quickly to get it over with, Cal messaged back, *Thanks, will pass that on*, then put the phone down and went in to meet Bea as she emerged from the bedroom in a robe, glowing with as much natural beauty as the scenery outside the veranda doors. 'Morning, beautiful. There's no almond milk here, so I made you a cup of black decaf tea. Hope that's okay?'

Bea smiled. 'You're funny. Thank you.'

They sat outdoors and drank their hot drinks. 'I can't wait

to meet your family.' Bea wrapped her hands around her tea. 'Do you think they'll like me?'

Cal was walloped with a realisation of what he was doing. He was taking Bea, a woman he was having a no-strings fling with, to meet his family. They'd love her, but then she'd go back to the US. Why was he pursuing this so doggedly? He'd justified it to himself as being to show her Scotland and to show his father he could get a good woman, but those reasons were flimsy now.

You're playing with fire.

'They will absolutely love you,' he told her because it was true. How could anyone not? God, maybe he should tell her he was failing at this no strings thing. Just come clean and get this weight off his chest.

But then Bea's attention was diverted by the sound of her phone that she'd just turned on and a message that made her frown.

'You okay?' Cal leaned towards Bea.

'What?' Bea glanced up from her deep concentration. 'Oh, um... yeah. Just a message from my best friend back home.'

'You missing her?'

'Oh, for sure. Friends like Amira are one in a million. She's been monitoring my scheduled social media since I've been here. I do some check-ins from time to time, but mainly she's been doing it. Telling them I'm fully focused on bringing them the best book possible.'

'And how's that going?'

'Good. Maybe not quite as quickly as I'd like because of being distracted but, you know, a girl's got to research.'

Cal hoped she meant researching the scenery and customs of Scotland. The last thing he wanted was to be the centrepiece of some racy book. He enjoyed listening to Bea read them and being racy with her but being in a book was another thing altogether.

'So, that's why it's great that we're here.' Bea motioned to the horizon. 'How could a girl not be inspired with all this in front of her?' She diverted her gaze to Cal and ran her toe up his leg, giving the sentiment a double meaning.

'It's pretty spectacular.' Lifting Bea's leg onto his lap Cal skimmed his hand to above her knee. 'So are things okay with Amira?'

'Oh, yeah, yeah. Well, I think so. I don't actually know. All she said was "call me, I have something super important to tell you" but she sent the message several hours ago and she'll be asleep now.

'Right.' Cal considered the message on his own phone and wished Elisabetta was in a different time zone. Australia preferably.

'Well, I guess by the time we get to Kinshore, it might be waking hours where she is,' he suggested.

'Yes,' Bea agreed. 'I guess I'll need to be patient and wait to find out what the fuss is all about. At least I have you to keep me distracted.'

Cal smiled and rubbed her knee. 'Exactly,' he said. 'I'm happy to add that to my to-do list.'

Chapter Forty-Six

Cal and Bea checked out at around 11 a.m. after a light breakfast platter delivered to the lodge door. Cal said it was another three-hour drive to his family home, but they would stop off at a few places along the way and arrive at the Butler residence late afternoon.

Once they were out on the road, Bea thought about the message from Amira. Thankfully, Amira had said it was nothing to do with her banking/romance crisis, so that only left something to do with Bea's family or the books and the website. But what could have gone wrong? Had readers left her a hundred bad reviews online? Were her fans fighting with each other? Maybe they weren't happy with her taking a vacation and were demanding the new book ASAP. But that wasn't like her fans; they were unwaveringly supportive. She could look and see but the thought terrified her.

'Are you alright?' Cal clearly noticed Bea's distraction. 'You're very quiet. And you've been watching that phone like a hawk since we left the lodge.'

'I know.' Bea turned the phone face down on her lap. 'I'm

sorry. It's rude of me. I'm just worried about Amira's missed call and hoping she might be awake and call me.'

'I'm sure it's all fine. If she called you now, you'd only get cut off due to a dodgy signal. And she's probably asleep, like you said.'

'Yeah, you're right,' said Bea. 'I need to relax and enjoy the day. I'm sorry. You've been pointing things out and I've only been half-listening.'

'Don't worry, you've not missed too much. Just a couple of pheasants and an old man skinny-dipping in the loch.'

'What?! I missed that?' Bea peered out the window.

Cal laughed. 'Nope. I just wanted to get your full attention back.'

'Okay, well you have it now.' Warmth encircled Bea's heart. She loved Cal's company and his humour, and that was what she needed to focus on today. Amira was asleep, so whatever it was would have to wait. She put her phone back in her purse and tried to bring the customary perk back into her voice.

'So, what's next on the agenda?' she asked.

Cal pointed out lots of fascinating Scottish sights as they drove on through winding roads alongside what seemed like an infinite number of lochs. More pheasants popped up with their plump autumnal plumage, blue-green necks and cute red faces; shaggy brown Highland cows or 'hairy coos', as Cal referred to them, grazed in green fields, and copious russet and crimson trees lined the way.

After an hour or so, they stopped for a break and walked through a wooded glade where Bea photographed the tranquil surroundings, remarking on her inner peace. Cal took her hand as they strolled along the woodland path and she squeezed it to say, thank you for bringing me here.

At around one o'clock Cal parked up at a long building with a gabled roof set against the backdrop of a rich green mountain. The signage across the gable end said Oyster Bar and Restaurant.

'Oh, wow, it's so pretty,' Bea remarked. 'And I love oysters.'

'Phew,' Cal said. 'I took a bit of a gamble. Best oysters in Scotland here. Come on, I got in early a few days ago and booked us the best table.'

At these words, an inkling of unease set in again. Cal had booked this place, so it wasn't going to be cheap. Bea had rankled at not being allowed to pay for things, but could she even afford half of this, especially since much of her funds had gone on helping Amira? She didn't want to bring it up before they even sat down and ruin Cal's good intentions, because he wasn't doing any of this out of anything but a desire to please her, but her enjoyment was cancelled out by the concern that she couldn't pay her way.

'Hey.' Cal glanced up from perusing the menu. 'You're not still worrying about Amira, are you?'

'Hmm, oh a little,' Bea lied, when, in fact, her mind was focused entirely on the prices here. It would be stupid if she asked Cal to pay for it all. There was no way she could do that. So, after he convinced her to order oysters to share, Bea decided to have another starter as a main.

'Are you not hungry?'

'I don't have to be hungry all the time, do I?'

'No, of course not. It's just that...' Cal appeared little taken aback and a cut of guilt sliced through Bea.

'I'm sorry,' she said. 'I...' But she couldn't face bringing up money again. All it would do was to elicit guilt in Cal for wanting to please her by choosing a nice place for lunch and she'd have to admit that she'd given most of her money away. It didn't matter that had she not done that, she might be able to pay; the inadequacy ran far deeper. Tears nipped at Bea. This was such a frustrating situation. She hated feeling like all she could give Cal was her company and sex. Despised the cheapness of it all.

'So, I know you wanted to go Dutch, but I am more than happy to pay for this as it's quite pricey and I didn't give you a choice of venue.' Cal paused to let his words settle and searched Bea's face, as if expecting an argument, but she knew that she couldn't offer one. It was so frustrating. She worked her butt off in the bar then wrote for hours, yet she had so little money.

'Sure.' Bea bit back tears. 'Thank you so much.' She thanked him again when they were out in the car park and she'd gathered herself a little.

'You're more than welcome.' Cal wrapped his arms around her and kissed her. 'Thanks for letting me spoil you. You know, I'm worried. You don't seem your usual vibrant self.'

Bea forced herself to look happy. 'I'm good.' She hated that the ordinarily divine experience of being held in Cal's arms was making her sad and low. She tried to tell herself that she could easily be an earning woman and still let a man treat her for the weekend, but it was no use. Josh had inflicted damage too many times. Damn him. How was she going to get over this?

The best thing, she decided, was to remind herself that this thing with Cal was short-term. It wasn't like they were laying the groundwork for the future. When pay day came round, she would have some money. All she had to do right now was hold it together for the rest of the weekend.

Chapter Forty-Seven

Two hours later, following a scenic drive along a coastline adorned with lush moss-covered crags and a shimmering blue expanse of sea, Cal drove past a small white sign that said, 'Welcome to Kinshore.'

'As the sign says, welcome to Kinshore. The distillery and house are up there.' Cal gestured to the left. 'But I'm going to swing into the village and show you around, if you'd like to see my wee toon?'

'I'd love to see your wee toon.' Bea genuinely couldn't wait to see Cal's home village. To understand more about the man and what shaped him.

'Well, let's start with the beach to your right.' Cal nodded to the grassy dunes which partially shielded a wide expanse of sand leading down to a shoreline where foam tipped waves tumbled in. 'We all learned to surf there, taught by our dad. It's looking like good conditions today.'

'Oh, it's beautiful, Cal. No wonder you don't feel the cold. Growing up surfing in these waters could not be for the faint of heart. And it goes on forever.'

'Aye, it's about five miles long. There are longer beaches in

Scotland, though. Right, let's go to the high street. I'm not going to bore you with my life history or anything, but if you want to go home saying you saw a quaint Scottish village then this is one of the best.' Cal swung left at a roundabout with a cross in the middle into a street lined with an array of shops and cafes. 'And this is Kinshore's central business district,' he said.

'Really?' Bea thought of central business districts as places like Wall Street.

'No, it's the high street, but I'd leave it at that. We've got the usual fare of a grocer's, a fishmonger's, a florist, etc. There's a nice wee coffee shop that does incredible cupcakes that I can take you to tomorrow. And I might even show you the secret garden, if it's not raining.' He reached out and squeezed her hand.

'Ooh, that sounds enchanting.' Bea was entirely charmed by Kinshore already. 'Is the secret garden where you used to get drunk as a teenager?'

Cal laughed. 'No, I just did that at home. Perks of living next to a distillery. I'll take you past my old school so you can see where I used to hang out in shorts when I was young.' He turned off the high street into a narrow street. Bea noted all the small stone houses with colourful painted doors and delightful little gardens. It would be an absolute dream to live somewhere like this. But she wouldn't mention it to Cal, in case thought she was hinting that she'd like to settle down with him.

When they reached his school, Bea could hardly believe the size of the building.

'How many children went there?' she asked.

'About thirty of us,' he said. 'It's since expanded to a new building. And the high school in Campbeltown was much bigger. There was at least a hundred of us there.'

'Incredible! My high school had over 1000 students.'

Cal laughed. 'As I said, welcome to Kinshore.'

Moments later, they were heading back the way they had come and Cal turned the car onto a wide driveway. Bea tapped her knee, nervously. This was it now. No more preliminaries of looking at shops and schools. Cal was bringing her to his family home and business: to the heart of something hugely successful, which, Bea realised, only enhanced the seeds of failure germinating inside her. He came from such a prosperous and high achieving family. No matter how she tried, she hadn't attained anything near those levels of success. Sure, she'd written books and some people liked them, but she had zero money and her self-esteem was low. She admired Cal, thought he was an amazing businessman and that he deserved the fruits of his labour, but being around his success all the time only reinforced how far she hadn't come.

The trees lining the driveway to the Butler home were lush and copious in their autumnal canopy, and there were bright pink fuchsia, too, still blooming before the autumn frosts set in. Bea opened the window to inhale the fresh air.

'This is beautiful,' she said, entranced. 'What an enchanting place to live.'

'Aye.' Cal slowed down to let a rabbit bound across the road in front of the car. 'It's not bad. I sometimes can't believe I was so desperate to leave.'

The driveway to the distillery house went on forever. There was a deer standing by the side of the road that darted off when it heard the car approaching, then they drove onto a little bridge which ran over a delicate stream. Bea fell instantly in love. How she would adore, in another universe, to be part of this world.

Eventually, after what must have been a quarter of a mile, the abundant foliage dissipated, and the drive widened into an expansive courtyard in front of a sizeable stone house.

As soon as she heard the car, Cal's mother emerged from

the front door: she was a vibrant lady with a warmhearted presence who moved with an air of efficiency, no doubt borne of raising seven children. Her ash blonde hair bounced in waves around her shoulders, and her long floral dress billowed at her ankles, drawing attention to her French pedicure. That she lived a good life without wanting for money was apparent, although Bea wondered if she was being extra sensitive on this front.

'Hello, sweetheart.' Cal's mother enveloped Cal in a generous hug as soon as they reached each other. 'It's so lovely to see you.' She turned to Bea. 'And this must be Bea. Oh, you are as beautiful as Cal said you were. Hello, I'm Amanda.' She hugged Bea, and Bea cheered a little at knowing Cal had told his mother she was beautiful. 'It's wonderful to meet you,' Amanda went on. 'We are all delighted you could come to Jimmy's celebration. Cal, your brothers are here. Come in and say hello to them.'

'Okay.' Cal glanced through the open front door. 'I'm going to take our stuff to the room and show Bea the place first before inflicting that on her.'

'Inflicting?' Amanda lightly pulled on her son's ear. 'Those are your family, young man.'

'I'm not so young, Mum.' Cal pretended to flinch but his affection for his mother was undeniable. 'And we'll be back down shortly, I promise.'

The Butler house was old but with fresh décor that embraced the Scottish outdoors with an indoor cosiness. Sturdy oak flooring was complemented with tweed and tartan fabrics and walls in palette of heather, soft green and grey. Cal led Bea along a hallway decorated in framed pictures of dramatic landscapes, Scottish wildlife and family portraits. They climbed a period style staircase and walked along another longish hallway before stopping at a large Edwardian four-panelled door. The synthetic smell of furniture wax permeated the space, but Bea could also smell history and love in this house. She wondered how many people had walked in and out of here since the house was built.

Cal opened the door to reveal a huge room. In the centre was an enormous bed with a fresh white comforter, topped with cushions in shades of heather and moss, and an expansive bay window framed with heavy dusk-pink tweed curtains. The window overlooked a sprawling lawn that commanded views down to the sea.

'Was this your childhood bedroom?' Bea was fascinated at being granted a peek behind the curtain of Cal's life..

Cal put their bags down on the luggage rack. 'Ha! No. That's upstairs. But this one has a better view. It would also be a bit weird being with you in the place where I used to be a kid. I think we should share a more grown-up room. I can show you it later if you like.' He cocooned Bea in his arms and kissed her.

'I'd like that.' Bea relished his hold, but the wrench between being so at home with Cal yet feeling like she didn't belong was growing stronger. How was it possible to be falling in love with someone but know they were completely wrong for you? Bea had always thought these things just worked out, that love conquered all. Maybe that was not the case.

'So, as much as I would like to stay here, let me give you a tour of the house then you can meet the family properly.' Cal guided her by the shoulder to the door. 'We'll start outside. I'll sneak you out the back so we don't get called to mingle before we're ready.'

Cal led Bea down a different staircase at the end of the hallway. They exited into a courtyard with lawns that could have been manicured with nail scissors. A small path led down from the other side of the courtyard to a low stone building with a stream running alongside it.

'This is the very first Butler distillery.' Cal seemed taller and prouder, as he spoke. 'It's out of commission now, but it's the original and the best. Just like me, the first of the siblings. Come on, I want to show you.'

'Are you sure?' Bea asked. 'I feel bad when your mom is expecting us in the house.'

'Don't worry, I won't bore you with a full tour or anything. I want you to see where it all began.'

'Okay,' said Bea. 'I'd love to.'

'Great. So that's the barrel store.' Cal signalled a low stone building on the right. 'Barrels of fun, that place.' He moved on swiftly, taking and squeezing Bea's hand as he did so. 'And down here is the main building.' They walked down a gravel path to the main distillery where Cal explained the history. 'The distillery has expanded over the centuries, but this old building here dates back to 1798 when my dad's ancestors founded it. Impressive, huh?'

'It sure is,' said Bea. 'You're obviously super proud of all this, so why aren't you more involved in it?'

Cal quieted for a moment. 'I am proud of my family,' he said. 'And things might change now that my dad's unwell, but when I was younger I needed to step out on my own and prove I could be successful without them. Maybe that sounds daft, but inheriting a job wasn't enough. I don't know if you know what I mean. Most people think that's stupid, but--'

'I understand,' said Bea. 'I understand better than you think.'

'You do?' Cal brightened. 'Are you a secret heiress or something?'

'No. I get it, that's all. I'd much rather work to be successful with my writing than have someone put a load of money in my lap.'

'Yes, exactly,' said Cal. 'I guess it's called a work ethic.'

To Bea, it was also self-respect. Knowing that whatever she

achieved – which didn't feel like much at the moment – she had worked for herself.

'Although,' Cal added, 'Your writing sounds like it is already pretty successful to me.'

Bea knew she was still on the journey up the mountain, but she didn't want to get into a conversation with Cal about her self-worth, so she simply said, 'Thanks.'

'That reminds me,' said Cal. 'Let me show you something else. Come on.' He led Bea back up the path to the main house. Once inside, he guided her through several corridors to what may have been another wing where he opened the door into a large, airy but welcoming room filled wall to wall with shelves of books. The whole place smelled wonderful, like old faded pages, decades of knowledge and forbidden secrets.

'Welcome to my mum's library,' Cal announced like a tour guide.

Bea spun round taking it all in. 'Just your mom's? There are a lot of books in here.'

'Yeah. My dad has his own in his study upstairs. 'These are all my mum's books and these two walls over here are all your speciality.'

Bea paced over to the shelves. 'Romance? Really? These are all romance books? Oh my goodness, so they are.'

'Absolutely. I told you she loved romance. Can you see now why I got an appreciation of the genre, growing up with this within my grasp?'

'I certainly can.' Bea pulled a book out from the shelf and flicked through it. 'This is an extraordinary collection.'

'Took me nearly forty years to amass them all.' Amanda's voice came from the doorway. 'Been collecting them since I was seventeen and I haven't thrown a single title away. Although, I have to say I'm surprised that this is what Cal considers a highlight of our home. My book collection isn't normally what wins people over.'

'Bea has more of an interest in the genre than some,' Cal informed his mother proudly.

'You do?' Amanda stepped closer.

'Um, yes,' said Bea. It awkward being put in this position. It was as if Cal was leading her into telling his mother she was an author, but in amongst all these Jilly Coopers and Jackie Collinses, she was a very amateur pretender to the throne. Amanda was examining her with interest, and Cal wasn't doing anything to help her – the floor was hers –so she had to say something. 'I, er ... I write romance myself.'

'You do?!' Amanda's face illuminated with genuine interest. 'Are you published?'

'Well...'

'Don't be modest, Bea,' Cal said with the deadpan levity he managed so well. 'Nothing can be overplayed when it comes to my mother and romance.'

Amanda shot Cal a withering but playful look. 'Oh shoosh,' she said, before turning back to Bea.

'I self-publish,' Bea said.

'Under what name?' Amanda was forthright and to the point. 'Is it your own?'

'Um, no. My pen name is Calliope Birch.'

Amanda's mouth dropped open. 'Calliope Birch? That's you?'

Bea tensed. Why was Amanda so surprised?

'Yes,' she murmured.

'Well, goodness me. I've read all your books. I especially loved the Midtown Millionaires series. Rock Dagenham is an absolute god.'

Bea was almost speechless but spluttered out some words. 'You ... you've read some of my books?'

'Oh, yes, they are unputdownable. I love them. You're a very talented writer and you will go places, I am sure of it. In fact, from what I've seen online over the past twenty-four hours that you may be about to.'

'Sorry?' Bea had no idea what Amanda was talking about. Online? What was happening online? She might have thought Cal's mother was confusing her with someone else, but for the fact that she named one of her series and one of her heroes.

'We've not seen the internet since we left Edinburgh,' said Cal. 'What are you talking about?'

'It's her short story,' said Amanda. 'Wait, I'll show you.' She moved over to the desk to a laptop and turned it on. 'Come and look at this.' She motioned to Bea and Cal. You're the talk of this romance forum.'

'My short story?' Thoughts were fleeting through Bea's mind. She had written quite a few short stories in her time, and she often gave them away as freebies to her loyal fans. But she hadn't written a fresh one in a while. That was until... The story she had posted a couple of weeks ago, the one inspired by Cal and her travels to Scotland, designed to be a teaser for the novel. That had taken off? Was this what Amira was calling about?

'People are talking about it a lot.' Amanda brought up a thread where people were saying how much they couldn't wait for Bea's novel to come out and that they hoped she'd come back from her holiday soon because they needed to read the book and learn more about this hot Scottish hero, Hal Hunter.'

'Hal Hunter?' Cal was reading over Bea and his mum's shoulders. 'This story everyone is talking about has got a character in it called Hal Hunter?'

'Yes,' said Bea, absent-mindedly because she was still trying to read all the messages on the screen. Then she realised what Cal was getting at and stood to face him. He was staring at her with a kind of puzzled surprise. She couldn't work out what he was thinking.

'Can I read it?' he said.

'I'm not sure it's your cup of tea,' Bea mumbled.

'I'd like to read it, if you don't mind.'

'Well, go to her website and sign up for the newsletter,' said Amanda, not realising what was going on. But Bea knew. Cal suspected the story she'd written was about him, and he was none too pleased with the prospect of finding out he was right.

Chapter Forty-Eight

Cal took his phone out of his pocket and pulled up the website for Calliope Birch. Before now, he had no need to trawl the internet to find out about Bea. Googling her name felt like snooping, and he was in the privileged position of knowing her in person and being read to first hand from her books. But maybe he should have snooped because he suspected he may have been immortalised on the internet. It wasn't his place to make any wild and arrogant assumptions, but the name Hal Hunter was quite close to his own and, well, it was something of a coincidence if he had completely got the wrong end of the stick.

The website loaded, and Cal entered his email address. Less than thirty seconds later a message arrived with a short story attached, entitled *Hunting for Mr Scotland*. Cal pursed his lips, skimming through the story and getting the general gist. An American writer comes to Scotland seeking inspiration for her writing in the form of a sexy Scotsman. She orchestrates a meet cute with Hal Hunter, a local entrepreneur, and sparks fly. Cal didn't want to carry on beyond the illicit scene where the couple make love in Hal

Hunter's restaurant office, but he read enough to feel like this story was a re-enactment of his experiences with Bea. It wasn't an exact copy of events, but certain similarities were enough for a swooping rush of betrayal to fly in. Cal glanced up from his phone. He could see from Bea's face that she understood immediately what was wrong.

'Bea, what is this?'

'It's just a short story, Cal. Please don't think I would ever—'

'It kind of looks like you have.'

'I might leave you to it.' Amanda shuffled towards the door. 'Go easy, Cal,' she said, touching her son on the shoulder before she left the room. 'She's a very talented writer.'

'Aye, she might be, but—'

'Oh, Cal,' said Bea. 'It's not what you think it is.'

Cal frowned. 'Oh, come on. I don't have a big head, Bea, but this guy here' – he waved his phone in the air – 'I'm not imagining it, am I? Hal Hunter? I mean, you may as well have called him Bal Bunter or Mal Munter, for all the lengths you've taken to disguise that he's modelled on me.'

Bea stifled a laugh and refrained from countering that Mal Munter was not a sexy hero name. 'He's not modelled on you. Just inspired by. You've inspired me, Cal. That should be a good thing. I mean, I didn't think many people would read the story, and even for the few who did, well, I didn't think it would be a problem. None of them would know who you are and ... I thought you would take it as a compliment.'

'You were going to tell me about this?'

Bea shrugged. 'I don't know. Perhaps. Once I'd finished the novel. I mean, this story is a kind of promo for the longer work.'

'Oh, great.'

'Cal, I'm sorry, I am. But I also don't see why it's such a

big deal. It's not like I've said awful things about you and, like I said, no one will know it's you because once I go back to the States then, well, we won't be together so nobody will work it out.'

Cal considered this. She was right. It was unlikely anyone would ever know it was him. But still, his strong desire for complete privacy jarred with the story. His mother had read it, for goodness's sake. And probably now, knowing he was its inspiration, his siblings would too. His brothers would take the piss right out of him, which he could just about stand, but having Cara and Eilidh read it made him uneasy. And as for his father; he didn't even want to think. If Elisabetta parading her possible Butler baby all over the internet was enough for him to feel his son was bringing shame on the family, then what would this do? All it would take would be for one person to identify Hal Hunter as Cal Butler from the Butler distilling family, then post it on social media and he'd be self-conscious every time he met a business contact.

Bea was watching him, nervously. 'You know, you're right,' she said. 'I should have given Hal a different name. I can easily change that.'

Cal shrugged. 'Sure,' he said. 'That'd be good, thanks.'

'It's not that big of a deal, I don't think,' she said. 'Honestly, it's not like I'm a big star and anyone will care to find out who you are. And besides, the longer novel doesn't bear that much resemblance to our experiences together.'

'Okay,' said Cal, still feeling far strange, although he wasn't sure why this provoked such a sense of betrayal. Bea was right, it wasn't that big a deal.

'I'm not sure if you are okay,' said Bea, sensing his unease. 'Believe me, nobody cares about my writing.'

'Of course they do,' said Cal. 'Of course people care. Maybe not millions of people yet, but you'll grow in traction,

Bea. This is just the beginning. You're a talented writer. People will care. They should. I care.'

And with a jolt at his own words, Cal realised why he was so upset about Bea's having written about him. It wasn't to do with his privacy or even his father's approval. It was because he cared. It was because he cared more than he ever expected he would. It was because when they'd gone into this thing together they'd both been on the same page, both wanting a no-strings fling. Bea had taken those experiences and used them as material for her writing, helping to advance her career. And what had he done? He'd gone and fallen in love with her. That's what. He'd let himself get attached to someone who was only interested in a short-term arrangement without ties, fallen head over heels while she had remained detached. God, he was a fool.

'Thank you,' said Bea. 'I appreciate that you care about my writing. Honestly, Cal, I used a little of our experiences to pepper things up a bit. I'd never spill everything onto the page. That would mean I'd be exposing myself as well, remember.'

Cal nodded. 'I guess you're right.' Bea hadn't noticed the subtext behind his words: that saying he cared meant he was in love with her. Well, he wasn't going to drive home the matter. Not if she was able to remain detached. And what she said next cemented that fact.

'If anything, it's a great advertisement for what a swell lover you are.'

'Um, whilst I'm flattered by the sentiment, Bea, that's not something I've ever felt the need to advertise, even if it were true.'

'I was kind of joking.' Bea smiled. 'About advertising it. Because it is true. But, you know, when I'm gone, you'll have a memory of our time together, immortalised. Not many guys can say that.'

Gee, how many times was she going to drive the point

home? That she was leaving, and that it didn't bother her at all?

'Okay, okay.' Cal sunk his hands into his pockets. 'It's fine. I'll try to see it as flattery. But if you could maybe change the guy's name to something that doesn't echo my own. I'd appreciate that.'

'I'll do that as soon as I am back at my laptop.' The tenderness with which Bea looked at him then melted his heart and frustrated him to the core. He wasn't sure how he was meant to hold these feelings in much longer.

Chapter Forty-Nine

It wouldn't be an understatement to say that Bea's emotions were a mess. What should she be feeling? There was the good news that readers were responding favourably to her short story. That brought the possibility the book would be popular. She'd been waiting for validation like this for years. But the fact that she appeared to have upset Cal by using him as inspiration completely took the edge off. Bea couldn't understand why it bothered him as much as it did. Did he like to be in control of things? Was it about power? He liked to pay for things. Maybe it was more to do with him not wanting a woman who was successful: he wanted to show he was the boss, even if it was only for a short period of time. Cal first decided when they would kiss, he'd shown her his country, paid for the lodge and lunch. But she had decided to put him in one of her stories, and he hadn't had a choice. *Is he bothered by the lack of control he had over that situation? Well, if that's the case, then I feel sad.*

'By the way,' Cal said. 'Really well done on the story. As much as I'm peeved at certain aspects, I know this is a massive deal for you, and I don't want to chuck water on your bonfire. You work hard and deserve every success you get.'

Holy moly. Cancel all those thoughts about him being a power tripper. Cal had the good grace to congratulate her and be pleased for her. He wasn't a control freak; he was one of the good guys. It was Bea who needed to get a grip and get over the fact that her experiences with Josh were colouring the way she saw Cal. Cal was more than honourable. The paying for things was generosity, the deciding when they kissed, well that was him trying to maintain professional boundaries but being unable to resist the physical chemistry so evident between them. And as for why the story upset him: well, that was the only thing she couldn't work out. Wouldn't most guys love being immortalised in a complimentary way in the pages of a novel. It was surely an ego boost, and the perfect memory of a short-term but fun fling. But maybe Cal didn't want any memory of their time together, but instead to move on and forget about it once she went back to the States.

A new feeling grew inside Bea. A slow tearing in her heart. What had she done by writing this story, by committing to the novel? That's right, she'd made a deal to write about Cal Butler and relive the time they spent together for a long time. She would have to talk to fans about him, discuss her inspiration, remember every moment, except only on the page because she would be long gone from the man himself. The thought of it was devastating. In a few weeks' time, the only part of Cal she would still have would be the memories. Memories that would be too upsetting to recall because of what she would have lost. Bea had come here to get over a broken heart, and all she had done was head towards another one. She was in love with Cal Butler and destined to make one of two dreadful decisions. Either go home in a few weeks and have to relive the book for a long time but potentially find success as a writer, or go home but start the book again with a different male lead. The latter option would mean less heartache, but it could also mean stymieing her career the minute it might be going places.

There was one other option, but Bea wasn't even going to entertain that. There was no way she would step out on the line and tell Cal that she was in love with him, that the thought of heading back to the States and leaving him filled her with a sorrow heavier than the Edinburgh rainclouds.

'Hey, are you okay?' Cal noticed Bea's faraway thoughts. 'Come here.' He slipped his arms around her waist and drew their bodies together. 'You're beautiful, talented and my mum likes you. How am I going to let you go?'

What did he mean? Was he going to find this as hard to let go of as she was? Bea bit her lip and scrutinised Cal's face for signs he felt the same way she did, but she couldn't work anything out.

'Hey, sorry.' He clocked Bea's confusion. 'I didn't mean to sound possessive or like I want to try to keep you in Scotland against your will. It's just that you've lit up my life and I want you to know that you won't be forgotten in a hurry.'

Cal's words were lovely, but they made Bea's pain worse. Knowing he'd had a good time with her was great. But she needed to hear more than that. Bea needed to know that he liked her like she did him, that he was besotted with her too. But if Cal carried the same sentiment in his heart, he didn't reveal it. And Bea was a staunch believer that if a man had strong feelings for a woman, he admitted them. She clearly wasn't enough for Cal Butler, and she didn't want to be with another man for whom she didn't meet his criteria; she would settle for nothing but complete adoration from now on. But the most heartbreaking thing of all was that Bea wasn't sure if you ever felt that way about someone more than once in your life. Was this chance – the only chance that she would get – going to slip through the net and be lost forever?

Chapter Fifty

Cal showed Bea to her bedroom with adjoining en-suite.

'I'll let you freshen up and do the same myself along the corridor. I'll call back for you in an hour and take you down to dinner.' He planted a soft kiss on her cheek then headed off to change.

An hour later, Bea opened her bedroom door and Cal's jaw crashed to the floor. She looked like she'd been sewn into a deep-red figure-hugging dress, her lips were stained crimson and she wouldn't be out of place on a red carpet. He sucked in a breath. Blood was rushing around his body in a way that was most inconvenient when he was about to introduce her to his family.

'Bea, you look stunning. Did you manage to talk to Amira?' Hopefully a change of subject would keep his body in line.

'Thank you. I did and it was exactly what your mom told me. It really is true.' Bea glowed.

'That's incredible.' Cal planted a congratulatory kiss on Bea's cheek so as not to smudge her lipstick, although if they hadn't been going downstairs he wouldn't have given two hoots about smudged anything. 'Your books are going to be known and loved all over the world, Bea. So, can I take this famous author to meet my family?' He held out his arm for her to link into. His family would love her; she was beautiful and charming and a delight to be around and could talk to anyone about anything. His brothers might even try to flirt with her, but they wouldn't get anywhere, because he wouldn't let them. But there could be questions from certain family members about what their future held. Which was a good point – what did the future hold? Well, maybe tonight was the time to find out. Cal decided that after dinner, he would take Bea down to the beach and tell her he was in love with her. He had to hang onto her. Letting her go couldn't be an option anymore. She was far too amazing to be a holiday fling this passionate, dedicated American goddess.

The other topic that was bound to arise was the family business. Jamie was the only Butler sibling employed by Butler's whisky. Working alongside their father was not a job for wimps. Jimmy Butler was a workaholic and expected nothing less of his son, but he was also vulnerable now and coming to the stage where he would need to think about passing the reins over. This would mean a gap in the executive arm of the business. There were people who could easily fill it, but Cal knew – and he knew that Jamie knew – that his father would prefer if one of his children filled the post. And both Jimmy and Amanda deserved that reassurance.

Cal wondered, as he entered the large drawing room where glasses were clinking and friends and family congregated, if Jamie might remind him how much this all meant to their dad, might question how Cal could get involved, somehow, to give Jimmy confidence that his company was in good hands.

'Lovely Bea,' Amanda chimed. 'Come and let me introduce you to the family.'

'It's fine, Mum, I can do it.' Cal would far rather he be the one to introduce Bea to his siblings and father.

But his mother was off, and Bea, being polite and having no apparent choice in the matter, was following her. Cal didn't pursue because he knew he would end up a third wheel while his mother paraded Bea around the family, clearly set on the idea that this was her future daughter-in-law.

Instead, he watched from afar and chatted to a family friend, casting glances when he could to see how Bea was doing. The answer appeared to be thriving. But Cal knew she would. Bea could charm a stone into doing the Highland Fling. She had certainly worked her magic on him, and he'd been stone-like for a long time.

Cal sidled up to Jamie when he saw his brother was free.

'How's it going, J?'

'Aye good, thanks.' Jamie squeezed Cal into one of his trademark bear hugs. 'How's you? Like I need to ask, obviously excellent after meeting your date for the evening.'

Cal nodded but said nothing more. He was close to Jamie but he didn't want to comment until he'd talked to Bea and, hopefully, had good news. Otherwise, all he'd hear would be people telling him that it would be hard to let her go. So, instead, he asked after Jamie's girlfriend of ten years.

'How're things with you and Katie? She not here?'

'She'll be along later. And we're the usual. She keeps busy with her book group and cocktails with friends, and I keep busy with work and hiking and a dram by the fire. Can't complain.'

'Aye, I suppose you can't complain about a dram by the fire. And is business alright?'

'Aye, I think so.'

'You think so? Is everything okay with the company? With

Dad.' Cal worried that maybe his father had taken a downturn, and this was why he hadn't yet shown face at his own party.

Jamie reassured him. 'Aye, things are fine with the business. I mean, we always want sales to be as strong as possible so we're looking at ways to maximise those, but nothing that isn't another day at the office.'

'Right. And how's Dad doing? You know, his health?'

'As well as can be expected. Still trying his best to work as normal, but it's early days. He's only recently got the diagnosis.'

Cal nodded.

'We're all worried, but you know Dad; he's got this way of making out like you're the one that *he* needs to be worried about.'

'I know. So then we have double the worry. We're worried about his health and worried about how much he's worrying about us and what we can do to stop that worry.'

'Aye, something like that,' Jamie chuckled.

'I know you don't fall into that category since you fell into line and didn't let him down.'

'Ah, well, it might surprise you to learn that I still feel I've let him down on a daily basis. I think it might be a hazard of having such a successful father. You never quite believe you can live up to his reputation.'

'Tell me about it.'

'You know, he is proud of you.'

Cal shot Jamie a look of surprise. 'Aye, right.'

'Of course he is. He's always talking about his son who runs the bar – soon to be bars – in the city and how you've made sure the folks in Edinburgh are drinking Butler's.'

'I don't think I'm the reason people are drinking Butler's, but okay.' Cal was glad he was having this conversation with Jamie. It was going some way to improving how he felt.

Although he couldn't take Jamie's word for things. He would need to talk to his dad.

'Speak of the devil.' Jamie nodded to the door. Cal turned to see that his father had entered the room. He seemed smaller and more vulnerable, his tall frame diminished somehow, although to those who didn't know him so well, such as Bea, he probably looked like a man of seventy rather than sixty. Cal could have sworn his father had shrunk a little. Seeing him like this, an incredible sense of guilt swooped over him. It didn't matter what Jamie said, Cal wasn't sure he could shift the niggling that he'd let his dad down somehow. This, compounded with the looming loss of Bea, made the foundations of Cal's life disconcertingly unstable. And if there ever was a legacy of his childhood, it was that Cal would do anything to avoid that feeling, even if it meant painting over the cracks with the wrong colour of paint.

There were toasts to Jimmy Butler before the meal. As the eldest son, Cal was seated next to his father at the top end of the main table, Bea to his left, Eilidh to the left of her. The room buzzed with loud chatter.

'How're you doing, Dad?' Cal asked as he watched his father watching everyone else.

'Aye.' Jimmy turned his attention slowly to Cal. 'I'm ... alright. Pretty much ... the same as ... the last time we spoke, which ... could be good ... or it could be bad.'

Cal noted that the protraction evident in his father's voice was something new since he'd spoken to him on the phone a few weeks previous. It unnerved him, seeing his dad as anything less than robust and invincible.

'I see you're doing well though.' Jimmy nodded towards Bea, having been introduced to her at pre-dinner drinks. Cal had only seen the conversation from across the room, and Bea hadn't had time to fill him in on how it had gone. 'And can I say that I fully approve? This woman is going to keep you on your toes, I can tell.'

Cal turned to Bea, who was smiling at his father's words. He was right; they did like her, and she would appear to like his family, too. It was great, but it also wasn't since it was a temporary fling and he'd have to let his dad down again and tell him that his firstborn couldn't hold on to a woman.

'Did you get a chance to look at that list I sent you? Of the therapists and stuff?' Cal asked.

'Aye, I looked.' Jimmy nodded and met his son's eyeline square on. He wasn't avoiding the topic but he was also telling Cal that giving the list a cursory once over would be all he would do, or admit in public to having done. Cal couldn't push the matter, certainly not in this context. He reached for his wine, hoping that something in the glass might help make this situation better.

'How's business?' he asked as a detour that would hopefully lead back to the previous topic.

'Things are grand,' said Jimmy. 'Jamie's heading up a great team … and we're expanding further into Japan. And, closer to home … maybe turning some of the old distillery cottages into holiday accommodation.'

'That sounds great, Dad. Are you sure you can keep working, though?'

'For the time being, aye.' Jimmy reached for his glass of water and Cal could see that he didn't have a firm grip on the glass. 'I could do with a real drink, though.'

'Want me to get you a wine?'

'Your mother says I'm not allowed.' Jimmy smiled. 'And to keep her happy I'm going along with it. For now, anyway.'

Cal was glad of his father's humour, but he took a sip of water rather than wine, so as not to rub it in. 'So, Dad, listen, about BDL—'

'What about BDL? Are you alright, dear?' Jimmy addressed Bea. 'I don't think Bea came here because she wanted to hear a conversation about business.'

'Oh, I don't mind.' Bea flashed her knock 'em dead smile at Cal's father. 'I'm sure you don't get to see each other too often and if you've business things you need to talk about, that's fine with me.'

There were business things Cal wanted to talk about, but his father didn't care to listen. All the kind words in the toasts had brought goosebumps up on Cal's skin, so proud was he of his father and all he had achieved, including his fine reputation in the community as a no-nonsense businessman but also a committed father. Cal wasn't sure he would have it in him to do all his dad had done. But listening to it all, he knew he had to try.

Cal took a deep breath. He was going to do this. No point thinking about it too hard; just go for it. He seized his moment, tapped his glass with a spoon, the chime seeming to splinter the air, stood up and surveyed the room. Everyone stopped and turned to see what was happening.

'Good evening, everyone. I thought I would add a few words,' Cal said. Public speaking didn't sit well with him, but this was important. He cleared his throat. 'There's a lot of pride in this room, a lot of love. And rightly so. My father has amassed a lot in his time. A lot to be proud of and a lot to make him worthy of all the love here today. I'm not one for lengthy speeches, so I'll keep it brief. I wanted to make a wee announcement, that as of this year I hope to become more involved in BDL. It will be an honour to be part of the family company. I think my bar, and soon to be bars, could manage on their own now so, well, I'll be focusing more on the family business from now on. If you'll have me, that is.'

Cal caught his father's eye and noticed a flicker of confusion.

'That was all I wanted to say,' he turned back to the guests. 'I just wanted to make it public.' *So he can't change the subject.*

As Cal sat down again, he said to his father, 'We can talk later about the finer details.'

'I don't think we've any details we need to talk about.' Jimmy shook his head.

Cal stared at Jimmy Butler, wondering if it really was his father. For as long as he could remember, every time he'd come up here from Edinburgh, Jimmy had pressured him about his business and whether the bar was going to work out and how he was always welcome at BDL. Now, he didn't seem interested in talking about it.

'Are you sure you're okay, Dad?'

Jimmy laughed. 'I'm fine,' he said. 'Are you worried because I'm no that bothered about you about working for me?'

Cal shifted in his seat. 'You could say that, aye.'

'Look, Callum, I might not be ready, or all that keen, to see a fancy therapist, but if this illness has taught me anything – and it's early days yet, so no doubt it will teach me plenty more – it's that life is precious, and we should enjoy every moment.'

'You've always thought that,' Cal countered.

'Aye, true, but I've always meant spend most of it enjoying working.'

Bea laughed at this. 'Sorry,' she said, slapping her palm to her mouth.

'No need to apologise,' said Jimmy. 'I like her, Callum. Hang onto her.'

'Um, okay, Dad.' Cal wasn't sure he understood this new version of his father, but he did quite like him.

'You dinnae want to work for me; you've made that perfectly clear in the past. I've spent half my days trying to convince you you've made a mistake, and I can see now what a waste of time that was. You've no made any mistakes. You've done very well for yourself, and I couldn't be prouder. So stop all this worry about working for BDL, just to make me happy, and keep doing what you're doing, which includes keeping a hold of this one here.' He tilted his head towards Bea.

Cal couldn't quite believe his ears. He'd wanted so badly to do well by his father, but what Jimmy valued most wasn't Cal working at BDL or even his own health. What mattered most to Jimmy Butler was Cal's own happiness. Why had that not been obvious all along? Cal noticed Bea's hand on his knee and turned to her. She was beautiful inside and out. It was no wonder his father had seen her wonders straight away.

'Are you okay?' he asked Bea. 'Sorry if my family are a bit intense.'

'They aren't at all. I'm having a great time.' Bea leaned closer and lowered her voice. 'Although I'd rather be alone with you, of course.'

Warmth rushed in. 'Maybe after the meal, we could go for a walk down to the beach if it's still light,' Cal said. 'I'd love to show you. We can be alone there.'

'Sounds lovely.' Bea's voice was as seductive as whisky liqueur. And Cal was sure he saw a glint in her eye that suggested she felt the same way he did. Maybe things would be alright.

But then the room hushed as chatter dimmed to a far lower level. Cal scanned the space. People were staring at the door which wasn't in his direct line of vision. He turned to see what they were all looking at.

Then he wished he hadn't.

Chapter Fifty-One

Standing in the doorway was a very visibly pregnant Elisabetta.

Bea looked at Cal and caught him shooting his brother Sean daggers for letting Elisabetta in without getting his elder brother first.

'What?' Sean shrugged. 'Am I meant to leave a pregnant lady standing outside?'

Cal sighed and stood up from the table. He made his way over to Elisabetta and said something in hushed tones Bea couldn't make out. Then he led her out of the room.

Bea dropped her gaze to her plate, her hunger departed. Why had Elisabetta travelled all the way up here, to Cal's parents' home on the Kintyre Peninsula? You didn't make all that effort unless you really needed to make someone understand.

'Are you okay?' Cara asked from the other side of Eilidh, her face drawn with concern. Bea knew that Cara wasn't a fan of Elisabetta, but it didn't make the slightest bit of difference if Elisabetta was the most unpopular woman in the world; she was still probably carrying the child of the man Bea was in love with, and that meant she had a hold on him that Bea could not have. What had Bea been thinking? That she was the sort of woman who could cope with this scenario? Or even more ridiculous: that she wasn't in love with Cal at all and that the no-strings affair they'd agreed on was working out? She'd been such an idiot, she truly had. And now, here she was, trapped at a family dinner – a highly personal affair, seeing as Jimmy Butler was unwell – with the family of the man she was head over heels in love with while he discussed who knew what with the mother of his child somewhere else in the house.

She had to get out of here. But this wasn't her party, and she shouldn't make a scene. So, fixing the politest of smiles on her face, Bea said to Cara, 'Oh, I'm doing great, thank you. It was so nice of Cal to invite me here to your father's celebration.'

It was negligible whether Cara was convinced, but to stem any further questioning, Bea took a sip of her wine and turned her attention back to her meal.

'This is so delicious,' she said to her plate. She truly was enjoying the meal but directing the comment at anyone in particular would mean looking at them, and if she did that they would see tears begging to be unleashed.

Unfortunately, Bea caught the eye of Cal's brother Jamie and she could have sworn shades of sympathy passed across his face. Nausea swept in. This was the last thing she needed: Cal's family pitying her. She finished her food, then turned to Eilidh and said, 'If you'll excuse me, I'm going to freshen up.'

Out in the cool air of the hall, Bea was emboldened. She had fully intended to pop to the restroom for five minutes, but now she was out of the dining room, the hardest part was surely over. The part where she got away from Cal's family. She'd made it out without creating any histrionics; nobody was offended, and neither was Cal's father upstaged. But now she had to do something for herself. Get out of here. Get away from Cal's family home, away from Kinshore, from the Kintyre Peninsula, away from Scotland. Bea was fully decided. She was going back home. Proper home, that was. Not to the chilly flat in Edinburgh, except to get her things. No, she was heading back to where she belonged, back to New York City.

The tricky part would be leaving this remote location without enlisting the help of anyone or alerting Cal, who would surely try to change her mind. But Bea had a plan.

She crept up the stairs and into Cal's room, found his keys on the dresser, made her way back to her own room, changed into jeans and a hoodie, then grabbed her holdall and headed down the back stair to the car. All the while, her heart was thundering in her chest as she knew she could get caught at any moment. She had no idea how long Cal would be engaged in talking to Elisabetta, but as soon as he found her missing, he would surely come to find her. She knew he'd be worried, but she couldn't stay here a moment longer. So, by way of compromise, Bea found a pad of paper in a drawer in the bedroom and wrote a note.

Dear Cal, I am sorry, but I have had to leave. Please don't come after me. It isn't what I want you to do, and you won't change my mind. I know we had an arrangement, but I think it's time we both focused on the things that are most important: my writing and your impending child. I've taken your car and for that I apologise, but I will leave it in Edinburgh. Thank you so much for showing me Scotland. I've fallen in love with the place and leaving is a wrench I never anticipated being so difficult. But I must go and look to the future. Thank you once again. I will never forget you or the hospitality you have shown me. All my love, Bea xxx.

Bea wiped a tear away as she folded the note and scrawled Cal's name on the blank side of the paper. She knew that she was taking the coward's way out, but she couldn't risk having her mind changed. She deserved better than being second best.

As she slid out the back entrance of the house and across the gravel towards the car, a sideswipe of guilt hit Bea. Cal was good to her; his family were good to her. And here she was repaying him by stealing his car. But what else could she do? If she went back indoors and told him she wanted to leave, not only would she be causing a scene, but he would inevitably try to stop her. And she couldn't allow that to happen.

It was difficult enough driving on the left-hand side of country roads, not to mention in the dark with no streetlights, but compounded by the tears blurring Bea's vision made this one dangerous escape mission. And so ridiculous, she considered, that she was running from the most wonderful man she'd ever known. Women didn't run from men like Cal Butler; they ran towards them, and that's what made her, Bea Gracie, such an absolute fool. How had she got herself into this situation? She'd come here to mend a broken heart, and she would head home with another fracture, except this one was bigger and deeper than the last, and she wasn't sure how she would heal this time as there would be no running away to escape the pain. The simple act of running home would have to be enough and Bea hoped, as she got miles and miles further away from Cal and Kinshore village, that by focusing on her writing she could push him from her mind and her memory forever.

Chapter Fifty-Two

Half an hour. For half an hour, Cal had struggled to end this pointless conversation with Elisabetta. It was like she knew exactly what she was doing, exactly what she was keeping him from by making sure he stayed in this room with her. But enough was enough. He had a guest, and he had to get back to her. *What must Bea be thinking?* He wanted to go to the dining room, sit next to her and take in her warmth, absorb her joy, hear her feverish laugh and watch his family fall for her too. He couldn't bear to think of her sitting out there alone wondering why this demanding blonde woman had turned up and insisted on monopolising his time.

'Betta, I'm going back to my meal now. I don't think there is anything else we can say on this matter. In fact, I don't know why you came here today. There's nothing that couldn't have been said in Edinburgh.' Could she have known Bea was with him? He wouldn't put it past her to have found out somehow and come up here intent on sabotage. Either that or she wanted to take some shots for her Instagram, which she'd done last time she'd been here.

'Okay, fine.' Elisabetta shrugged. 'I can't say I'm exactly delighted, but I said what I came to say. All I can hope is that you'll do the right thing.'

'I've told you I'll support you if the baby is mine. Now, I'll walk you to your car and that's that, okay?'

'Sure.' Elisabetta swept out of the room, taking a selfie against the piano as she went.

Out in the drive, Cal spotted Elisabetta's sleek white Porsche, immediately. In fact, it was sitting next to where he'd parked his own car. Except the spot he'd parked his car was now empty.

'What the…? Where's my car?'

Elisabetta shrugged again. 'I don't know. It was here when I arrived. I parked right next to it.'

A paddle of fear hit Cal. Bea! Oh, please say it couldn't be so. Surely not. He would go back inside and find her chatting away with his family as if nothing had happened.

'Betta, I have to go. Drive safely.' Cal watched as she got into her car and deliberately took her time getting comfortable, putting her seatbelt on, slowly reversing out of the parking spot before stopping to apply some lipstick and face mist, then finally driving out of the grounds of the house. Cal's brow furrowed, and he was fraught with angst. He knew if he showed any sign of going back in before Elisabetta was out of sight, she would find a reason to return, but the minute the white of her car disappeared from his vision he strode back into the house.

Cal's heart sank as he entered the dining room and saw that Bea's place was empty. It confirmed all his fears. She had gone.

'Where's Bea?' he asked Cara as she was most likely to know. But on this occasion, his nosey sister let him down.

'She went to freshen up about twenty minutes ago, but

she hasn't come back. I thought she would have found you, so I didn't want to interrupt.'

Cal scraped his hand through his hair. If it weren't for the fact that his car was gone, he'd have accepted Cara's theory as the probable truth, but something in his gut told him otherwise. He'd messed this one up.

He left the dining room and took the stairs two at a time, burst into Bea's room and shot his eyes to the dresser. The car keys were missing. And in their place was a piece of paper. A tightness built in his throat as he read the note. Yep, she'd taken his car and gone. Cal slammed his hand on the dresser, then reflected that he deserved that more than the furniture. What an absolute idiot he'd been. There could be only one reason Bea had left like this, and it wasn't simply because he stepped away from the table for a little too long. No, this was about feelings – unequivocally – how she felt about him. It must match how he felt about her. Cal knew it now. He had to find Bea and get her back. No way was he letting her leave the country without telling her what she meant to him.

But it was his father's party. This was important. Really important. His father meant the world to Cal and upping and leaving his celebration on a melodramatic whim was not an option. In fact, it would mostly upset his mother. He couldn't do it. There was no way that Bea would leave the UK in the next twenty-four hours. First thing in the morning, Cal would get himself back down to Edinburgh, find her and tell her she wasn't going anywhere, not until he could be open about his feelings. She had to know. And he had to know if it was mutual because he was sure that, had she not been in love with him too, she wouldn't have disappeared in such a hurry when Elisabetta had arrived. God, he'd been a fool.

The rest of the evening dragged like a slow ocean trawler out on the horizon. Cal tried his best to enjoy himself and make sure that his father had a wonderful evening. Was he annoyed at Bea for having put him in this position? No. She hadn't stormed off in a blaze of histrionics; she had subtly made an exit after what must have been quite a difficult situation for her. Elisabetta, conversely, with her unwanted entrance, should have known better. The conversation she wanted to have was one they could have had in Edinburgh; but Betta had wanted to ingratiate herself with Cal's family. She was unable to accept that he didn't want her to be part of his life. No, Elisabetta was the rude one here, not Bea.

Cal took it easy on the alcohol, mindful of the fact that he to get up early and drive to Edinburgh. He considered getting a flight, but he couldn't bear the waiting time at the airport. He'd far rather be on the road and moving to give the illusion of getting to Bea as quickly as possible, even if it worked out roughly the same amount of time. Already he missed her. He'd so cherished the promise of having her by his side this evening, of watching her win over his family, of being warmed by her presence, hearing her laughter and seeing her listen intently to whoever she was locked in conversation with. Then he'd wanted to be in bed with her, pull her to him, her soft, warm skin against his own, kiss her, make love to her again and again. They'd have stayed up all night but woken up entirely enlivened from the drug that is each other's company. Not exhausted from a restless night alone, unable to sleep from worrying about where she was and if she'd got back to Edinburgh safely. He'd tried calling her mobile but it rang forever or went straight to voicemail. Bea either didn't want to talk to him or the lack of signal denied her the right.

At 5 a.m. Cal forced himself under a cold shower. Nothing less than he deserved for putting Bea through that last night and hopefully enough to ready him for today. He repacked his barely unpacked bag and made his way downstairs to the kitchen. As anticipated, his mum was already up and sitting at the large kitchen table reading the news online.

'Morning, Mum.'

Amanda Butler didn't look too surprised to see her eldest son up at such an early hour. Cal hadn't said too much the night before, but Amanda was astute enough to work out that Elisabetta's appearance and Bea's disappearance were not entirely unlinked.

'I have to go back to Edinburgh,' he told her. 'I'm taking a spare car, so I'll come back up next week again with the car and spend some quality time with you and Dad.'

'Okay, Love,' said Amanda. 'I hope Bea is okay. Have you heard from her?'

'No, I haven't. I hope she's okay, too.' Cal rubbed his chin. 'This is all my stupid fault, Mum. Please tell Dad I'm sorry.'

'You've nothing to be sorry for, Cal. Your dad had a great time last night, but he was in bed by nine so he wouldn't have noticed much. He went to sleep a contented man and will wake up one too.'

Cal nodded. 'Thanks. Are you okay? We didn't get to talk much about Dad's illness and what it means for you.'

'I'm good, sweetheart. Don't worry about me. I was planning to take a step back from the business anyway, so I'll be doing a gradual handover of the reins. And we're lucky enough to be able to afford extra help at home, so please don't worry about us. We can talk more next weekend. I'm looking forward to it already.'

'Me too. I'll see you then.' Cal gave his mum a tight squeeze, kissed her on the cheek and told her he loved her. Then he went outside to get in the car and journey back down south.

The drive back to Edinburgh was a blur. By the time he reached the city's outskirts, Cal was alert on adrenaline and thanking his lucky stars that he'd arrived safely, considering he didn't remember much about the journey. He recalled the speedometer hovering around maximum and over a lot of the way though, although it was hard on the smaller, more winding roads.

It was now 11.30 a.m. Where would she be? Surely at her apartment. Cal swung the car towards the south of the city. Fifteen minutes later, he was parking outside Bea's flat, just as two days earlier. Only now, he had no idea if she would be there or not, and so much more rested on the hope that she was. Cal rubbed his eyes. Exhaustion weighed on him, but he had to find the energy to go out there and fight for this woman. He'd never shied away from hard work, always believing you could achieve whatever you wanted if you put your mind to it, although he knew that Bea was a living, breathing person he couldn't make behave whichever way he wanted. There were feelings to consider. He only hoped that hers were the same as his.

Cal knocked on the door of the flat and waited, heart in his throat, for Bea to answer. He noted the flaking paint and empty crisp bags at his feet and shook his head at the fact she had to live somewhere like this. She deserved so much better.

Chapter Fifty-Three

Bea heard the knock at the door and her hands trembled around the cup of camomile tea she'd been drinking to calm her nerves. It was a fruitless endeavour. Those nerves had barely subsided since she'd left Kinshore, and her whole body had tremored all through the booking of a flight back to the States; how could a cup of tea help? The uncertainty terrified her. It was like some part of her didn't want to leave Scotland, wanted things to work out with Cal. Returning to the States felt like going somewhere foreign and unknown and filled her with dread. How could leaving a place you'd been for barely two months be so difficult? Bea knew why and it was the same reason that she was shaking at the thought of opening the door: Cal. Cal made Scotland more than just a place; he'd given the country a heart and made her so welcome. And now he was on the other side of the door. Bea considered not opening it, but seeing as she had already stolen his car, she didn't have the heart. She would have to play a part here to get through this. The part of a heartless woman.

Cal's face was drawn. Like a man who'd lain awake all

night worrying. He was still handsome, but a slightly careworn handsome. It was less than twenty-four hours since she had seen him last, but with the journey and distance travelled since it could have been days ago in another land. Bea was discomfited. Now she was distant from this man to whom she'd been growing closer; he was almost a stranger again. The initial reaction was one of sadness, but she tried to tell herself that, if she was going to make the break from him, this was a good thing. Although it would be damned difficult if he kept staring at her with those hopeful green eyes.

'Morning.' Cal's voice was a little hoarse and somewhat muted.

'Morning.' Bea found it hard to look at him for long. Because if she had to stare at his beautiful face, she would end up admitting what he meant to her and, subsequently, what she'd have to walk away from. And then she might not walk away from it, and that would mean being stuck in a scenario where she was reminded how substandard she felt because he was having a child with another woman. In her heart, Bea knew she should be bigger than this and accept that Cal had to do the right thing, and how much he wouldn't be the man she loved if he hadn't. But it was more complicated than that. Everything was entangled in the worthlessness Josh had made her feel and the added kick in the gut of Avery's baby.

'Do you mind if I come in?' Cal asked, and Bea realised that she must have been standing deep in thought for some time.

'Um, yes, do, sorry.' She fumbled her words slightly as she moved from out of the doorframe to let Cal enter the flat. 'I'm sorry about taking your car. How did you get here?'

'I borrowed a family car. And don't worry about it.'

'I'm sorry, again.' Bea handed Cal his car keys. 'Would you like a cup of tea?'

'I'm all right, thanks.' Was there the tiniest little flicker of amusement on his face, at her attempt at what she supposed was the done thing in this country – to offer tea in times of crisis? 'Look, Bea—'

'Would you like to sit down? You look tired?'

'No. I'd rather just say this. That's the most important thing. And I don't need to be sitting down to say it.'

'Well, I have a flight to catch so if you could make it quick.' Bea shocked herself at how short she was being with him. Cal started, taken aback too.

'When is your flight?'

'Um, eight tonight?'

He looked at his watch. 'Right, well, I'll try to wrap this up in the next four hours.' He was joking, but Bea remained steadfast.

'I have to pack,' she said.

'Aye, all right. Look, Bea, I'm sorry. I'm so sorry. I had no idea Elisabetta was going to turn up last night.'

'I know you didn't.'

'Okay, but I know how embarrassing it must have been to see her there.'

Embarrassing? Bea frowned. He was oblivious to how much it cut her up to see him with his ex. Bea wasn't merely embarrassed; she was struggling in foreign waters, lost, away from a sinking ship that she thought was sailing towards a bright horizon. But no way would she would admit that. Not if he thought it was only a bit of social upset.

'You were my guest, and I left you so I could talk to her and that must have been uncomfortable for you. I'm so sorry.'

Bea said nothing. She couldn't. It was too hard. She would sound spoiled and silly. How could she explain without sounding ridiculous? Then he would try and convince her it would all be fine and she'd be trapped in a scenario that was against the better wishes of her heart. She wrote all the time about characters being true to themselves; for once in her life, she needed to do the same.

'Bea? Are you going to say anything? I really am sorry.'

'It's fine, Cal, you didn't embarrass me. Well, you did a little, but it's no big deal.'

'It's not? Then why did you drive off like that?'

She searched his face. He didn't understand and she couldn't bring herself to explain. It hurt too much, and, in her deepest centre of truth, Bea knew she was scared that Cal would see that what she was saying made total sense and that she wasn't a proper woman, and what had he been thinking?

'I don't have anything more to add,' Bea said, in the most detached tone she could muster, but boy was it hard.

'Really?'

'I don't know what you *want* me to say, Cal.'

'I don't know either. But I do know I don't want you to leave here like this.'

'Like what exactly?'

'Like this. All cold and anonymous. I think we have more than that. Look, I know that you only ever wanted this to be a fling, and that's all I ever thought it would be too...'

Bea glanced up at him. Where was he going with this?

'Bea, I knew you were more than a fling when we decided to have a fling. It was the single daftest and smartest decision I ever made, to do the "three months and bye bye" thing with you. The three months was the smart bit because if I only had five minutes with you, I'd take it. It's probably all I'd need to be honest, the amount you turn me on. I'm joking. But I'd be happy sitting holding your hand. Anyway, the "bye bye" bit was never going to work. Not recognising that you'd be impossible to let go makes me Scotland's biggest numpty. Bea, I have never met a woman that has the effect on me that you do. This country can be so gloomy and dreich and it's winter about 340 days of the year, but you waltz in and it's like ... I don't know, the two weeks we get in May when the sun shines and everyone says summer's arrived and takes their tops off. That's you. Sunshine and ice lollies and taps aff. And, Jesus, just as well I don't write greetings cards for a living.' Cal shook his head and raked his palm through his hair. 'Welcome to romance, Scotland style.'

Bea pursed her lips and tried not to laugh. Or cry. What he'd said was beautiful. And he looked as edible as an ice lolly. *This is so hard.*

Cal continued. 'Before you came along, I thought I could only ever have vacuous women because that is all I ever had. I'd decided to be alone and focus on my work. I never thought it was possible to experience job satisfaction *and* have a woman like you in my life. A woman whose company I can't get enough of, that I thrive on being around.'

Bea bit the inside of her lip hard in the hope that it would stop the tears coming.

'I want to be with you Bea. I want those two weeks in May all year round. I want to ride a wave at Kinshore and see your sunshine smile next to me, I want to see your laughter make little clouds on the baltic air, I want to make you so happy that you don't care that it's snowing in March. I...' Cal stopped, his voice wavering on the edge of possible uncertainty. He stepped towards her and softly but assertively grasped her face. Bea was so taken aback that she froze on the spot.

'What?' Her voice wobbled.

'I love you, Bea. I love you, so, so much. Please, don't go back to the States. Stay with me and make a life here, if you can stand the drizzle and the biting wind. I'll keep you warm. Or at least tell me you feel the same and then we can decide what to do.'

There were tears fighting for presence in Cal's eyes, too. Bea hadn't been about to speak but his words took her breath from her and for a moment, she struggled to inhale. Despite

Cal holding her cheeks she had to stop herself from falling over. Cal Butler loved her. He was in love with her. Just as she was in love with him. He was touching her and searching her face now with those yearning and sincere eyes. He was so close, the familiar cedar and the lime scent was trying to trick her into believing she was home. There were his lips, so incredible to kiss and able to elicit feelings she had never known with any man before. She could almost swear she heard his heartbeat. Heard his love. She could see it, she could feel it, so blinding now that she wondered how she'd never noticed it before. Why had she thought he was completely detached? It was glaringly evident that he wasn't that person at all. Not one single bit.

'Bea.' Cal stroked her fringe from her face then reached down for her hands. Bea's instinct was to slide her fingers in between his, squeeze tight whilst gazing into his soul and admit she was besotted too. Then she'd collapse into him and to let herself be held. She didn't give a damn about the weather. She cared about Cal Butler. But she couldn't. She just couldn't. So, instead, she held her arms fast by her side and remained unresponsive. Cal took in her rigidity, flicked his gaze back up, then asked a question that broke Bea's heart.

'You don't feel the same way?'

Oh God. She did. She did. But she couldn't do this. 'No, no, I don't,' she lied, the hurt on Cal's face ripping her heart in two. It didn't matter if she was in love with him and he was in love with her. Bea had always thought that was all that mattered, but she could see now it wasn't enough. She needed more. Needed for it to be her and Cal alone. No shadows from the past. He couldn't see it, but when that baby came along everything would change. His priorities would change.

'I don't believe you, Bea. God knows, I've never professed to be amazing at reading women, but look at you, you're stiff as a board but your hands are trembling. What are you hiding from?'

Cal was right. And it was insightful of him to notice her behaviour. But he wasn't being insightful in the slightest. If he truly was, he'd have worked out that it was the baby that upset her. Why he hadn't clicked about this, she wasn't sure. She could come right out and spell it out for him, but that would mean admitting why his having a child with another woman bothered her so much – because she was in love with him too – and she couldn't risk losing him when he saw her for who she was. A silly woman who wrote books for a living and that was it.

But then Cal said something that knocked Bea sideways.

'It's the baby, isn't it? Jeez! Of course. How could I have been such an idiot?' He took a step towards her and placed steadying hands on her shoulders. 'Oh, Bea. I am so, so sorry.'

Bea stepped back to dislodge his hands from the position where they felt far too comforting. 'No,' was all she managed to say. She couldn't have him pity her. 'No, Cal.'

'No? No, what?'

'Just no. I am not doing this.'

'Just because there might be a baby doesn't mean there isn't a future for us. You do love me, don't you, Bea? I can see it in the way you look at me. I can feel it in the space between us. I always have. I can't be feeling this on my own.'

'You're wrong.' Bea couldn't admit it and risk him persuading her. She couldn't take that chance on being left again like Josh had done to her, but this time by someone who was truly amazing. She had to go. She had to make him leave, then get out of here herself. 'I'm not in love with you,' she said. 'This was only ever a temporary arrangement. I'm sorry if you've gotten more caught up in things than I have, but I was only ever here in a professional capacity and—'

'Does that include writing about me?' Cal was hurt and

Bea wanted so badly to ease that hurt. She never wanted to cause him any upset.

'I would never exploit you for my writing, Cal. I have only ever been inspired by you, but if you think you see yourself in my writing to an extent that you would be recognisable to someone who may know you, then please know that I will rectify that so that no upset is caused.'

Cal shrugged. 'It doesn't matter. But, please, you can drop the formalities. We're not in a court of law here. I think we know each other well enough by now.'

Bea shrugged, too.

'Okay,' she said. 'Look, if you don't mind, I need to get on with packing and cleaning this place.'

Chapter Fifty-Four

Cal regarded the room Bea was talking about cleaning. It would take more than a few hours to get it anywhere near hospitable. He hated that she had to live here. Why hadn't he done something about it before? Helped her to get somewhere better? Offered her the use of his own place in town? He was ashamed of himself. Not only for that, but for not considering the baby thing until it was too late. The selfish truth of it was that until he'd realised that he was in love with Bea, Cal hadn't thought the baby would matter. And he certainly hadn't considered how it might feel for a woman to be in that situation. The truth of it was, he'd thought he would have sex on tap for a couple of months and after that he wouldn't have sex on tap. The truth of it was that he was an idiot.

'I'll drive you to the airport,' he said. Maybe he could change her mind. 'We can talk on the way.'

'No, Cal.' Bea picked up a duster and turned to the mantelpiece, her body stiff. Cal could see it was forced; she was shutting him off and the pain of that broke him. He wanted to take her to him, hold her close and tell her it would all be okay, that they would find a way together and that he would always love her, no matter what happened. But when she sensed him standing there, she turned from the mantelpiece, walked out of the lounge and opened the front door.

'Please, I think you should leave now, Cal. Thank you for everything. Every single moment has been wonderful, and I will never forget you.'

Cal couldn't believe this was happening. The woman who was so free and open with him – who had taught him how to let go and to love – was shutting him out, denying her own heart. How could he get her to be the one to let go and love? Cal had no idea. He wasn't armed with those skills. He studied Bea for a time, willing her with his stare to see how serious he was, but she merely stared back with a tenacity that surpassed his own.

Against his feelings, Cal, reluctantly, leaned in and kissed her on the cheek, inhaling one last waft of that sweet amber and honeysuckle scent. An aching thud hit him and tears pooled in his eyes.

Bea darted her glance away. Maybe she didn't want to see him so vulnerable. Or maybe she felt the same and didn't want him to see her welling up, too. He didn't know and he couldn't make her admit anything.

Cal examined her for a moment longer, willing her to meet his gaze so he could convince her intuitively that they belonged together. But when she looked at him again, although her eyes were glistening, he saw a resolve that he knew he had to respect.

'I will never forget you either, Bea,' he said. 'And I will never, ever stop loving you, no matter what. If you ever change your mind about us, I will be here for you, in my little corner of this rainy wee country.'

'Okay, goodbye, Cal.' Bea's words were choked but she was holding herself together, which, if she was dealing with the emotions he was, he had to commend her for. She was a woman of principle and the fact that she knew exactly what she wanted from a relationship only made him love her more. He wondered how he was ever meant to forget her but accepted he probably never would.

Chapter Fifty-Five

Things continued to go well in the bar. Business was steady. Christmas and New Year were mayhem, although nothing Cal and his team couldn't cope with. Edinburgh got busier every year around the Hogmanay celebrations. Cal was grateful as it had given him less time to dwell on the hollow emptiness hanging around ever since Bea had left.

As they always were, January and February were long, cold, hard months with no highlights besides Cal's birthday and the hope that spring might bring some sunshine. He kept himself busy with work and going for a run most days. It was too cold for surfing so he contented himself with quick dips in the sea to wake himself up in the mornings. He swore it was good for the immune system. There was also an element of torturing himself a little, although he wouldn't admit that.

In late March, the baby was born, and word came from an exhausted but ecstatic Elisabetta that both she and the little boy were fine. Cal was torn between wanting to visit the child and not wanting to have his heart broken again. He knew that if he met the baby, held him in his arms, he would want him to be his son, fall in love on the off chance he was and if he discovered that he was not, it would be unbearable. So he told Elisabetta that he needed the paternity test done before anything else. She was surprisingly accommodating and couriered a swab test to him.

The phone call came forty-eight hours later.

'I'm so sorry, Cal. I was almost certain. I believed instinctively that he was yours.'

Cal resisted the temptation to tell her that her instincts had never been especially finely tuned. It would have been the wrong thing to say. He was a swirl of emotions already and throwing bitterness into the mix would not be productive for anyone. It was sad the baby wasn't his. Although he had done his level best to keep his emotions in check and not get too attached to being a father, he was only human and it was natural that certain thoughts had crept in: playing football with his son or daughter, teaching him or her to surf. It would take a little time for him to become accustomed to the fact that this would not be happening imminently. It would hopefully happen someday, but this was not his time to be a dad.

When Cal did become a father, he knew who he wanted it to be with. But that dream was gone. So, why couldn't he shift her from his mind? The frustration at having lost Bea and also not being a dad was crushing. He had lost her for nothing. Now he was alone. And, if he was honest with himself, it was nothing less than he deserved. But that didn't stop him from wanting Bea, from wanting to win her back. So, never one to back away from a fight he had even the smallest chance of winning, Cal knew what he had to do.

Chapter Fifty-Six

Bea was an overnight success: one who had worked eight years to get to that point. Her latest novel was a smash hit and even those who did not normally read in the romance genre were reading it and talking about it. She was being invited to conventions and book readings and her reader group on social media was always full of questions and people thanking her for writing such an awesome book. It was her dream coming true at last.

Healthy sales of the book and her back catalogue also meant a more robust bank balance for Bea. It was such a blessed relief to focus on her writing without having to work bar at the same time. Of course, there were no guarantees that the next novel would be as successful as the current one, but if she had to, she could always go back to bartending. Bars weren't going anywhere.

The one downside to the popularity of her latest book was that it meant Bea could never push the memory of Cal from her mind. He was there in her hero. Sure, she had changed the name but all that did was stop the public from knowing who she'd based him on. Bea couldn't shield herself from that knowledge. But how she missed him. No matter how hard she tried to forget it, the time they had spent together was too special, too wonderful. She had fallen head over heels in love with him and you didn't fall out of love like that, especially not from someone like Cal Butler.

It was early April and Bea was having lunch with Amira at their favourite Chelsea deli. Since things had taken off, Bea had found that there weren't enough hours in the day to get all the writing done, as well as the admin, so Amira had taken on a bigger role in helping Bea with monitoring and filtering her emails as well as some social media scheduling.

'So I finished the book,' said Amira, referring to the second book in her latest series, which Bea had given her to read for feedback.

'Oh.' Bea was nervous of what Amira thought of it. 'Great. Or is it?'

'It is. I loved it.' Amira tucked into her avocado salad. 'I'll message over the notes this afternoon. But I think Gil Painter's brother is going to be as popular as Gil.'

'You do?' Bea let out a breath she didn't know she'd been holding in. 'That's great. I've been a bit worried this one might fall flat as it's more from my imagination than the last one.'

'No way will you fall flat, Honey. There's too much spirit in these books. Real issues that real people experience, like toxic relationships, guys with kids already. I'm fielding loads of emails from people who don't want to talk on the public group but want to share how much the story touched them. I've put them in the fan mail folder, but I've flagged some of the ones you'll need tissues for.'

'Really? God!' Bea had always imagined what it would be like to get fan mail like that, but she hadn't been prepared for if it did happen.

'Yeah, I guess when you talk honestly about life it means a lot to a lot of people.'

'Oh, my goodness! I didn't ever think my stories would affect people in such a way. I will be reading those with a box of Kleenex this evening.' Bea took a large gulp of wine; such was her excitement.

'And before I forget,' said Amira. 'I've transferred you back that money you lent me. I'm sorry it took so long.'

'You didn't need to worry about that. You know I'm going to add it back into your pay packet. And lunch is on me. Should we order some more wine?'

The conversation flew like a runaway train. Bea and Amira never ran out of things to say to one another. Then when they were on their third glass of white, Amira broached the thing she knew must be on Bea's mind and Bea sobered up fast.

'It's around about now, right, that the baby's due?'

'Mmhh. How on earth did you remember that?'

'Well, as your assistant, it's my job to keep track of everything in your life. Also, it's written all over your face. My guess is you're thinking about it a lot?'

There was no getting anything by Amira, but Bea wouldn't have expected anything less from her closest friend.

'Yep, the baby's due around about now and I'm finding it difficult to stop thinking about it. That'll be one lucky kid having Cal as its dad.'

Amira topped up Bea's glass. 'Have you thought any more about getting in touch with him?'

'No, I don't think so,' said Bea. 'I mean, I have thought about it, but I don't see what's changed. I still don't think I could cope with being a half mom or something.'

'Well, that's a shame. He did sound like Mr Perfect.'

'He was pretty damned perfect.' Bea wondered if she would ever find anyone quite so wonderful again.

· · ·

When Bea had said she'd read the fan mail with tissues, she hadn't anticipated needing a whole box. There were so many moving messages and she was truly humbled. That evening, she sat up until two replying to each one with heartfelt gratitude to her wonderful readers for sharing their stories with her. But there were two messages in particular that stood out. One was from a reader called Andrea:

It means the world to have my concerns over being a stepmom reflected back to me from the pages of a novel. Thank you for putting what is in in my heart into a character, so eloquently and accurately. I should also say that although being a stepmom is darned hard at times, I am so glad I chose to go down this route. My love for my husband is stronger than ever and his kids are amazing young people who fill me with so much pride.

There was also a message from a reader called Laura:

Having lost the love of my life – the bravest and most selfless man I ever knew – on what should have been a simple tour of duty, I have to say that I treasure your books for both the escapism as well as hope that one day I might love in that way again. Never stop writing your beautiful stories.

These messages were truly heartbreaking and uplifting at the same time. Bea was reading this last message again and nearly choked on her tears when the realisation hit her. What on earth was she doing? These women were inspired by her: women with problems that they had overcome. Overcome with love and hope and strength. Why did Bea think she was any different? Cal loved her, she loved him, yet here they were living on separate continents because Bea was afraid that an innocent little baby might impede him loving her enough. What an absolute fool she was. All the emails and messages people had written telling her that her stories had given them hope in a world where they thought they could never find true love, and there she was having found it, but thrown it away like a perfect winter coat with a small pulled thread in the fabric. Not a day went by when she didn't long for Cal: to feel him envelop her, to have his hot skin burning with hers, his fingers linked through her own. It didn't escape her attention that she was pining as if it were impossible to have any of this. Yet, that was not the case. Oh, what an idiot she was. What an absolute fool.

Bea opened up a blank email and started to type. She might not be able to get Cal back, but she owed him a proper explanation.

*Chapter Fifty-
Seven*

Cal's flight landed at JFK on a sunny April morning. He hoped this was a good omen. Although, he had a fair bit of work to do before he could even find Bea, never mind win her back, armed with only the address on her driver's licence she had used as ID when signing up to work at the bar, and the name of the Manhattan bar she worked in, or once worked in. *Not at all like hunting for a needle in a haystack*, he thought ironically. But he would do it. He would find her. He hadn't flown all this way to give up after a morning.

She wasn't at the apartment and he couldn't see a buzzer marked Gracie. Cal rang the other buzzers until he got a response, but the neighbour wasn't forthcoming apart from to say that Bea had moved out. Cal felt like he was in a Hollywood movie. He made his way across town to the bar she had worked at. A sleek, modern building with full glass frontage and a gunmetal interior. Impressive stuff. Not only the bar itself, but the fact that Bea worked here, or had used to. It would definitely get busy on evenings and weekends. He imagined Bea handling each customer with aplomb, mixing the most complicated cocktails and delivering them with a million-watt smile on her face, breaking customers' hearts left, right and centre. Just as she had broken his.

He asked at the bar.

'Bea? Yeah, she worked here, but she packed it in a few weeks ago. Her writing is taking up all her time now.'

Cal nodded. He knew about Bea's writing success. He'd followed it online, delighted for her hard work to be rewarded at last, although sad at being unable to help her celebrate and enjoy her achievements. He went to a nearby branch of a coffee chain and drank a latte while thinking about what to do next.

While he was drinking his coffee, Cal pulled out his phone and read Bea's email for what must be the hundredth time.

Dearest Cal,

This is a message I should have sent a long time ago. In fact, this is probably something I should have said to you in person last time we saw each other. But my head was in a different place then. Allow me to explain.

You were right when you said I was upset about you having a baby with someone else. I was upset, but not because I was jealous, more I was terrified because it brought up such feelings of insignificance for me. So much so that I didn't think I could cope with being with you when the child was born.

The reason I found this so difficult – and found it almost impossible to share with you in person – is because of my previous relationship. I told you my ex was controlling and that he left me. What I didn't mention was that the woman he left me for fell pregnant as soon as he and I broke up. This gave me a huge inferiority complex on top of the one already cultivated by him – feelings of worthlessness around not being a mother yet, of not being a 'proper woman', which I know are nonsense, but I couldn't help it. I simply couldn't cope with those emotions again but this time with a man I had fallen head over heels in love with, more than I ever have for anyone in my life. That's you, by the way, in case you were wondering.

I guess you will know by now whether you are a father or not. I wish you nothing but health and happiness, whatever the outcome. I can only apologise that I was not more open with you at the time. I was struggling immensely and could not work out my feelings to articulate them. Please believe me when I say that I am truly sorry, and I hope this helps you to understand why I may have behaved in a way that came across as irrational or cold. Trust me when I say it was not at all what was going on inside.

Yours regretfully but warmly and with love, always.

Bea

Cal sighed and pulled up Bea's author website on his phone. For a few moments he gazed at her photograph, still stunned by her beauty although nothing compared to her actual real-life luminescence. He wasn't sure exactly what he was searching for, a sign, perhaps, but whilst scrolling down her *Latest News and Events* page something arrested him. 'Meet Me. Talk and Book Signing, Amour Amour Book Nook: a romance book store.' And the date of the event was today. Cal's blood pumped hard. The event started ten minutes ago. He googled the address on his phone. It was far away, but if he was fast, he could make it.

Cal sprinted to the nearest subway station. A couple of trains and he would only have a block to walk to the bookstore. He peeled off his jacket. The light cotton shirt he was wearing was sticking to his back, partly from weather far warmer than Scotland and partly from nerves. A few months ago he was so at ease in Bea's company. Now so much was at stake and he wasn't sure she would even want to talk to him.

Chapter Fifty-Eight

The reading was going well. Bea hadn't expected the bookstore to be so packed, and it was both a pleasant surprise and somewhat intimidating to see so many expectant faces waiting for her to stimulate and illuminate. But she needed to try to enjoy it; this was what she had waited and worked for all these years.

She started with a reading from her novel, which even garnered a few laughs in some places. Would she ever get used to this after working alone for so long and never knowing which parts evoked which reactions from her readers. It was fulfilling. What if she got used to it and took it for granted? No, that would never happen. Not after all this time.

As she read, Bea realised her heart was pounding, and it wasn't the adrenaline from reading in front of an audience. It was what she was reading. Every word Gil Painter spoke, every loving gaze he gave her heroine, every embrace and every kiss was a weapon through Bea's heart. She had read and re-read her work so many times now that she was sure any impact the words could have on her would have worn off, but it was not so. The legacy of Cal Butler lived on and on. He simply wouldn't leave the residence he had taken up in her being. Bea choked a little on the words as she read them. She should have chosen a different passage. But this was one of the best, it was one of the readers' favourites; it showcased her writing well and somehow – she knew in her heart of hearts – it brought her closer to Cal. And that was why she chose to read it, even though it made her well up with emotion.

'I'm so sorry.' Bea hardly dared to lift her head as she spoke to the crowd. 'This bit always chokes me up a little.' She met the eye of some of her readers, a few of whom were weepy themselves. Others watched on with admiration. One of them – a woman in the second back row – raised her hand. Bea nodded at her as if to say, please ask your question.

'Are you okay?' the woman asked.

'Oh, yes, I'm fine. I think maybe I haven't detached myself well enough from my subject material.'

'This is based on your own experiences?'

Bea nodded. 'Well, some of it is. Inspired by, shall we say? With all the names changed.'

Another woman cut in. 'Are you still with him? With Gil?'

Bea steeled herself. 'Um, no, no I'm not.'

'I'm sorry to hear that. He sounds perfect.'

'He kind of was. But he is a long way away now, somewhere in Scotland.'

'I might go there and see if I can hunt him down,' one woman joked.

Bea chuckled. 'He stands out from all the rest. He shouldn't be too hard to find.'

'Certainly not, considering he's right here.'

Bea's gaze shot to where this deep, resonating voice had come from. It was so different from the others in the room. Scottish. Male. As she hit the location of the sound, the back of the room, her jaw lost its battle with gravity. Standing in the doorway, as devastatingly handsome as the first time she laid eyes on him, green eyes reaching out to her like daytime stars, was Cal Butler. Live in the flesh in New York City. In the exact same bookstore in which she was conducting a book reading. With an expression of such intense adoration on his face that Bea's whole body quaked.

'Cal?' Bea couldn't get out any more words.

'Bea.' Cal stood still like a Scottish mountain, just looking her, his ardent gaze holding such depth, so many questions, torrents of unspoken emotion.

'What? What are you doing here, Cal?'

'Is that him?' Bea could hear voices in the audience whispering and rising up, wondering if what they thought was happening was really happening. Were they seeing their author's inspiration live in the flesh?

'I came to find you.'

'You did? But why?'

Cal strode down the corridor between the two columns of seating. 'Because I wanted to tell you something.'

'Oh, Cal.' Bea didn't know what he was about to say, but she knew that she had to say something first. She owed him that.

'Cal, please. You don't have to––.'

'Bea, I came all this way. I've eaten some dreadful airline food and slept about three hours. Please let me tell you what I came to say.'

'No, I insist!' There were gasps from the audience at Bea's tenacity. 'I don't know what you've come here to say, and I'm sorry about the airline food, but I've been doing some thinking and, although I never thought in a million years that you would end up here in this bookstore, now you are here, I have to tell you.'

Cal frowned. 'What? What is it?'

Bea glanced at the audience, ready to apologise, but it was unnecessary. They were clearly rapt. She turned back to Cal.

'I've been selfish and silly, Cal. I don't care if the baby is yours or not. It doesn't matter one bit. What matters is that I miss you so much that I can't even sit here and read about Gil Painter without my whole body cracking in pain that I don't get to see you anymore.'

Cal's mouth lifted in amusement. 'Gil Painter? Is he ... the new Hal Hunter?'

'Yes. He's you. Basically.' Bea shrugged and managed a small affectionate smile.

'He sounds kind of hot.'

'He is.'

'Sounds like the sort of guy who would fly eight thousand miles to tell you how much he loves and misses you.'

Bea's heart soared. 'That's exactly how he is.'

Cal was right in front of her now. 'Because he wants so much to be with you. To give his entire heart to you.'

'He does?'

'He does. I do.'

Bea's eyes filled up. 'Oh, Cal. What about the baby?'

'The baby... It isn't mine. Look, Bea, I won't pretend it hasn't been an emotional wrench, detaching myself even from the idea of having a child, but I'm determined to focus on the things I already have that matter to me. And one of those things is you. I can never make that baby be mine, but you and me, Bea, we could be something. I'm sorry I didn't understand exactly what you were going through, but your letter helped me to "get it". So, I've come here today to ask if you'll give me another chance. Will you be my girl, my woman? I love you so much, Bea. This time apart from you has almost killed me. I don't care where we live or if you put me into all of your books—'

'Yes, please,' called out a voice from the crowd.

Cal smiled. 'All that matters is that you say yes, you will be with me.'

'Oh, Cal...'

'You do love me, don't you, Bea?'

'Cal. I kind of have a book reading to do here. Maybe we should have this conversation afterwards.' Bea's professional obligations took over. She worried her audience would be getting impatient.

'Oh, okay. Sorry, everyone.' Cal addressed the crowd, all of whom shook their heads and called out in various ways that he had nothing to apologise for and that this was even better than the book reading. 'We can talk after,' he said. 'I'll go up the back and mind my own business.'

'No!' a vociferous reader cried out.

'Well, they don't seem to mind.' Cal turned back to Bea. 'Although, if you'd rather do this in private afterwards, I completely understand. I'm not normally one for public displays of affection, but you do this to me, Bea. Know that.'

'I don't think this can wait,' said another audience member, and some others pitched in and agreed.

'Well, it appears I'm outnumbered.' Bea laughed.

Cal scooped her cheeks into his wide palms. 'I think you might be. You've got an audience here who want a happily ever after and you're depriving them of it.' He winked softly and gazed at her with such pure love that she could do nothing to resist.

'Yes,' she said.

'Yes?'

'Yes, I love you, Cal. Just as much as you say you love me. I have done from about five minutes into our no-strings affair. So yes, I'll be your girl. Your woman. And, no, I don't care either where we live, as long as we can be together.'

'Oh, Bea.' Cal pulled her to him, placed his lips on hers and indulged her in the softest, yet most passionate, kiss she'd come to know as trademark Cal Butler. 'You've made me the happiest guy alive, you know that? I am so glad you jumped in front of me in the queue that day. So happy you came to work in my bar, and over the moon that you feel the same way I do. I love you, Bea Gracie. More than anything.'

The audience let out a collective 'Aah'. There were some sniffles, suggesting the scene had moved some to tears, then a collective chanting began, which soon became clear was the audience demanding Cal read from Bea's novel. 'Gil Painter, read! Gil Painter, read!'

'Really?' Still with Bea in his arms, Cal turned to face the audience. 'You want this guy to read?'

They did. So, a little reluctantly but glowing from the fact that his precious Bea was his at last, Cal sat down in a chair next to the love of his life, in front of her adoring audience, and read them the story that had brought them together, looking very much as if he was finding it hard to keep the smile off his face as he did.

THE END

Thank you for reading *A Cask of You*. If you enjoyed this book, please consider writing a review so more people can find the book. I know writing reviews can be a headache and it's not always easy to know what to write, but it makes such a tangible difference when you do.

Thank you

Amber

Free Prequel and Secret Scene

If you enjoyed this book, you can download the free prequel to the series at my website, www.ambercooperbooks.com or here. Email sign up is required but you can unsubscribe any time you like.

You can get a secret steamy scene for *A Cask of You* entitled Chapter 44 1/2. It fits between chapter 44 and 45, funnily enough. This scene tells a bit more of Cal's backstory and gives spoilers to the prequel to the series, thus is not included in the novel. You can download it using this link: https://BookHip.com/LRZFRTQ or here. Again, email sign up is required, but you won't be added more than once and you can unsubscribe any old time you like.

Acknowledgments

There have been many people who have propped me up while I've worked on getting this series off the ground.

This book began its life on the 2019 romance writing course of the PWA. Thank you to Heidi Rice for her input on the initial incarnations of Cal and Bea. Thank you also to all the lovely ladies on that course for their initial feedback and support. I don't know where you are now but I hope you are still writing romance. The consensus then was that Cal was hot. I hope he still is.

Thanks to my 2021 RNA NWS reader for all the invaluable feedback on the first full draft. A thank you also to my initial beta reader, Callaborde. She's ace, speedy and very affordable.

A million thank yous to Ash for basically being my unpaid mentor and championing me to everyone from your sister to the lady who does your eyebrows. Also a million thank yous to Jo (Josfeen) for your incredible input on the original covers and patience with my constant questions about whether the sky should be a darker shade of pink and whether the buttons on someone's coat were wrong. Thanks to Lauren for falling in love with every Butler man I've sent your way and making me believe others could too. Thank you to my parents for all their support to make this happen. And to my Scotsman, Chris, for your love through it all.

Huge thanks to all the friends who may not have read this specific book but who've had a role in supporting my writing journey, from reading other books, to offering publishing advice to generally being enthusiastic about the whole thing: Susan, Trudy, Maureen, Jess T, Jenny, Sheena, Kristy, Becky, Elspeth and Jess W. Thank you!

Oh, and special thanks to my cat for getting me up at 5am most days so I can write my books. At least I think that's what she's doing.

My editor is the awesome Aimee Walker. Find her at www.aimeewalkerproofreader.com

The covers for this series are designed by Hellie Cory who saved my cover bacon. Thank you!

And thank you to you, lovely reader, for reading this book and all of this bit, too. I hope you will come back for more. Jamie is next so I'd better go and sort him out.

Until next time,

Amber x

About the Author

Amber Cooper is Scottish lady who lives in a wee flat in Edinburgh, Scotland, with a Scotsman and a Scotscat. She took to writing when chronic illness put paid to too much physical action – and she loves it (writing, not chronic illness - chronic illness sucks). Romance writing is even better.

When not writing, Amber can be found searching the internet for vintage furniture to upcycle, watching Eastenders (British soap where everyone is always shouting at each other), and going for walks whilst listening to her Spotify playlists and imagining dreamy scenes for her next novel.